SERIAL CHEATERS

SERIAL CHEATERS

OLIVIA FLAGGERT

Thriller Book Lover

Thriller Book

Lover

Serial Cheaters by Olivia Flaggert

Published by Thriller Book Lover™
www.thrillerbooklover.com

Printed in the United States.

First Edition: July 2021

To my wonderful mom, Lisa Flaggert

"Be careful who you trust, the devil was once an angel."
- Ziad k. Abdelnour

"Sometimes I'm terrified of my heart; of its constant hunger for whatever it is it wants. The way it stops and starts."
- Edgar Allan Poe

Part 1

I

Victoria

March 3, 2007

The championship game was over. It'd been a blowout. Again.

The gym filled with congratulatory cheers as all Victoria Henderson's teammates celebrated the victory with their family and friends.

"We won, we won!" her teammates chanted all around her. Victoria scanned the bleachers for her mom, Cindy Henderson, and for a moment, allowed herself to imagine her mom here, with the rest of the parents, rejoicing over their championship basketball game victory.

"Great job tonight, Vic!" Mr. Daniels, Victoria's history teacher, called out. She only played for twenty-nine seconds in the fourth quarter of the game, but she managed a smile and a thank you before she slid out the gymnasium doors.

Darkness filled the parking lot except for the glow of her mom's SUV headlights. Quickly, with her head ducked down, she walked the rest of the way to the parked vehicle. She didn't want anyone else to congratulate her. Victoria got inside the car and slammed the door shut.

"I'm sorry, Victoria. I cannot believe that coach of yours," Cindy said as they sped off. Victoria agreed but stayed silent.

"Leslie—is that her name? You know who I'm talking about. The girl who can't shoot the ball to save her life." The car picked up speed as they soared down the road.

"Yeah, Coach says she's more consistent than me. I think that's why she plays her so much," Victoria replied, knowing this wasn't what her mother wanted to hear.

Her mom laughed hysterically. "Your coach sucks."

"I thought you said you weren't going to get upset about it this time."

Her mom looked straight ahead as they drove down the long stretch of a highway. "Nine seconds. Is that how much she played you?"

"Um—I think it was twenty-nine seconds."

"I refuse to let that idiot coach bench you and ruin your scholarship opportunities. You're way too talented to have it all go to waste." Victoria's mom slammed down on the accelerator, tailgating the car in front of them. "This is the fast lane, fucker!"

When the car finally moved to the other lane, her mom flipped off the driver, giving the guy in the busted-up Chevy truck the dirtiest of looks before they drove past. Her mom took a deep breath. "We're not putting up with this anymore. I already sent an email to the coach at that other school. You're still okay with transferring, right?"

"Sure." Victoria didn't need to think about it much; she hated her coach just as much as her mom did. Not only that, but it wasn't like she was leaving friends behind. She didn't have any.

2

Victoria

Fourteen Years Later, Present Day

Another superb performance, Victoria thought as she stood at the foot of the bed. Dr. Dave Anderson lay naked in his condo bedroom. Dead. Moments ago, she'd slit his neck and watched the life evaporate from within him. Blood had gushed out violently and soaked into the bed-sheets. As always, it had been truly captivating to watch, but Victoria knew time was of the essence, and she needed to hurry and bring it all to completion.

Now that step one was finished, she looked up and scanned the room for the castration knife, which she remembered she'd placed on the end table. Yes, there it was. Exactly where she'd left it. She gripped Dave's motionless legs and dragged his body closer. Next, she flipped him over like a pancake. His hairy ass now filled up her view. Arranging him in this position was critical for what she planned to do next.

Momentarily, Victoria stepped away from him and walked toward the end table to grab what she needed. With glove-protected hands, she gripped the castration knife tightly in her palm and proceeded to finish what she'd started. This was her favorite part. She glided the blade right up against his dangling testicles, holding it there for just a moment, and then sliced off his entire ballsack. Carefully, of course. She had much practice and knew how to do it without making a mess of things.

Victoria held his balls in her gloved hand, admiring the prize before she placed them inside a Ziploc bag. She secured them in her red Louis Vuitton purse, the same one Dave had bought as a gift for her a few months back. A thoughtless gift, really, considering she'd told him that she hated the color red. Oh well. It would serve as a suitable ballsack carrier for tonight, but she'd trash it later.

After Victoria packed up the balls in the purse, she placed the rest of her tools in there and then inspected the entire room, which had been thoroughly sanitized and cleansed down to the very last crevice and corner. Everything looked as planned.

To create even more confusion, Victoria left behind a stolen ID, a different identity from the one she'd given to Dave. The name that Dave had known Victoria by was Mary. Little did he know that Mary was just a temporary character she'd played with him. A step in the action plan. Mary was a nobody. A secret, just as Dave had suggested.

Before Victoria made her final exit, she did a double-check to make sure the Grindr app was still installed on Dave's phone, displaying all the past records of his messages to other men. Well, her messages. She'd sent them regularly, pretending to be Dave, since the day they'd first started their secret affair.

It wouldn't take long for the detectives to connect the dots with this new cheater.

3

Holly

Present Day

Never again, Holly Anderson thought as she tumbled out of bed. Last night had been memorable and forgetful all at the same time. She walked over to her nightstand and checked the package that contained those new Delta 8 Gummies one of her clients had suggested she try. The label said one gummy had thirty milligrams of THC, which was apparently a single serving. She had mistakenly taken three, which explained the profound effect they'd had.

Holly pulled on her silk robe and walked toward the kitchen for breakfast and coffee. As she made her way down the halls, she flipped off all the lights that she'd left on. The previous night, paranoia had rippled through her. She'd thought a book she was trying to read had been giving her strange secret messages. A similar occurrence happened when she tried to watch a funny television show. At one point, she'd even called 911, thinking her limbs had turned to jelly. Fortunately, the dispatcher had been patient and stayed on the line until Holly realized that her body parts were, in fact, still intact. Mostly, from what little she remembered, she had done her best to distract herself until the effects of the substance wore off.

After the terrible experience, it suddenly made sense why society was so divided over whether weed should be legalized in every state. She hadn't been herself last night by any means. Thank God everything felt back to normal again today.

As Holly's coffee brewed, she pulled out her phone to learn more about why she'd had such a bad reaction to those gummies. In the search engine, she typed in "paranoid after delta 8 gummies" and clicked on the first result that came up. It was a Reddit post where a user had asked a similar question. She read her way through all three of the comments on the post. The first comment mentioned that it could happen if you got too high or were a new user. The second comment said that maybe another substance could have interacted with the Delta 8 to cause a bad reaction. The third comment, from a user named, Druglover15, said that the intake of Delta 8 later resulted in an emergency room visit and a diagnosis of schizophrenia. After Holly read that comment, she decided that was enough research. She had plenty of anxiety and stress these days and didn't need to worry about a sudden onset of Schizophrenia on top of everything else. Just when Holly was about to set her phone down on the counter, the doorbell sounded. Reluctantly, she rushed to the front door to see who it was. She wasn't expecting any visitors this morning.

A woman in business casual clothes stood on her front porch. She showed Holly a badge and introduced herself as a detective. "I need to speak to Holly Anderson, please. Is she home?"

Holly wasn't sure what a detective badge even looked like, but the badge seemed real. Had it been a man at her door, she probably would have spoken through the window, but there was something about this woman's face that suggested she was telling the truth.

"I'm Holly. Is everything okay?" she asked, feeling as if she was in a strange new world. This was the first time a detective had ever come to her house. For the most part, Holly didn't experience unexpected surprises or events. Most days, she went about her everyday routines, and her life carried on as expected. The last time she'd experienced a shock was when she found out about her husband's affairs. That news had devastated her at first. However, by now, she accepted the fact that she had married a deceitful person.

As the detective stood there, Holly suddenly realized that she was about to experience another life-changing disturbance. Detectives never showed up abruptly with good news. Holly prepared for impact. Instinctively, she thought of her dad, mom, sister, and nieces. *Please not one of them, please*, she pleaded silently to herself.

The detective looked down toward the cement porch briefly and then met her gaze with sorrowful eyes. "It's about your husband, Dr. Dave Anderson. I don't know how else to tell you this. He's been murdered; I'm very sorry..."

Holly's heart beat rapidly in her chest, and tears began to spill from her eyes. This couldn't be real. She was still trying to shake off the peculiar events from last night and now process this tragic news.

Even though Holly's husband had destroyed their marriage and she had yet to forgive him, that didn't stop the despair she suddenly felt. Yes, her husband had broken her, but the love she had toward him still remained. The longer Holly absorbed the shock, the more she began to reflect on the fuzzy memories from last night. She couldn't help but ask herself: *did I have something to do with this?*

* * *

After she answered what felt like an endless amount of questions from the detective, Holly was alone again in her house. Her first instinct was to call her husband, Dave, but then the reality of the situation sank in. Her husband was dead.

Tears streamed down her face, and her fingers trembled as she dialed her sister's phone number. Holly and her sister, Layla, were extremely close.

"I was just about to call. What are you doing?" Layla asked. In the background, the sounds of little voices echoed. Layla, a stay-at home mom, had the life Holly had always envisioned for herself. A faithful husband, two perfect kids, and a beautiful home. A flash of all the arguments with Dave suddenly replayed in Holly's mind. The infertility. The cheating. The falling out of love. Slowly but steadily, Holly's entire life had been crumbling away, and now, her husband was dead.

Holly cried into the phone, unable to find the words; the hand which held the phone trembled frantically.

Her sister spoke next. "Holly? What's wrong—Are you crying?"

"I don't know," Holly said as the tears poured out. "I don't know exactly how it happened, but there was a police—I mean a detective came by just a second ago. Dave—he's, um...Dave's dead. He's been murdered."

The phone went silent and then, "Hold on. Mark," Layla yelled to her husband. "Please watch the kids for a second."

Holly heard the sound of a door shutting and then her sister spoke again to her this time. "What happened? You can't be serious right now. Did you—please don't tell me you had anything to do with this."

As Holly tried to get a grip on her emotions and explain the situation, she recalled all the prior conversations she'd had with her sister about Dave's affairs. When she first found out about them, Holly had been overcome with emotions. She'd even wished him dead. Holly had told her sister about how she could kill him—that was how angry she'd been. It had only ever been all talk, though. She'd never actually do that. Obviously. At the time, her sister probably understood it as a coping mechanism. Although now, Holly wasn't so sure what her sister thought.

"I don't know. I don't know..." Holly repeated, her voice shaky and intermittent with sniffles and heavy breathing.

"Don't you dare say a thing to that detective until Mark is there. I'll call Mom and explain everything. She'll come watch the kids, and we'll be right over."

Holly had never been more thankful for Mark, Layla's husband, and a successful defense attorney. He'd be able to fix this in case the detectives started to view her as a potential suspect, which they likely would if they got access to her and Dave's recent text message conversations.

"I didn't do this, Layla. Please tell me I didn't do this. I—I don't know what happened. But I—"

"Take a deep breath. Just calm down. I know you didn't. I know. Relax. We'll be right there."

Holly did what her sister said. She couldn't stop the tears from flowing down her face, so she figured she'd just wait until her sister arrived before she explained how she'd already spoken to the detectives and probably made the situation much worse.

While Holly was still doing her best to collect herself, the doorbell sounded. Although she wished that her sister were here already, she knew that wasn't possible. Her older sister lived a good thirty minutes away and it had only been about five minutes since they'd gotten off the phone.

Holly blew her nose with a tissue and then went to answer it. She prepared herself mentally, in case it was the detective, returning with handcuffs and all the evidence that Holly had murdered her husband.

From the far end of the hallway, Holly looked through the window but didn't see anyone outside. She walked the rest of the way down the hall and opened the door. A warm blast of air greeted her. She looked around. No one.

Holly looked down to find a brown cardboard box. There wasn't a label or any way to indicate where it had come from. Seeking answers, she grabbed the box and returned inside. She locked the door behind her.

In the kitchen, she grabbed a knife to open the mysterious box. Inside, there was a typed note.

All it said was:

You're welcome

4

Amy

Present Day

After a long day of work, a wave of fatigue swept over Detective Amy Carson as she sat at a table for two near the back of Hickery's Bar and Grill, waiting impatiently for her Tinder date to arrive. Although she'd planned this meet-up weeks ago, she couldn't help but to think about how it was the worst possible time to be trying to meet a new guy.

In a way, she felt guilty over it. She'd finally been assigned the most important case of her career, and here she was, on a dinner date. To help relieve some guilt, she reminded herself that she hadn't eaten anything all day, and based on the hunger pangs in her stomach, she desperately needed food. This was just a convenient way to throw some food down her throat while determining if this new Tinder match had any long-term relationship potential.

A quick glance down at her watch revealed a time of 6:47 pm. *Where is this guy?* She wondered. He was supposed to arrive seventeen minutes ago. The guy she'd agreed to meet seemed like a potentially decent match for her—well, based on Zodiac sign compatibility. He was a Scorpio and she was Gemini, which apparently meant they could have intense physical chemistry.

"Are you ready to order, or are you still waiting on someone?" the waiter asked kindly.

Amy looked up, immediately noticing the man's tall stature. At five foot nine, Amy stood well above both men and women alike and naturally found tall men irresistible.

Just when she was about to respond to the waiter's question, her phone dinged. On the screen display was a text message from the guy she'd planned to meet:

Sorry, got held up at work. Reschedule for tomorrow?

Amy tossed the phone back in her pink leather purse. She wouldn't respond now. Or ever. *His loss*, she thought, and then looked up at the waiter. "I'm not waiting on anyone. I'll go ahead and order. Could I please get the baby back ribs? I'll take another Miller Lite, too, when you get a chance." *Screw it*, she thought, she was going to treat herself and get the ribs, and she wasn't going to have any regrets about it either. Initially, she'd considered the house salad to play it safe on a first date, but now, dining solo, she really didn't care.

"Sure thing," he said, graciously taking her menu.

"Thanks."

While waiting for her food, Amy dug into her purse for her pink laptop. Early on in her career, she'd learned that the men she worked with didn't take a homicide detective with a pink laptop as seriously as the other mostly male detectives with basic color laptops, such as black or grey. However, now as a more experienced thirty-three year-old woman and a fairly accomplished detective, she no longer cared what they thought about her.

Amy made use of the spare time, remembering what her dad used to say: "Every time you choose not to work is more time that someone else is suffering or dying because of it." Her dad, Shawn Carson—a well-known workaholic—had been one of the best homicide detectives in

Philadelphia. All the long hours, stress, and cigarettes eventually caught up with him, though. In the end, it was the lung cancer that killed him. Amy missed him every day but knew that he'd be proud of what she'd accomplished so far in her career. Well, overall speaking, he'd be proud. Would he be turning over in his grave right now, knowing she had wasted time squeezing in a Tinder date on the day she'd been assigned the biggest case of her life? *Probably*. But despite the need to live up to her father's expectations, Amy also had goals of her own, which included finding a husband and starting a family someday. *It shouldn't be a crime to want such a thing*, she reminded herself.

Amy buried herself in the review of key details and photos related to the ongoing investigations. She'd been given access to case files of the connected homicides, which at this time the FBI believed were all connected. However, it was her job to perform all the groundwork and ensure they proceeded in the right direction. Any loose ends had to be determined and accounted for.

This serial killer had a level of sophistication uncommon among most criminals. Thus far in Amy's career, most of the homicides she'd solved were motivated by drugs and money. The offenders were violent, but not pure evil. This was the most difficult case she'd ever been assigned. And she had to figure this out by herself. In the past, whenever she'd been stuck or needed help, she could count on her dad's insights. The conversations she'd had with her father always forced her to think outside of the box and observe everything from multiple angles, which was how she planned to approach this investigation.

5

Amy

Present Day

The following day, after hitting her snooze alarm for the third time, Amy woke up. She hurried over to her medicine cabinet to pop an Ibuprofen and down a large glass of water. A yawn escaped her mouth as she realized she had less than twenty minutes to get ready if she wanted to get a Starbucks latte on the way to work.

Amy browsed through the clothes in her closet to find something to wear. Her job required business casual attire, and thankfully she had gone shopping recently. She settled on a purple button-down blouse and black slacks. The outfit was cute, yet very breathable, which she needed today since it was forecasted to be another humid day in downtown Philly.

Next, Amy swiped mascara onto her lashes, coated her lips in a hydrating gloss, and applied foundation and concealer to her face. She liked to look nice and put together just for herself—no one else. It amazed her how many men assumed women applied makeup to impress them. As a last-minute effort, she gave herself a hasty glance in the mirror to make sure there weren't any makeup lines and then shoved her work stuff into her bag before she finally headed out the door.

Unfortunately, the Starbucks drive-thru line had been much longer than anticipated, and Amy arrived at work five minutes late. She subtly walked to her desk, trying to conceal the coffee in her hand. If it weren't for the Starbucks, she would have made it on time. However, she reminded herself that life happened sometimes and not to beat herself up over being a few minutes late. She just hoped her boss wouldn't make a big deal of it.

The other detectives, including Brad McDonald, her least favorite of them all, were huddled together around his desk, laughing themselves to tears about something. The insecure part of her thought maybe they were making fun of her, but she quickly pushed that thought aside. Although she wasn't certain, she had an inclination that Brad was still jealous about how she'd been promoted to homicide detective first.

"How's the investigation going, Amy?" Brad called from across the room. Brad was the kind of guy who at first glance appeared like a decent person, but once you got to know him, it became clear how much of an asshole he truly was. He acted like he knew everything and always claimed to be right, but Amy had worked with enough men like that in the past to know how to stand her ground.

"Great," she said with a friendly smile. She took a sip of her latte and turned back to her computer screen, hoping he'd get the hint. Instead, he walked toward her desk and pulled up a chair.

"Clearly, your Monday is not as busy as mine," she said.

"That's right—I forgot. You're balls deep in work these days with this new homicide investigation." Brad winked at her.

"Ha. Ha. Funny. You should really consider a career as a comedian. Might be a good change for you, since you can't stop throwing a pity party over the fact that I'm working the biggest case this department has ever seen. Here you go." Amy handed him a tissue from the Kleenex box on her desk. "Why don't you go dry your tears back at your desk? Because some of us, actually have real work to do."

"If only we could all sleep our way to the top like you, Amy." Brad spoke so only Amy could hear it. Amy wanted to punch Brad in the face and tell him to find something better to do with his time. But she'd had enough past conversations with him to know that he had the sort of ego which demanded the ridicule of others to feel better about his insecurities. Unfortunately, his motives would never change.

"Are you stupid? I already told you to leave me alone," Amy snapped, looking him straight in the eye. Despite his condescending personality, Amy was reminded of how superficially good-looking Brad was. He stood tall with thick, black hair, a five o'clock shadow, and those sparkling blue eyes. Surely, he possessed all the physical traits of what most women desired in a guy.

Before he could say anything else, an office door toward the back of the building swooshed open. The Department Chief of Police Wesley Jenkins stood in the doorway and looked at her coworker first, then her. "Brad, back to work. Amy, please see me in my office."

Amy proceeded into the chief's office and took a seat in the chair across from him. Long, vertical white blinds blocked off the natural sunlight. Bright, fluorescent lights lit up the entirety of the room. The place had an exhausted and worn look to it. The only sentimental object in the room was a photo of the Chief's ten-year-old daughter. He'd used to have a family photo on his desk, but that was before his divorce.

"So, there's been a slight change in the case."

The coffee hadn't kicked in enough to deal with any sudden changes. "What do you mean?" Amy asked.

"I want you and Brad to work it together. With all the media attention we're getting right now, I need my two best detectives on this one."

"Yeah, that's why I'm planning to work with Charles."

The chief shook his head in disagreement as he delivered the news. "Not anymore. Charles is taking a short leave of absence."

"Since when?"

"As of today. He's not doing well—health wise. I asked him to take some time off, and he agreed."

"Okay, so why not me and Jake then? We work well together. I'll work with him."

The chief sighed. "Look, Amy, I know you and Brad don't always see eye to eye, but believe it or not, you two work the best together."

"I honestly don't need his help. The FBI's already involved. We have a full-force investigation already in progress, and I don't need any distractions or drama. Brad's a drama queen, and you know it."

The Chief sat back in his chair and looked at Amy gently. "Your dad was like that. He preferred to go at it alone. We hated each other at first. But then—"

"You guys became the best of buds. I know the story."

The Chief smiled, clearly reminiscing. A few tears tried to form in Amy's eyes, but she blinked them away. She didn't want to linger on the conversation about her dad.

Amy stood up. "Not all stories have a happy ending, you know. Brad and I will never be friends, not even acquaintances—but I'll take one for the team and suck it up."

"Thank you, Amy."

"Are we sure this is the best decision? This serial killer has evoked a lot of fear within the LGBTQ community, and I don't think Brad can sympathize with that."

"His sister's lesbian."

"Is that the lie he fed you?"

"Maybe if you took some time to get to know Brad on a more personal level you'd realize there's a lot more to him than what you see on the surface."

Amy crossed her arms. "I don't have time to study the complexities of Brad's personality or life history. Have you told him yet, or do I get to do that fun part?"

"He's been briefed," he said, looking down at his watch. "It's already getting late in the morning. I'll let you both get to it. Please keep me updated on everything."

"You know I will," Amy said, and then turned to walk away.

"Oh, and there's one more thing," the Chief called. Amy turned back around. "If you're going to be late, make sure you don't walk in holding a Starbucks in your hand next time. We have a room full of detectives out there. And trust me—they take notice."

She nodded her head in agreement. "I understand. I'm sorry; it won't happen again."

"Please make sure of that. I put you on this case for a reason, Amy, but you have to do your part to show the other guys that you're serious about it. They all would love to work a big case like this, and when they see you walking in late, they assume I'm playing favorites. "

"I understand. Like I said, it won't happen again."

Amy walked out of her boss's office and met Brad at his desk. "You ready?" Her voice was devoid of any excitement.

"Glad the Chief updated you on the good news." Brad closed up his laptop and smiled.

"I wouldn't call this good news." Amy waited as Brad locked away paperwork in the drawers of his desk and gathered his things. After Brad had what he needed, they exited the building together in silence.

"I'll drive," Brad suggested, once they reached the parking lots.

"That's okay. I can drive us—I'm right over there." Amy pointed to where her SUV was parked.

"I'd like us to get there in one piece."

Amy rolled her eyes. "Oh shut up, and get in." As Amy started up the car, the song "Candy Shop" by Fifty Cent blasted out of the speakers. She reached for the knob to turn the volume down.

"I didn't realize you listened to rap. I thought Taylor Swift would be more of your thing."

"Well, you thought wrong."

Amy began the drive and handed Brad her GPS. "Can you put in the address for the hospital please? That's where we're heading first."

Brad turned the device around in his hands. "You still have one of these? You know your phone has a GPS, right?"

"Yes, I know. I like to use this one though." Her dad had bought this GPS for her a long time ago.

"Do they even update the software on it anymore?"

"I don't know, but it works fine."

"Hm. I don't trust it. We'll use my phone," Brad suggested.

"Fine. Whatever," Amy agreed, but only because she didn't want to waste another second.

For the next ten minutes, Amy stayed focused on the drive. The only audible noises came from the highway sounds and the soft hum of the radio until Brad finally broke the silence, "So, what happened yesterday?" he asked.

Amy adjusted her sunglasses. "Nothing. The guy never showed. Such a waste of time."

Brad looked perplexed. "I'm talking about the case. When you spoke with the victim's wife? What were you talking about?"

"Oh, shoot, my bad. Yeah, with that. It was interesting."

"How so?"

"She seemed a little disoriented. I mean, not in the usual sense of what we'd expect. Something just felt off."

"Did she have an alibi?" Brad asked.

"Not a strong one. She was home that night. Alone. When I interrogated her in the kitchen, she had newspaper articles related to the Homophobic Killer. She was clearly familiar with the style of murder."

"That's not any cause for concern. The only people who haven't heard about this serial killer are the people living under a rock. The last murder was—what, about three months ago? It's a high-profile case. Everyone's reading and talking about it."

"True. But I plan to look at this from every angle. I'm setting all assumptions aside. I think she's hiding something." The car swerved to the right as Amy rounded the curve to exit the toll road. "We should have more to go off soon. The digital forensics team is examining the phone records. Once we get access to that information, we'll have a better idea of the relationship Mrs. Anderson had with her husband—she let me perform an exploratory search of the home, though."

"And?"

"Based on everything there, the guy was definitely in the closet. I don't know if he was bisexual, or maybe maintaining these other relationships with women to cover the fact that he was gay."

"What'd you find?" Brad asked.

"In his office, he had several locked storage trunks. Our team was able to break into them, and they found a double-ended dildo and lots of butt plugs. I mean, a whole trunk full of them—and several magazines of gay porn. I bagged all the evidence so we can test it for DNA."

"Lots of women like butt plugs. We don't know for sure these items belonged to the victim. They could have just as easily belonged to the wife."

"Yes, I know. I looked that up. Apparently women use those, too," Amy added.

"You've never tried one?"

Amy raised her eyebrows. "No."

"You're missing out."

"You've used one?" she asked.

"No, of course not. But I've known some women to like them. That's all."

"Well, anyway, back to what I was saying about the case, I know that's not evidence in itself to be used as anything. But when I questioned Mrs. Anderson if her and her husband had ever used sex toys, she said no. She's Catholic, and so was he. I guess vanilla was more their thing. There wasn't any hesitation with her answer either. So, as you can imagine, these findings are making me believe we're dealing with the Homophobic Killer, but I'm not ready to omit her as a potential suspect. At least not yet."

"The wife had nothing to do with it. This is the work of that serial killer; but I'm sure we'll have more definitive answers soon," Brad said as they turned into the hospital parking lot.

6

Victoria

Present Day

The day after the most recent murder, Victoria woke to the sound of her mother's voice. Her mom had a habit of letting herself into Victoria's home. The multi-million-dollar property was secured by a wrought-iron gate and passcode, but her mother knew how to gain access to almost every area of Victoria's life.

"Where is she?! My crime fiction, best-selling author of the year!"

Victoria eased out of bed and shouted back, "I'll be right down." Winning author awards had become as ordinary as brushing her teeth, but she loved how her mom still gloated about her accomplishments. Her mom had always known Victoria was destined for success, and all of her success came from the many sacrifices her mother had made to get them to where they were at today.

Victoria found her mother in the kitchen opening up a bottle of champagne. "Mimosas?" her mom asked.

"Sure," Victoria replied, stifling a yawn as she took a seat at the kitchen table. Cindy poured Victoria a mimosa and then handed it to her before yelling for the maid. "Anne, can you take a break from the laundry and come cook Vic some breakfast, please?"

"She's off on Saturdays, Mom," Victoria reminded her mom for what felt like the thousandth time. Her mom always forgot that the maid didn't work weekends.

Victoria's mom took a sip of the mimosa and then said, "Oh, that's right. Oh well, not to worry. I'll make my little best seller some breakfast. What do you want, sweetie?"

Victoria wasn't that hungry yet, but she knew her mom wouldn't take no for an answer. "Eggs sound good."

Cindy shuffled through the pots and pans before she found the right one and placed it on the stove top. She sprayed some oil into the pan. "I thought you were going to call me once you landed in Dallas. It worries me so much when I don't hear from you."

Last night suddenly felt like a blur. The night after a murder always did. "It was late, I didn't want to wake you."

Her mom cracked an egg into the pot. "I can forgo my beauty rest every now and then—thanks to Botox. How was your trip and the flight back from Philly? Everything go okay?"

"Yeah—got a lot of writing done." An image of Dave's dead body popped into her head for a second.

"You're not too tired?" her mom asked, "because your brother and his fiancé are supposed to be coming over for dinner to celebrate your latest book. We're all just so excited for you!"

Victoria did her best to concentrate as her mom blathered on about random topics. She nodded and engaged in all the body language cues that suggested she was paying attention to the conversation. "They're flying in from California—they loved your engagement gift by the way, been talking my ear off about their trip to Sonoma—I'll let them tell you all about it when they get here." Cindy turned to face her, holding the spatula in one hand. "Or I can tell them you have an author event or something like that if you want to reschedule—the two of them can always catch another flight down here. Your brother won't mind."

For a brief moment, Victoria considered her mother's offer before she agreed to their dinner plans. Although Victoria wasn't in the mood for a social get-together, she didn't like to reschedule pre-committed plans with family members. Her brother, Jeff, and his new fiancé, Ted, were engaged with a wedding date right around the corner. She hadn't even met Ted yet. It probably was about time that she did.

7

Victoria

Present Day

Before long, her brother, Jeff, and his fiancé, Ted, showed up. Like every other guest Victoria had invited over, Ted was in awe of the house. Indoor and outdoor pools, sky-high ceilings, crystal chandeliers, original stone architectural features throughout the main rooms—all on top of fifty acres of iron-fenced land. The custom-built, 6,135-square-foot home had a mid-century modern exterior with a timelessly designed interior. Conveniently, it was also located within the same town where Victoria grew up. According to Home & Style's most recent article, it was "a paradise in the Southern heart of Texas."

From where they now stood in her living room, looking out the floor-to-ceiling windows, she watched one of the Thoroughbred stallions graze near the pond; his shiny black coat glowed in the Texas sunshine. The horses were one of her and her mom's more recent hobbies.

Even though it was the first time she'd met Ted in person, Victoria figured he'd be somewhat familiar with, or at least aware of, all the wealth she'd accumulated over the years. Her brother's continual and failed attempts at an acting career didn't pay for itself, either did his expensive new home in California. Victoria paid for everything he owned: the Ferrari, the acting lessons, his newest house (1.7 million dollars), the vacations, the flight here to Dallas to visit her. The list was endless. Victoria handled all the family expenses—whatever they needed or wanted. After all her success as an author, the book to movie adaptions of her novels, and all her various investments, it was impossible to run out of money.

After more small talk and once the tour was finished, they all made their way into the extravagant dining room for dinner. Once seated, Jeff's phone vibrated loudly. He pulled it out of his pocket, staring at the iPhone screen. "OMG. Did y'all hear about this?" His jaw dropped as he looked around the room at everyone.

"What?" her mother asked. Victoria looked up from her plate, patiently waiting for whatever gossip her brother planned to make tonight's topic of conversation. Jeff looked to Ted and then back at Victoria and Cindy, clearly shocked that they didn't know. "The Homophobic Killer—there's a new victim."

"Oh geez, Jeff, honey, you had me worried. I thought you were going to say you had cancer or something horrible like that," Cindy said before shoveling a scoop full of mashed potatoes in her mouth. Victoria continued eating in silence.

"Um, yeah—we should all be worried. This guy is nuts—literally! Me and Ted have been following the coverage extensively. The story is all over the news lately. Last night they were saying how rare these kinds of violent crimes are these days, so of course, all the news reporters are talking about it, and what this means for the LGBTQ+ community. I mean, we all know the gay community has always been under attack—don't even get me started on that—but this is far beyond attack, in my opinion. It's so sickening; I just hope they find him soon so we can all start sleeping again at night. I mean, look at these bags under my eyes. I've hardly slept, and this is not ideal for my next audition." Jeff pointed to the skin underneath his eyes. "I really need a better eye cream."

"Oh, please, Jeff. You don't look a day over twenty. If anyone has bags to worry about, it's me," Cindy remarked.

"They're going extinct. Serial killers. It's why everyone can't stop talking about it," Ted informed the table.

"Hm—I don't know about that, but Victoria would know. She does tons of research into serial killers for her books. Is it true they're going extinct, Vic?" Cindy inquired, curiously.

"There aren't as many today as there were back in the 60s and 70s, but I wouldn't say they're a dying breed. They've just gotten better at their craft," Victoria answered.

"Oh, and get this. Apparently, the killer has suppressed gay feelings or something like that, and that's why he keeps their ballsacks. It's, like, his trophy, which is so disturbing!" Jeff exclaimed. Victoria didn't say anything but suddenly thought of all the frozen ballsacks she had stored in her freezer. No one in her family cooked, so she didn't find it risky to keep them in there. The only person who ever went in her freezer was Anne, the maid, and Victoria already made up a lie about how they were bull testicles she was saving for a special occasion.

"Jeff and I were just in Philly last month," Ted chimed in again.

Jeff nodded in agreement, and then said, "That's where they found the latest victim. That could have been us. We could have just as easily been killed by this psychopath."

"So they haven't found him yet?" Victoria asked, already knowing the answer as she knifed into her medium-rare filet mignon.

Cindy threw back a sip of wine and then looked at Victoria, interrupting Jeff before he could reply. "Vic, you know what I was just thinking? This would be a great story for you to write about for your next book."

"It would. Everyone's talking about it," Ted agreed with a mouthful of breadcrumbs tumbling out as he spoke. Crumbs had scattered all around his section of the table. The disarray bothered Victoria, and she wanted to clean it up but chose not to make a huge deal about it. She didn't want to come across as rude while Ted was here. Her mom or the maid could clean up the mess later.

Victoria pretended to consider the idea her mother suggested. "Maybe, but that sounds familiar—I'm sure I've read a book like that before. I'm known for originality, and I'm not about to destroy my career with a been-there-done-that storyline." The truth was that she'd be way too good at writing a story like that.

"Uh, actually there's, like, none. I've never read a book about a serial killer who targets gay people. Gay men are way under-represented in literature. And you have not had one gay character in any of yours, Vic. Not one!" That was probably true. Her editor had brought something like that up at their last meeting when she was half-listening.

"I can't even remember all the characters in my books. There's been so many, but I'm sure at some point I included a gay character," Victoria insisted, and then took another bite of her perfectly cooked steak.

"Mom, has she included a gay character? Oh, wait, never mind. Mom doesn't read them." Jeff and Ted laughed in unison.

Cindy looked over at Victoria, smiling. "I read every word of them. Everyone loves Vic's books—especially me! They're the best books out there." Victoria was Cindy's favorite child; she'd always agree with Victoria—even if the evidence suggested otherwise.

"Hey, who wants to hot tub and watch *The Bachelor*? Vic, can you turn the TV on out there? The season premier starts tonight at nine. I know we all could use some eye candy," Cindy suggested, and with wine bottle and glass in hand, she started walking toward the outdoor patio.

Just like Victoria, her mom had a relationship status of single. Victoria's biological father had been out of the picture for almost all of their lives. And the last guy her mom dated had turned out to be a dick. Many men these days were exactly that. Unfortunately, Victoria knew first-hand what it was like to date those kinds of guys. That was one of the many things Victoria and her mom had in common. Cheaters. They couldn't stand an unfaithful guy. Whereas her mom simply hated and left them, Victoria hated, killed, and then castrated them.

8

❧

Amy

Present Day

Amy and Brad took a seat in the waiting room of Anderson Plastic Surgery Center. As they waited to speak with Dr. Dave Anderson's clinic partner, Amy glanced around the room. A platinum blonde with large lips and breasts sat in a chair directly across from them. Like a Barbie doll, her body and face had been scrupulously crafted and molded to fit today's beauty standards. Although Amy wasn't a fan of plastic surgery, it never bothered her that women chose to get work done. If this helped a woman become more comfortable in her skin, then Amy didn't see any problem with it. Amy checked the time on her watch and then looked over to Brad. He was looking down intently at something on his phone. Surprisingly, he didn't seem the least bit interested in checking out the attractive women in the room.

After a short period of time passed, the front desk attendee led them toward the back of the clinic. Amy and Brad followed the young woman down the long hallway as she directed them into Dr. Benjamin Brown's office.

Amy took in the entirety of the office space. The walls were covered in a luxurious, glossy wallpaper. The executive desk was mostly empty except for a few clipboards filled with paperwork, a tablet, Clorox wipes, hand sanitizer, and a decorative flower piece. Large windows overlooked downtown Philadelphia and allowed an abundance of natural light to fill the room. The design had a feminine flair and a sense of intention to it.

Dr. Benjamin Brown spoke first: "Hi, come on in. What can I do for the two of you? I take it you're not here for a surgery consultation."

Amy grinned at his attempt to introduce a note of levity to the situation, but quickly got back to business. "That's correct. We're with the Philadelphia Homicide Division. We're here to ask you some questions related to the murder of Dr. Dave Anderson, your clinic partner."

"Devastating. I couldn't believe it," he said as he clasped his hands together and paused for a moment before he continued. "It's been quite hectic here. We've been working around the clock to notify his patients and find a place for them on my schedule. That's the temporary plan for now, until we're able to hire a new surgeon to help."

Brad spoke next. "What kind of relationship did you have with Dr. Dave Anderson? You must not have been that close, considering—"

"It's what he would have wanted. This clinic was everything to Dave," Dr. Brown interjected and then continued speaking. "It didn't matter what Dave was dealing with, his patients always came first."

"Okay, so it sounds like you had a friendship with the victim. When did that begin?" Amy asked as she prepared to take down notes.

"I first met him during my plastic surgery residency. Dave was always extremely ambitious and wanted to work for himself, so he started this private practice, which took many years of hard work to get to this capacity. He'd gotten so busy and needed help, so he reached out to me to see if I was interested. At the time, I needed a change and so agreed to a partnership."

"When did you start working here?" Brad asked.

"I've been working here for about a year. Since then, I've established my credibility and have patients of my own. But most of the patients that come here, they come for Dave. Well, came for Dave." A look of despair swept across Dr. Brown's face, and upon closer observation Amy noticed the puffy, swollen bags beneath his red-rimmed eyes. "Many of his patients have been seeing him for years. Some of the women we work with, have low self-esteem, body-image issues, things of that nature. Not all of them, of course. But many do. Dave wasn't just a surgeon to them, he was someone they trusted. A friend. I'm only doing my best to do what I know Dave would have wanted, and that involves being here to notify his patients as soon as we can, so they hear it from us first, instead of the media. It's extremely challenging for me to be here, but again, anyone who knew Dave would know this is what he'd want. You can ask the staff. They'll tell you the same thing."

Brad sat up straighter in his chair. "We'll have questions for them next. Can you give us any insights into Dave's state of mind before he was murdered? Since you claim to have had a friendship with the victim, surely you must have had deeper, more personal conversations unrelated to work." Both Amy and Brad waited attentively for the answer to the question.

Dr. Brown sighed. "We did."

"Go on," Brad urged.

"There was stress at home. From his wife, Holly. From what he told me, she nagged him constantly about work. Said he didn't spend enough time with her."

"Okay, when did he first start mentioning that?" Amy inquired.

"Right around the time when I first came on board. It's why he helped Holly start her interior design company. Something to keep her busy."

"Did that help at all?" Amy asked.

"From what I can tell, no. He still complained about how she was nagging him constantly. She wasn't happy. A few weeks ago, he told me she wanted a divorce."

Amy considered everything Dr. Brown had to say. "Did he want that, too?"

"I'm not sure. I don't think so. As much as he complained about

Holly, I know he still loved her very much. He'd surprise her with flowers. Vacations. Whatever she wanted."

"One last question: can you confirm if Dave had any relationships with men?" Amy asked.

Dr. Brown looked puzzled. "He never disclosed such information to me. If I had to guess, it wouldn't entirely surprise me if he had. With age comes wisdom. Nothing surprises me anymore. But I can't give you an absolute answer to that. The last thing I'd want to do is mislead you two."

* * *

After they finished interrogations with the rest of the medical staff at Anderson Plastic Surgery Center, Amy and Brad exited the building and proceeded to the parking lots.

A short walk led them to where Amy had parked the vehicle. "That could be our guy," Brad said as he closed the passenger side door shut.

Amy put the car in reverse and pulled out of the parking space. "I don't think so, but I'll have our task team pull his financials. See if he had any kind of financial motive."

"No, I mean he fits the killer profile. White male in his thirties to forties. Organized."

Amy disagreed. "Did you see the gym bag next to his desk?"

"No. What gym bag?"

"You probably couldn't see it from where you were sitting. Well, I got a good look. He had gym clothes balled up in there. Empty protein bar wrappers. Mismatched socks. The serial killer we're looking for wouldn't have a gym bag that looked like that."

Brad turned his head slightly to look out the window as they drove down the road. "He's a plastic surgeon. He would have the knowledge of how to perform a castration, I'm sure of it."

Amy considered what Brad had to say. "That's true."

"Doctors, CEOs—men in high power positions often have psychopathic behaviors or tendencies. As far as suspects go, he may be worth looking into."

"I understand, but my gut's telling me he's not our guy," Amy replied as they drove past several fast-food restaurants. "You hungry? I was thinking about swinging by that Chick-fil-A near the office."

"Nah—I don't eat that processed shit anymore. I have grilled chicken and vegetables waiting for me back at the station. But go right ahead and swing by if you want it."

Amy laughed. "Is your girlfriend on a new health kick or something?"

"No, but I am. I haven't had anything fried in over a month. And there's no girlfriend anymore either—we broke up."

"What happened?"

Brad shrugged. "She wanted more. Marriage. Wedding. A family. And I wasn't ready to commit to all that."

"Well, I'm sorry to hear that."

"There's nothing to be sorry about. Not everyone can handle being in a relationship with a detective."

"It's tough. That's for sure." Amy was suddenly reminded of how her mother had left her dad when she was sixteen years old. Although Amy's mother still tried to stay in touch, Amy didn't have much of a relationship with her anymore, and she had mostly stopped returning those calls and messages.

"You know how it goes. Whatever happened with that guy you were seeing a while back? I take it that didn't work out either."

Amy could count all the men she'd dated on a single hand. It didn't take long for her to determine which guy Brad was referring to. "You're right. It didn't," she said.

"Is that when you and the Chief decided to go at it?"

"I don't know what you're talking about. But I'd appreciate if you'd stop bringing that up. There's nothing going on between me and the Chief. Nothing at all."

"Oh come on, Amy. I saw the two of you in his office. Together. That night. Don't play dumb with me. And you're lucky I haven't said anything to anyone about it. If there's a relationship of any kind going on between the two of you, it needs to be disclosed."

The sound of a phone vibrating cut into their conversation. Amy was thankful for the interruption. She didn't want to explain that incident to Brad or anyone for that matter. It had been nothing and it would never happen again.

A new text message appeared on Amy's cell phone screen. It was Dan from their homicide investigations team.

We were able to access the victim's phone records. It's pretty interesting stuff. It's on your desk. If you have any questions or anything, you know where to reach me.

Amy shot Dan a quick thank you text and then said to Brad, "Let's review the phone records during lunch. We have them now. Then we'll head back out. Sound good?"

"You do know it's illegal to text and drive, right?"

Amy chose to ignore Brad's question. They'd finally arrived at the Chick-fil-A drive-thru, and she wasn't about to get into an argument with him. He didn't understand the concept of efficiency, and nothing she said would make him change his mind. "You sure you don't want anything?"

Brad looked out the passenger side window. "I'm sure. Feel free to clog your arteries with that junk though."

Amy took a deep breath. Brad was stressing her out already. She wasn't sure how much longer she'd be able to put up with him. Hopefully, the phone records would give them more certainty of what happened to the victim. Because right now, this investigation was off to a bumpy start. And the longer it took to solve, the longer she'd have to put up with Brad criticizing everything she did.

That was how many of the men Amy worked with behaved. Any time she suggested an idea or made a good point, they'd all completely criticize or ignore it. Then, later, when a man suggested the same idea, everyone would praise him and say how great of an idea it was. It often felt like she couldn't do anything right. However, Amy wasn't going to let the cynics bring her down. She had too much on the line. She'd show everyone just how capable she was. No matter what, she planned to solve this case. Maybe then she'd finally get some respect from the other detectives, and instead of everyone talking about how great of a detective her dad had been, they'd say something about her, too. She loved her dad and didn't mind living in his shadow of greatness, but she also wanted to make a name for herself. It was about time that she did.

An hour later, Brad and Amy were eating lunch and reading over Dr. Dave Anderson's text and call records. Amy looked into the almost empty Chick-fil-A French fry package. Only two remained. She regretted not upgrading to the large size. She finished the last couple of bites and then wiped her greasy hands on a napkin. With a full stomach, she felt more focused, but she still decided more coffee wouldn't hurt. She was one of those people who drank coffee all day long. Compared to Starbucks, the coffee they brewed at the office tasted horrible, but at this point in the day, all she cared about was the caffeine.

Once she made herself a cup of coffee, she returned to her desk. Brad looked up from the paperwork. "I'll take one," he said, directing his gaze at the cup of coffee in her hand.

Amy took a seat in her chair. "You have two working legs down there."

"Three actually." Brad winked and stood up.

"You're gross."

His laugh echoed in the room. A moment later, he returned with his coffee and took a seat.

"Did you see this?" he asked Amy, pointing to an exchange of messages between the victim and his wife.

"Yeah, I saw it." The particular message that Brad pointed to was from Holly to her husband.

How many have there been, Dave? You're such a piece of shit. I could kill you. I really could.

"That's a little incriminating. Don't you think?"

"I mean, it definitely isn't an ideal text conversation to have with your husband a few weeks before he's murdered. On the other hand, her husband was cheating on her. She was upset."

"So, you'd say something like this then to a guy after you found out they were cheating?" He asked.

Amy tossed the idea around in her head. "Probably." Although Amy had never experienced such a betrayal, she could relate to how Holly must have felt. Men these days didn't have a commitment bone in their body, and they were always in search of the next best thing. Well, that was what Amy suspected the issue was. "You've been around the block, Brad. I'm sure by now, you've seen the crazier side that most women have. The only reason that women are so crazy, though, is because of men. You guys are stressful. And confusing."

"I've never cheated. If I didn't want to date her anymore, then I'd break up. It's as simple as that."

"Okay. Emotional cheating is cheating, too."

"Same concept. I would break up with her first before I moved on with someone new."

"Right."

"I'm not as big of an asshole as you think, Amy."

"I never said you were. The whole point I'm trying to make is that when a guy hurts a woman, especially if it's her husband, it can sometimes result in arguments like this. Shoot, if I had a husband and he cheated on me, I'd want to..." Amy was just about to say 'cut off his dick', and then it suddenly hit her. Could they be wrong about the killer? Could this be a woman serial killer? But if that was the case, then why did all the victims have evidence that suggested they were engaged in relationships with other men? She didn't want to mention the thought yet. Especially since that would throw a curve ball at this entire investigation. However, she planned to keep the possibility in the back of her mind. Anything was possible. That was something her dad reminded her of all the time.

"What?"

"Oh, nothing," Amy replied. "I just wouldn't be happy. That's all."

9

Victoria

Present Day

It had been a few days since Dave's murder, and Victoria had already started to feel refreshed and back to her normal energy levels. As fun as it was, the process of finding and researching her victims—and all the preparations and time that went into killing them—took a significant amount of effort. Like a drug addiction withdrawal, it sometimes took months to fully recover after a murder, but like everything in her life, Victoria improved at it. Nowadays, it only took about a week for her to get back into the swing of things. On the plus side, the killing was a good outlet for whenever she was experiencing writer's block. She'd already had a spark of new ideas for the latest novel she was writing.

The early morning sun rays shone through the windows giving off a heavenly glow, as she strolled into the kitchen. She looked outside, admiring her beautiful back yard. Everything was always bigger in Texas, so they had to go all out on the pool design. Stone steps led up to a fifty-meter long slide that curved elegantly into the twelve foot deep water. Curved, rocky stone edges surrounded the entirety of the massive pool. A bridge with elegant arches led to the iridescent indigo-glass-tiled island, where the reclining lounge chairs offered an idyllic position for sun-bathing.

Further down the sprawling acres of land, near the steel-framed barn, stood their part-time handyman, Rex. On this blistering hot day, he wore just a cowboy hat, a pair of dark blue jeans, and his work boots. Even from the considerable distance, one could make out his 6'4" stature and deeply defined six-pack abs. Victoria watched as he effortlessly picked up a haystack and tossed it over the fence for the stallions. Most women would kill to wake up to a sexy cowboy like Rex working in their backyard. His sort wasn't tough to find either. Thankfully, Texas wasn't in short supply of men like him.

All the animals on her ranch, including the horses, cattle, chickens, and goats, all needed care, and Victoria sure as hell wasn't going to do it. She loved the beauty of the animals and the fun they provided, but she hated the monotonous effort of taking care of them. That was why her mom had hired Rex for the job. The guy couldn't tell a pencil from a pen, but he knew how to take care of a farm, and that was all she needed him to do for now.

"Mom, did the pool-cleaning guy show up yesterday?" Victoria yelled over the blasting sounds of the television. "Can you turn it down a little?"

The television's volume lowered, and a few seconds later, her mom walked in the kitchen, wearing silk pajamas and holding a cup of coffee in one hand and the remote in the other. The mug was one that Victoria had designed back when she aspired to start an e-commerce business. Most people would have considered that business a success, but not Victoria. She'd always been destined for more. After her first novel's success, she sold that business and abandoned a few others to focus full-time on her writing career.

"I couldn't hear you. Did you say something, Vic?" her mom asked, pouring herself another cup of coffee.

Victoria reached for a mug in the cabinet. "I won't be able to think straight if you keep blasting that TV all day."

"It wasn't that loud, but I'll turn it down a little so you can concentrate. How's the new book going?!" Cindy asked eagerly.

"Fine. Did the pool guy show up yesterday?"

Her mom paused for a second to think about it. "I had the arborist over to look at those trees in the front yard, and then Glen and his crew came over to mow the pasture and pull weeds. Pool guy never showed. I forgot his name. Was it Lance—no, Leonard, maybe? The guy wasn't very memorable, I can't even remember his name now." Her mom laughed. "You want me to have Rex do it? I'm sure he won't mind."

"Yeah, sure. He can do it if the other guy doesn't show."

"Okay, I'll call him over once he's done with the stables. Anyway, I have your social media posts all planned out for this month. You've been getting so many emails about brand partnerships now that you're about to hit one million followers. Oh, which reminds me. Tarte—you know, that makeup brand you love?"

"You mean the one you love."

Her mom smiled and then said, "The one we both love. Well, they want to pay you ten thousand for a partnership post. They wanted to do a TikTok video, but since you're booked out with partnerships for the rest of the year, I told them we can only do an Instagram post. That's it. And that's us being generous to squeeze them in."

"I hate it when brands do that. Act like we don't already have a bunch of other partnerships lined up."

"It's incredibly selfish of them. I almost wanted to tell them no, but I know we like their makeup products, so I agreed. All they're asking for is a photo of you wearing their new lipstick product. It's a shade called Serial Killer—such a cute name. It's red. I know you hate that color, but you look so good in red. We need more photos of your beautiful face on your Instagram, Vic. You get so much engagement when you're in the posts. All the book posts we do can get a little boring. Don't get me wrong, your followers love to see posts about your amazing books, but your followers want to see more of you, too."

"Okay, that's fine. We can do them once I'm back. But I don't want to go overboard with it—you know I don't like my personal life broadcasted all over social media. More fans will start recognizing me in public, and that's the last thing I want to happen. It's why I purposely don't let our publishers include a photo of me along with my author bio."

"I know. I know. Don't worry. It'll be fine. So when you're back from Philly, you'll have photoshoots with Edward. For all the other partnerships this month, we already have those photos done and ready to go. I'm way ahead on the marketing, as I always am."

"Okay. I'm heading up to the cottage to write, so I need to start packing and get going before I miss my flight."

Cindy walked over to Victoria and kissed her on the forehead. "Have a safe flight, Vic. Be careful, please. Call me the moment you land. And if you forget, I'll fly up there to check on you like I did last time ."

10

Victoria

Present Day

Victoria drove her Ford F-150 down the long gravel road to one of her secluded investment properties. She'd planned this short pit stop on the way to the Dallas airport. As Victoria continued down the driveway, a squirrel darted in front of her vehicle. The animal crunched beneath the tire as she ran it over. From the rearview mirror, she gazed back. Guts and blood smeared across the gravel. Even though most people would feel distressed over accidentally killing an animal, she didn't feel sorry for the squirrel; it should have stayed out of her way.

As Victoria rounded the final turn, she saw Larry, her eccentric cousin—who'd been in and out of jail for most of his life—waiting for her. He wore dirty cowboy boots, a plaid shirt, and tattered overalls. The outfits he wore always reminded her of scarecrow attire. He smiled and waved at her with those hideous buck teeth. The genetic similarities between her and Larry weren't apparent; he hadn't received the genetic blessings that she had.

Victoria parked the truck and got out to greet him. "How'd it go?" she asked, as she followed Larry inside the large metal building. Adrenaline surged through her veins. This punishment wasn't too closely related to her usual undertakings, but it was something she had to do, and it was finally happening. Like a lion in the wilderness, she'd vigilantly stalked her prey, and she was now ready to dig into that first bite.

Larry looked proud of himself as he answered in a thick southern drawl, "Good. He didn't leave the backdoor open like you told me he would, but I worked it all out. Everything went smooth for the most part."

"How'd you get inside then?"

"One of the windows in the back of the house."

A welcoming blast of air conditioning greeted them as they walked inside the large metal building. The tiled hallway appeared bare as the Texas plains. The only noticeable feature was a massive see-thru windowpane. From their side, they could see through, unlike the person on the other side of it.

Victoria glanced through the glass to observe the guy. A short, redheaded, pale-as-a-ghost man with freckles was passed out on the floor.

"What the fuck, Larry?" Victoria fumed as she stared back at her cousin. The adrenaline and excitement she'd felt moments ago had evaporated. Confusion swept over Larry's face.

She grabbed Larry by the overalls and pushed him up against the windowpane so he could get a better view. "Does this look like my father?" Victoria's shoulders tensed, and her forehead felt as hot as a sauna despite the gusts of air conditioning circulating the room.

He looked closely at her and then the man he'd kidnapped. "Uh—I don't know. I mean, I was wondering about that the whole time, but you said—"

"Where'd you get this guy?"

"At the address you gave me. I did everything exactly as you said."

Larry stepped back a little to create some space between them and dug into his front overall pocket. After a long second, he handed her a crinkled-up piece of paper. Victoria tore it open. "3459 Dickerman Drive. That's where you got him from, correct?"

"Yep, I followed all them instructions you gave me. Wait, no, the address was 8459—"

Victoria pointed at the first number on the sheet of paper and held it up to her cousin's face. "That's a three!" she screamed.

The window was soundproof, so the guy who was supposed to be her father couldn't hear them. Victoria took a deep breath before speaking again. In all her years, she'd never made a mistake, especially not one of this magnitude. But then again, this was the first time she'd recruited someone else to help her with a job. This only reminded her of how she could only rely on herself for anything. "We need to fix this. Immediately. You need to return him. Tonight."

He shook his head. "I can't tonight. I'll take him back first thing tomorrow morning. My back's killing me from getting him in the trunk—he's heavier than he looks, and I can barely keep my eyes open. It took me all night to get him here."

"Listen here, Larry, you're not doing anything else until you fix this problem you created, and this problem requires solving immediately. Understood?"

Larry looked like a child who just had a chocolate chip cookie stripped from his hands. "I ran out of that syringe stuff," he mumbled.

Victoria dug into her purse to pull out one of the propofol injections. "Here," she said, throwing it at him. She'd only brought an extra one with her today because she wanted to perform the punishment if time permitted. Now, unfortunately, Victoria would have to waste it on this random guy, so Larry could fix this disaster before it was too late.

"But the Cowboys game is on tonight. I was—"

"I don't care. Are you sure you can handle returning him? Or do you need me to take care of it? I'd hate to see you back in jail again."

He sighed. "No, I got it under control."

"Good, I'm glad we're on the same page. Even though you screwed this up in every possible way, I recognize you put in a little effort. You'll get some of what I owe you later tonight, but only after you fix this." Victoria gestured toward the man on the other side of the window and then continued. "We'll have to sync up later this week to discuss next steps. Then, once you do what I actually hired you for, you'll get the rest of the money—as long as there are no more slip ups. There won't be any other second chances, Larry, so you better get it right this next time."

11

Victoria

Present Day

Victoria sat comfortably in her first-class seat on the flight to Philly. She took a long sip from her champagne glass and scrolled through her father's Facebook page. Her father, Mic Henderson, must have some-how struck a deal with the devil with all the splendors that fell into his lap after leaving his family behind. Her father—a loser, red-neck, beer-bellied, cheating asshole, as her mother liked to describe him—hadn't been much of a man until he won the Mega Million Lottery. Since his miraculous lottery wins a few years ago, everything had been handed to him on a silver platter. And he didn't deserve it.

After Victoria had become famous and wealthy, her dad should have crawled back to their family, got on his knees, and begged for forgive-ness. But that never happened. If her father had never won the lottery and all the money that came with it, he would have come back.

Because of the unfortunate win, Victoria had been unable to punish him properly. It had become clear to Victoria that money made the world go round—it put people up on thrones, made them kings and queens. With it, her dad had happiness, but Victoria couldn't allow that for him. Although Victoria couldn't strip him of his money—well, she could but that would take longer than she'd want to wait—there was one thing she could take away from him that was sure to make him suffer for the rest of his pitiful life. Serial cheaters were a significant problem to society, and it was essential that someone made them pay for their heinous crimes. All of them had to pay—especially her father, the very worst of them.

Victoria looked up from her reverie and unintentionally locked eyes with the man seated beside her.

"Who's your favorite serial killer?" he asked, looking down at the *History of Serial Killers* book she had in her lap. The reading was research for her books, although she already had a thorough understanding of serial killers.

Myself, she thought, but replied, "Ted Bundy."

"Hm, interesting choice. Why's that?"

"He's the first one to come to mind," she answered truthfully and then turned to look out her window. She hoped that he'd stop with the questions.

"Are you going to ask who's my favorite?" he asked.

"I wasn't planning on it, but since you seem desperate to share, why not? Who's your favorite?" Victoria's tone came out as harsh as she intended. Maybe now he'd get the memo.

"Well, I couldn't tell you. I don't know much about serial killers. I've heard of Ted Bundy, though. You must be one of those true crime junkies."

"I wouldn't so easily define myself as that, but I'd watch a show like that over something lame like *The Bachelor* any day."

"Fair enough."

Victoria flipped open the book and began pretending to read, hoping that would shut him up. She wasn't in the mood for small talk. She was never in the mood for that. Over the years, she learned that most people weren't great conversationalists and had nothing interesting to say.

"I'm Henry, by the way." *I didn't ask, fucker*, she thought, but she still shot a smile at him. Upon closer observation, she noticed he had deep brown eyes, broad shoulders, and a killer smile with adorable dimples. In a strange way, he reminded her of a much older version of Drew. *Probably a cheater*, she thought, but perhaps he would be a good candidate for her next kill.

"I'm Daisy. It's nice to meet you, Henry."

Midway through the flight, Henry got up to use the restroom. Once he was out of sight, Victoria glanced over to his seat. He had left his tray down, and on top of it, next to his water, was his wallet. The temptation gnawed at her.

Victoria stood up, pretending to stretch while at the same time observing the activity of the two passengers seated in the rows behind her. Two businessmen. Both asleep. Quickly, she snagged his wallet. She flipped it open and observed his driver's license.

Henry Thompson. Date of Birth: December 3, 1986. Address: 3267 Paper Mill Road in Queen Village, Pennsylvania.

Million-dollar homes made up that part of town; she'd invested in properties over there. A full-time management firm had been handling all of that for her, but she was still familiar enough with the area to know that it wasn't cheap. First-class passengers didn't usually experience common-folk inconveniences like those flying coach—sitting shoulder-to-shoulder, in a seat that hardly reclined with cushion equivalent in comfort to the plane's metal exterior. Like Victoria, Henry had the monetary means to invest in the finer aspects of living, and it made sense that a first-class passenger like him would live in a coveted neighborhood, too. She made a mental note of his details, slipped his driver's license back into the same slot, and then returned the wallet well before Henry came back to his chair.

* * *

The three-hour flight had landed, and Victoria now stood in baggage claim, waiting impatiently. She hated everyday, tedious, and boring tasks like this one. But she wasn't sure if she could hire someone for such a role. What would the job application even state: 'Looking for an experienced and patient person to serve as a Baggage Claim Manager?' She'd have to ask her mom to look into that.

More and more bags circled around. Victoria's luggage was new and should be easy to spot among the other dilapidated bags. In her peripheral vision, she watched Henry from the plane approach.

He ran his fingers through his thick hair, and then clicked his cell phone off, turning to face her.

"It's a shame people don't take interviews seriously anymore. The interview was supposed to start at 5:00 and what do you know, they call in at 5:03."

"That's disrespectful of them. I can't stand people like that," she remarked, instantly regretting the words as soon as they left her mouth. She was supposed to be acting like Daisy, not herself. Like all her characters, Daisy needed to be the exact opposite of her. A free spirit who lacked attention to details. *Why is this guy throwing me off my game?* She wondered.

"That makes you and me both."

"You know, maybe this person just had an unlucky day, and something happened that prevented them from being on time for your call. Bad things happen to the best of us sometimes," she increased the pitch of her voice to sound more friendly, and she nervously twirled her long blonde hair. She couldn't make that kind of slip-up again if she planned to consider this guy for a potential kill. Although, right now, she thought it would be much too risky because she wasn't in any kind of physical disguise. Her hair, makeup, and outfit looked too much like her real self. She wasn't sure what her plans were for him, but she at least wanted to look into him. He intrigued her. Plus, the challenge thrilled her, and perhaps she could make adjustments to get this interaction back on track. But it was still too soon to tell.

A while later, Victoria spotted her luggage. She grabbed it and proceeded to the door. She knew Henry's name, birth date, and address. That was plenty enough information to find out more about him later—if she chose to do so.

Before she could get any further, a gentle yet firm touch stopped her. She turned around. It was Henry. "Wait, Daisy, pardon my directness, but I can't let you leave without at least getting your number. I enjoyed our conversation today. I'd really like to see you again," he held out his phone, ready to save her contact information.

A sense of warmth filled his dark eyes. A deep desire spread within her. *Why am I intrigued by this man?* He was attractive, but there was something else there. Maybe it was his similarity to her first love. She was familiar with what she suddenly felt. This lingering excitement of something more, but she told herself she'd never allow it to happen again. Not after what happened with Drew Mason back when she was a junior in high school. She'd made that mistake once before, and she'd accomplished too much to watch her success all slip like sand from her hands. Still, like a person on the edge of a cliff, with unknown dangers beneath her, she couldn't stop herself from taking the potentially deadly plunge.

Victoria plucked the phone from his hands and entered the phone number from a stolen iPhone device she made use of. After she entered the number, she saved it under the contact name of Daisy.

"There you go," she said, handing his phone back.

"Great, I'll call you later tonight after my board meeting."

We'll see about that, she thought.

In the arrivals area of the Philadelphia airport, a black limo waited for Victoria. The driver kindly placed her luggage in the trunk and opened the door for her. Discreetly, she looked around to make sure Henry wasn't in view before she got inside. It was always better for her to have the upper hand when it came to information. The less people knew about her, the better.

Once inside the limo, she pulled out her cell phones and proceeded to research questions she already knew the answers to. However, she liked to confirm by cross-referencing reliable sources on Google. In the search engine bar, she typed in: "what does it mean when a man says he'll call you later?" According to a blog called *Decode Men* this meant that he'd call at his convenience. *Typical*, she thought. Another blog called *Decipher Confusing Guys* said that it was unlikely he was going to call unless he'd already sent a text message. Victoria checked her messages. Nothing. If he didn't contact her back by tonight, she decided that, despite the risks involved, she'd have to kill him. It was disrespectful to lie to her like that, and she wasn't going to put up with that behavior—especially after she'd allowed herself to be so vulnerable with him. She suddenly regretted even giving him a phone number.

Only Drew had ever made her feel on edge like this. It was critical that she didn't allow that wild and uncontrollable energy to seep in as it had with Drew. That couldn't happen again. No matter what, she couldn't let the heartbreak take over. Everything had to be controlled. All the unknowns with Henry were distracting. At least she'd know by tonight what her plans were for him. In the meantime, she'd need to find the next cheater to release some of the built-up energy. However, before she could get to work on that, she had that meeting with her agent, Donald Fretter.

The limo made the final turn. Victoria checked the clock. 5:55 pm. As always, she arrived on time. She informed the driver that the dinner meeting would last an hour, and he should be back to pick her up at 7:00 pm sharp. No later. Once the pick-up plans were confirmed, she walked into the Italian restaurant.

The hostess greeted her and took her to the table she'd had reserved for months now. Reservations had to happen weeks in advance at places like this one.

Shortly after she was seated, the waitress approached the table. "Are you waiting for someone?" she asked.

Unfortunately, Victoria was constantly waiting on Donald. "Yes, but I'd like to order a glass of wine while I wait."

The waitress whipped out her pen and pad. "Of course. What would you like?"

"What do you recommend?" Victoria asked, staring at the menu. She didn't care to know much about wine and preferred the waitress to do her job and recommend the best one for her.

"Château Mouton Rothschild is what I'd recommend. It's two thousand dollars per bottle."

"Is that the most expensive?" Victoria asked.

"Yes."

Victoria handed the wine menu to the waitress. "That will work fine then. Thank you."

Finally, at 6:09 pm, Donald walked in the restaurant's front doors. Late, of course. The little wisps of white hair he had left on his head stuck up wildly like he'd just had an electric shock. In a way, he reminded her of Albert Einstein—a much less intelligent version though. Donald had the brain synapses of a sloth, and with such a gaunt stature, looked like he belonged more in the ICU than a restaurant. Victoria sometimes wondered how much longer she had until she'd need a new agent. Surely, retirement wasn't far off for a guy like Donald.

"Good evening, Victoria. I apologize for running a tad behind. The parking spaces were limited. I was driving around for a while trying to find a place to park."

Victoria always had a driver, so she honestly couldn't relate to his experiences, but she supposed the excuse made sense.

They engaged in some small talk about the weather and Donald's grandkids—two of Victoria's least favorite conversation starters—until the waitress came by to take their orders. Once the waitress departed from their table, Donald started up the conversation again.

"So tell me, how's the progress on the new novel?" he asked. Unlike the earlier conversation, this topic was at least of interest to Victoria.

"Great. I'll be finished well ahead of the upcoming deadline," she replied.

"Good. Good. It all comes so easy to you, doesn't it, Victoria? I mean that in a good way, of course. Natural talent like this in a writer is surprisingly uncommon. I'm sure so many other writers out there would love to know your secret. Have you ever considered instructing a course to teach your fellow writers?"

Victoria took a sip of wine and considered the idea. She wasn't sure how to teach her writing skills to other authors. Writing about murder wasn't fiction to her. It was her real life, and she knew that couldn't be taught. "No, my schedule is way too packed."

Donald nodded his head. "Of course. I understand. Well, hopefully one day you'll consider it."

"Perhaps," Victoria said, although she truly wasn't interested in helping other writers. After all, she didn't want to give away any of her secrets. Essentially, it was like giving the enemy additional guns and bullets. *Why would I want to make the competition stronger?* It made no sense.

The conversation dragged on. Mostly boring stuff. Victoria had gone into this dinner meeting like a fully charged battery. Now, she felt like she imagined those people in corporate America did after every pointless meeting which could have just as easily been an email. Eventually, they circled back to discussing her talent and the new book. The characters. The plot. The twists. As usual, Donald was impressed with her progress. She could finish the last stretch of the race here, as long as they kept talking about her. Victoria found discussions that centered around herself—especially her talent—the most interesting. It was much easier to pay attention to Donald when they discussed such topics.

Finally, dinner came to a close, and they said goodbye. Victoria departed to where her limo awaited her. She couldn't wait to get home to her cottage. She had so much to do and couldn't stand to waste another minute of her day.

The drive to her cottage took about thirty minutes. Although Victoria called the place a cottage, it didn't actually look like what most people would consider a cottage. Instead, it was a woodsy, mid-century modern-styled home of considerable size. With all the glass windows surrounding the perimeter, the residence itself offered limited privacy, but since it was located in a very secluded, high-end part of town, privacy wasn't an issue. Century-old trees with enormous trunks filled the entirety of the property. The open concept walls of glass that let in an abundance of natural light and lovely wrap-around deck made it feel like she was one with nature. The cottage provided both a place of peace and inspiration. It was a writer's dream.

Once they arrived, the limo driver carefully swung open the door for Victoria, and she stepped out. She dug into her wallet and handed the driver a wad of cash, which included a considerable tip. Victoria had learned that if you paid people well, they did the job well. Her driver knew too many details, such as where she lived, her schedule, and whom she was meeting with. Therefore, the establishment of trust and loyalty with him was critical. Of course, she had her own vehicles, but for work-related outings, she always preferred to use the driver and limo. Driving required energy and focus, and she understood the importance of outsourcing those kinds of tedious tasks so she didn't exhaust herself for the more important activities.

Victoria walked to the front door and punched in the numerical password on the digital keypad. The password was a random string of numbers that had no ties to her personal life whatsoever. Only idiots failed to ensure proper security measures were in place. Victoria would never make the careless mistake of using a password that was as obvious as her birthday or a pet's name. Before walking inside, she checked to make sure no one had messed with her Ring alarm. Nothing like that had ever happened before, but it was a habit of hers to look at it and make sure it still had all the pieces attached and functioned as it should.

Once inside, Victoria hung up her purse and locked the door. As she stood in the hallway, she pulled up her phone to check the Ring app activity. She clicked the history button, which showed nothing new, but she wanted to check the previous week's history. The only other recent activity had been a few days ago, and that was the pet sitter. The pet sitter stopped in three days of the week to take care of her cat and had a different code that allowed her access to the home.

The Ring alarm system helped to ensure that nothing was stolen when Victoria wasn't there. Additionally, Victoria had a full-blown interior surveillance camera system hidden inside every room. The pet sitter had been working for Victoria for a year now and so far had proved to be trustworthy, but as she always did, Victoria would check those cameras later tonight before she went to sleep to make sure.

Victoria proceeded into the kitchen to make a cup of coffee. The caffeine calmed her more than anything and soothed her busy mind. As the coffee brewed, she thought about how she should murder Henry. He hadn't called her yet, and Victoria was becoming impatient.

She held the coffee pot handle and poured herself a cup of black coffee. As she poured the fresh coffee into the mug, a vibration ring tone interrupted the tranquil atmosphere. It was her burner phone. With the cup of fresh coffee in hand, she walked down the hallway and proceeded into the home's entryway to get the device from her purse. When she flipped it open, a message from her cousin, Larry, appeared on the screen that said just two words:

Fixed it

Victoria typed a response back:

There's a grand in the glove box of your truck. Maybe if you didn't have so much shit in there, I could have included more. I'll message again soon. DO NOT CALL. In character mode for book.

Victoria suppressed a laugh as she reread her message. The stuffed to-the-brim glove box had nothing to do with the amount of money she'd left for Larry, but it served as an excellent reminder to him that he was at fault here. Not her. Just when Victoria was about to put the phone back, it rang. Larry's number appeared on the screen, but she immediately hit end call and then turned off the device.

She knew what he wanted to talk about, and she didn't have time to listen to his temper tantrum over the money. He'd get the nine thousand, which was the rest of his payment they'd discussed, after he did the job correctly. *How hard of a concept is that to understand?* she wondered.

Rewards only came to hard workers and achievers. Larry didn't even deserve anything yet. Victoria had kindly given him one thousand dollars cash out of sympathy because she knew he was homeless and had no money whatsoever. Failure had its consequences. Larry would learn a valuable business lesson from this experience. He needed to accept responsibility for his mistakes and fix them.

Now, thanks to Larry, Victoria had extra work on her hands. She'd have to revisit the logistics to ensure this next kidnap attempt was performed flawlessly. It occurred to Victoria that her cousin probably needed a more immediate update due to financial burdens. The money more than likely meant a great deal to him. However, Victoria was running the show here. Not Larry. Victoria wanted to allow some time to pass before she provided Larry with his next tasks. Make him starve a bit. In starvation mode, he'd perform better.

The more Victoria thought about it, the more infuriating it became that Larry hadn't listened to what she went over with him earlier today. She hated repeating herself. Her cousin had better clean out his ears and take some notes next time because Victoria wouldn't repeat herself any more with him. The directions had been clear as one plus one equals two, and she'd already repeated herself more than necessary. If he couldn't pull himself together and figure it out, Victoria would find someone else for the job. The only reason she'd even considered him for the role and still hadn't fired him yet came right down to the fact that, technically, he was family. That was the only reason.

Victoria returned the burner phone to her purse and then walked back down the long hallway to the office room. She needed to work on researching Henry and didn't need any further interruptions tonight. At present, the only things on her mind related to Henry. Everything else could wait.

Once Victoria reached the back end of the hallway, she pushed open the hidden bookshelf door, which concealed the office room. The office space had black glossy walls, which contrasted nicely with the pearly white and gray carpet. The luxury carpet was primarily gray with lighter colored wave-like lines throughout, which gave it a contemporary appearance. Toward the room's left side was a floor-to-ceiling bookcase with soft LED lights and glass floating shelves. Color-coordinated books of various topics lined the shelves. Back when Victoria had hired the professional organizers and interior designers, she had specifically requested color-coordinated shelves and made sure they aligned each book at a ninety-degree angle. Victoria had been adamant about that. It bothered her to see a book tilted in any other way.

Some of the books on these shelves were first editions and extremely valuable. Victoria didn't care much about these particular first-edition books. However, the expensive books reminded her of how priceless her novels' first editions would eventually become.

Across from the bookcase was an original Eames lounge chair. Every so often, Victoria liked to sit in that chair and read other best-selling crime fiction books. Over time, it had become apparent to Victoria that as much as these other authors tried, they couldn't even compare to the caliber of her work. Still, Victoria liked to buy their books and support their author dreams, especially since they most likely would never come close to the sales volume that she received. Every time she cracked open a new novel, she had to remind herself to prepare for the worst and that not everyone had her skillset and innate talent. These other authors were trying their very best. She especially had to remind herself of that when providing publicity quotes for their book covers. Usually, she strung together some long-winded blurb that praised the book in the same way everyone else had but with slightly different words. As of lately, 'irresistible,' 'page-turning,' 'compelling,' and 'cunning' were her go-to adjectives. It didn't matter what Victoria's quote said, as long as it was positive and followed with her name. Readers across the globe recognized Victoria's pen name. That alone would offer a spike in sales for some of these lesser-known authors.

Recessed lights overhead turned on automatically as Victoria made her way toward the desk setup. The high ceiling had been painted white to contrast with the dark walls, all of which further added to the stylized feel of the room. A series of large computer monitors covered Victoria's desktop. The monitors gave her full surveillance of every room. Despite the dark-colored interior walls, the room had a sense of openness thanks to the floor-to-ceiling glass windows behind the desk and monitors.

Victoria clicked the button that opened the shimmery white drapes. During the day, if the sun caused a glare on her computer monitors, which it often did at certain times, she'd close those drapes. At this time of night, the distant trees that spread for miles and miles were cloaked in blackness, but the nearest sky-high trees were still relatively visible upon close inspection. The unknown that lurked out in the darkest hours wasn't anything that Victoria feared, and she preferred to leave the drapes open at night.

Fear wasn't foreign to Victoria. Rather, she was quite familiar with the sense of authority and power that later came with it. The shock and confusion embedded within a wide-eyed expression. The realization that the trust, loyalty, and love that you thought existed inside another being was utterly non-existent. A lie. And then, looking back on the series of events that led to it all, the realization would suddenly make sense. That same look that asked: why? What went wrong? Like everything, fear had a beginning and an end. Followed by regret and wishful thinking and those same thoughts that asked: what if?

Untamed fear was deadly.

* * *

For the next hour, Victoria busied herself with interior surveillance checks. When she was almost finished with the task, the screen on her phone lit up. An unknown number. She answered.

"Hello?"

"Daisy, It's Henry. I hope it's not too late..."

"You caught me at a decent time," Victoria said, realizing now she wouldn't have to kill him.

"Great! So, what are your plans for Friday night?"

Victoria thought about it for a moment. She still had tons of research to do on Henry. Not only that, but she needed to work on her new novel and find a new cheater to punish. But, she supposed her schedule could have some openings on Friday. "I don't know yet. Why?"

"I wanted to see if you'd like to have dinner together. There's a boutique restaurant in downtown Philly. I'd love to take you. We'll have to dress up, of course. They won't let us in the restaurant otherwise. The food's worth it, though, I promise. You're gonna love it."

Evidently, he'd assumed Daisy was poor with a lack of experience in the culture of fine dining. If she hit it off with him, she'd have to figure out how to twist this lie so it didn't look bad. She could always tell him Daisy was her middle name and she preferred to give it out to strangers until she got to know them better. That lie would work. He'd understand. In the meantime, she'd need to let this play out and make sure he was someone worth her time. Until then, she'd keep up with the Daisy act. "That sounds great, Henry. I'll wear my Sunday best."

"Okay, great. What's your address? I'll pick you up at five."

"That won't be necessary. I'll meet you there."

"You sure?"

"Yes. What's the name of the restaurant?"

Henry provided the restaurant name and address, and they confirmed plans before they hung up the phone.

Just when Victoria was about to set that phone down and finally do the research she needed to, her personal phone buzzed. *What now?* she wondered. She'd been entertaining everyone else all day long. When Victoria looked down at the screen, she realized it was her brother calling, so she answered.

"Vic, thank God you picked up."

"Is everything okay?"

"Yeah—it's just the LGBTQ+ Pride Parade and Festival is tomorrow. I hope you're not too busy and can still come. Our outfits are phenomenal this year. A little on the wild side, but I think you're going to love them—they're a surprise. I can't wait for you to see them! What time should me and Ted meet up with you at the cottage? Because I was thinking we could all get ready there and then have your driver drop us off at the parade by eleven. What do you think?"

"Sure. That's fine. Why don't y'all get here at ten?" Victoria suggested. She wasn't looking forward to this parade at all. Parades brought together unsanitary, loud, and disorderly people, all in a single location. The LGBTQ+ community was a fun bunch, so it wouldn't be as bad as other types of parades she'd experienced in the past, but, still, she wasn't looking forward to it. At all.

Nonetheless, this event meant the world to her brother. She'd attended each year with him, and she wouldn't let him down. When it came to pre-made commitments with her family, Victoria did her best to follow through.

"Yay, that sounds great. We can't wait. Love ya, Sis. See you tomorrow!"

After Victoria ended the call with her brother, she finished reviewing the interior surveillance recordings and then attempted preliminary research into Henry. She typed variations of his name into the search bar of Facebook. After multiple revisions to the search filters, she finally found him. His strict privacy settings prevented her from extracting anything of value from his social profile. The only information that he'd made available to the public was his profile picture—a photo of him and a woman. Based on all the eye wrinkles, the woman was either his mom or possibly grandma, Victoria supposed.

Victoria stifled a yawn and checked the time. 10:13 pm. As convenient as it would have been to find out more about Henry tonight, she could wait. From experience, she knew where most men hid their secrets; either on their phones or in their homes. She'd have access to both of those areas of his life soon enough.

I 2

Victoria

Present Day

The following day Victoria's alarm went off at five in the morning. She removed her cat, Princess, from her face and spat out the fluffy hair and then reached to switch off the ringing alarm clock. Next, she grabbed her lint roller and rigorously cleaned the comforter. The hair shedding was the reason why Victoria only kept one indoor pet. Once she was sure every piece of cat hair had been accounted for, she began the rest of her morning routine.

Victoria walked over to the bedroom closet. She had various sets of black tights, V-neck shirts, and black cargo boots. That was what she usually preferred to wear. Deciding what clothes to wear was a time-consuming process and wasted energy, which was why she often wore the same outfit daily. The only time she ever dressed up was for author events, and she did her best to keep the number of those at a minimum. Although Victoria was thankful for her fans, she didn't care for the in-person author events that came with her level of success. Not only that, but those events took up much time. Victoria would rather use any extra time toward punishing serial cheaters.

Toward the back of the closet was where she reserved what she called the character attire. A variety of T-shirts, pants, sweaters, cardigans, and shoes filled the space. Most of them were randomly selected—in her size, of course. Today's character would be casually dressed. Jeans and a nice blouse. Nothing too fancy. That should get the job done.

Once dressed, she walked over to the back section of the closet to where her safe was located. She entered the code, and then pulled it open. Inside were wigs of various shapes and styles. She had yet to wear the short black wig with bangs and so settled on that hair style. After she put the wig on, she applied her makeup. In her everyday routine, Victoria never wore makeup. She was already naturally beautiful and didn't need it. Even for author events, the most she ever would do was a swipe of mascara and lipstick.

At first, Victoria didn't know much about how to apply cosmetics. So, she learned how, and by now, all the YouTube makeup tutorials she'd watched had helped advance her makeup skills exponentially. With the wig, outfits, and makeup on, she was completely unrecognizable.

Victoria grabbed her laptop and purse then made her way toward the six-car garage. Her car options included a Lexus RX, a Bugatti Chiron (her favorite), a BMW 3 Series, and a Toyota Corolla. She settled on the very ordinary and boring Toyota Corolla. She hated the slow and basic vehicle, but it was critical that she didn't attract attention when on the hunt for the next cheater. There wasn't anything special about a Toyota, so it was perfect for ensuring invisibility.

Following a ten-minute drive, Victoria arrived at a coffee shop. Even though she'd never been to this particular place before, she'd picked it specifically because she was sure that the shopping center lacked any kind of video surveillance.

Victoria parked the car, grabbed her laptop and purse, and then strode inside. After she ordered a large black coffee, she took a seat at the table near the front entry that overlooked the small shopping center and parking lot. Across the street was a grocery store and a few fast-food restaurants. Directly to the left was an independent bookstore called Thriller Book Lover. She'd ordered books from them online in the past and hated the pink wrapping paper and boxes. But the service had been slightly better than average, which had been unexpected. Perhaps, she'd give them another try in the future.

Since it was still early, Victoria buried herself in her work: the latest story for her best-selling series. Another book with a serial killer main character. She was already familiar with the characters in this novel, so she didn't need to perform much research. The research took the longest—especially when she included characters much different than herself. The development of likable characters didn't come naturally to Victoria. Fiction had taught her that she didn't behave or think like most people. The crime-fiction genre, however, meant that readers accepted unlikeable characters, which was why Victoria often preferred to write from the antagonist's point of view. She was good at that, and it felt instinctive to her. She wrote what she knew, and that was why her books sold so incredibly well year after year.

A few hours passed, and by then Victoria had completed close to ten pages of writing. She looked up from her laptop and took another sip from her coffee. That was when she spotted him. Her next victim. From the other side of the window panel, she watched as a man parked his red corvette, and walked inside, his phone glued to his ear. He wore a dark blue suit with a crisp, white button-down T-shirt underneath. The shaggy dark brown hair atop his head gave him an unruly appearance, as if he'd just woken up from a deep sleep. Even with the overgrown and slightly wild hairstyle, there was something charming about him.

As he stood in line to place his order, Victoria observed him more closely. On his left wrist, there was a Rolex watch. But he was clearly single or at least pretending to be, because he didn't wear a wedding ring. The way he carried himself evoked status. Statistically speaking, wealthy men were always more likely to cheat, and that likelihood increased considerably with a face like his.

Victoria pretended to work on her laptop as she watched his movements and listened to his conversation at the checkout counter. "Mm, you were right, this latte is delicious. I'm glad you talked me into it," he said to the barista.

"I'm glad you like it!" The cash register clicked opened. "Thank you so much, we'll see you next time, Karl."

"Go get yourselves something special with that tip, now, you hear? You guys are working yourselves way too hard in here." That was a lie; they'd been incredibly slow with Victoria's order.

The baristas chuckled. "Only the best for our favorite customer. Have a great day!" the other barista called.

"Bye, ladies. I'll see you both tomorrow, I hope." A regular. Interesting. Victoria filed the detail away for later.

Victoria imagined this guy, Karl, behaved this way with all women. Hopefully, the baristas here didn't actually think they were something special to him. *This guy is so pathetic*, she thought, as she waited for him to hurry his way out of here. Clearly, he was a slow walker. Any day now. *What is the hold up?* she wondered. Victoria had her laptop and coffee packed up and ready to go. She stared at her phone mindlessly as she waited. The clicking of business shoes against the tile floor told her it was time. Quickly, she stood up. As she'd planned, the man's shoulder bumped into her, causing her coffee to spill down her blouse.

"I'm so sorry—are you okay? Here, let me buy you another coffee," Karl offered.

Victoria's jaw dropped open in pretend shock, but then she laughed it off casually. On another occasion, she would have been pissed over a situation like this, but that kind of reaction would not get her to step two of the plan. She had to stay in character mode—and deliver a solid performance if she wanted to kill him. "You're so kind. That was 100 percent my fault though. I'm so clumsy sometimes."

Like a knight in shining armor, the man went to grab some napkins. He cleaned up the mess on the ground and then said, "Here. I don't know if it will help much. Again, I apologize."

She smiled. "Thank you, I appreciate it. But I can assure you, my shirt is the least of my worries. I have nowhere important to be." With the napkins, she dabbed at the coffee stains, knowing the effort was pointless.

"Well, at least let me buy you another coffee. I insist."

She waved his offer away. "No, no I can't let you do that. This was my fault."

"Okay, well, since you won't let me buy your coffee, I hope you'll let me buy you a new shirt. That bookstore next door has some nice apparel for women—my sister shops there all the time. Come on, I'll show you."

"Aw, you're too kind. Alright, but only because I actually have been wanting to check out that bookstore." Victoria flashed a playful smile at him and then followed him next door.

In the front of the store, all of Victoria's best-selling books were on display. All the bookstores always put her books on front display. That was where the best books belonged. "Do you read?" Karl asked.

"Occasionally," Victoria replied.

Karl pointed to Victoria's books. "Well, if you're looking for something good to read, I can assure you this author's series won't let you down. I highly recommend. I'm probably her biggest fan." He held up the fifth book in her series. "In fact, I lent my copy to a friend, and I've been wanting to reread this one, so I'm going to get it. One for you, and one for me," he said, his charm now on full display as he grabbed two copies of her book.

"You're too generous."

He waved the compliment away. "Like I said, I'm the one who owes you right now. I still feel horrible over this." He gestured at her shirt.

They proceeded to the section of the bookstore that had apparel. "It's honestly not that bad. You know, most guys would have probably just said sorry and walked away instead of taking blame for this. You don't seem like most guys," Victoria remarked. She shuffled through the t-shirts for a size medium.

Karl stood back and watched her admiringly. "You got that right. You know what I realized? We didn't even properly introduce ourselves yet. I'm Karl," he held out his hand with the Rolex watch.

Victoria met his gaze while shaking his hand. "I'm Sammie, it's short for Samantha."

"Beautiful name for a beautiful woman."

"Stop it, you're going to make me blush." Victoria laughed and brushed a strand of fake hair behind her ear. "What do you think of this shirt?" She held up a white t-shirt with the quote, 'A thriller book a day keeps reality away.'

"I love it."

Karl bought the books and shirt, and then they headed outside back to the parking lot.

He took out the copy of the book he purchased for himself and then handed her the bag. "Well, this was so sweet of you. Thank you," she said.

"Of course. So, what are your plans for the rest of the day?" he asked.

"Well, I'm new to the city, actually. I'm temporarily staying with my sister until I find a place. House hunting is all I have planned."

"No kidding. I'm a realtor. Are you working with an agent already?"

"No, not yet. I've just been looking at homes on Zillow."

"Well, let me give you my card in case you need someone to show you around town." They walked to where Karl's red corvette was parked.

"Wow, your car is amazing!" Victoria gushed, although she didn't really mean it. In a race, her Bugatti would blow this car away.

"Thanks, I'm glad you like it," he said as he opened the door and reached inside the center console.

"Here," he said, handing her his shiny business card. "I don't usually take on new clients, due to the demand I have with my existing clientele. But if you need someone to show you around, I'd be happy to. I know this area like the back of my hand. Born and raised here."

"Oh gosh, that would be fantastic. I still need to get pre-approved with a lender, though, which may take me a while."

"I tell you what, if you're willing to agree to dinner with me afterwards, I'll take you to some showings without the pre-approval. What do you say?"

"Wow, I'd love that!" Victoria beamed. She gave Karl a phone number from another stolen device she had before they said their goodbyes.

A renewed sense of energy swept through her. Naturally, she'd love to fast-forward the tedious, more boring steps involved, but she'd learned to enjoy the process. It only made the punishment and murder even more fulfilling in the end.

* * *

When Victoria arrived back to her house, an hour remained before her brother and Ted would arrive. Plenty of time to sharpen her kitchen knives, she thought. A sharp knife not only performed better when slicing food, but it also made cooking safer. Injuries in the kitchen could easily be avoided with regular knife maintenance. Plus, a dull knife was a huge pet peeve of Victoria's, so she regularly took the time to ensure her kitchen utensils were functioning as they should.

She only used a knife set at her cottage. This place was like her private sanctuary, meaning she didn't want a maid cutting into her alone time. When she was here, she cooked and cleaned herself, just like ordinary Americans. In a way, the chores kept her humble and reminded her how far she'd come in life. All it took to get from rags to riches was hard work. Her life was quite an inspiration, and she knew many people, especially those who dreamed of becoming successful writers one day, looked up to her because of it.

Victoria continued gliding her knives firmly against the sharpening stone until there was a loud knock at her front door. Carefully, she set her knives aside and then went to answer it. Ted and Jeff walked inside wearing their colorful costume-like attire.

"So, what do you think?" Jeff did a twirl.

"Very nice. Where'd you get that outfit?" Victoria inquired.

"Ted made it for me."

Victoria raised her eyebrows. "That must have taken a while."

"I'd do it all again a thousand times. He looks amazing," Ted gloated.

"Ted made something for you to wear, too. Here," Jeff said, handing her a bag with what looked to be an outfit that was just as colorful as what her brother had on.

"You really shouldn't have," Victoria replied, and she meant it. "This is so sweet, thank you, Ted." She leaned in to give her brother's fiancé a hug because she knew that was the normal social gesture to perform after receiving a thoughtful gift.

"Well, go try it on!" Jeff ushered her into the guest bathroom to change into it.

13

Victoria

Present Day

The parade was exactly how Victoria remembered from the years prior. She felt like that little leprechaun guy from the Lucky Charms cereal box. Rainbow flags. Rainbow outfits. Some people even had on rainbow makeup. It was as if she'd been immersed into some alternate rainbow-filled universe.

By now everyone, except Victoria, had had too much to drink. The cheers and rants had become even louder, and Victoria struggled to even hear, much less concentrate, as her brother talked to her about his upcoming wedding.

"Vic, what do you think of these? For bridesmaids dresses." Jeff showed her a photo on his phone of a red, sparkly dress.

She hated it, but said, "Pretty."

"Mom showed them to me. I'm not set on these yet. The color, yes. But I want to look around more, you know."

"That makes sense," she replied in what would usually be a shout. However, it was the only pitch her brother would be able to hear over the commotion from the crowd.

Victoria bent down and itched her thigh. The rainbow stockings that Ted made for her had been such a thoughtful gift, but they were also so uncomfortable and itchy. She couldn't wait for this parade to finish up. Between Karl, Henry, and the punishment she had planned for her dad, her schedule was jammed packed. Thankfully, the parade would more than likely finish up sooner than later.

The parade this year had also turned into a kind of civil rights event. Several attendees held posters that said, "Protect LGBTQ+ Stop the murders." Although Victoria wasn't for certain, she had the inclination these posters had been made in response to the person whom the media had named the Homophobic Killer.

Initially, Victoria hadn't realized how famous the Homophobic Killer would become. She'd only done what she believed would throw the police force and detectives off her tracks. It was the only way she could keep doing what she needed to accomplish. Without her work, cheaters would continue to cause great pain; she'd keep doing whatever was necessary to stop them.

As the parade carried on, Victoria remembered she needed to inform Larry of his next task. She pulled the burner phone out of her pocket and sent him a quick message.

"That looks like an old phone—wait, is that a burner phone?" Ted asked.

Jeff looked over to the phone in her hands. "Why do you have a burner phone, Vic?"

Thanks, Ted, she thought sarcastically. "It's for my book. Research. One of my characters uses one. They say write what you know, and it's the only way for me to get a better idea of how my character would use one of these things."

They both fell for the lie and then resumed watching the parade festivities. Victoria placed the burner phone back in her purse.

As soon as Victoria noticed some other parade attendees leave, she turned to Jeff, "Should we head out, so we beat traffic? I'll call for the driver." The statement was more of an update about their plans than a question.

"Already, Vic? It's not over yet," Jeff complained.

"Your sister's right, Jeff. We'll be here all day stuck in traffic if we don't leave now," Ted said.

Following Ted's input, Jeff agreed that it was the best decision to leave, so they scurried through the rainbow-colored crowd back to the parking spots. On the way back, Victoria spotted a deserted gay pride flag. "Hold on," she told Jeff and Ted. She put on gloves and pulled out a Ziploc bag from her purse.

"What are you doing?" Ted looked perplexed.

When Victoria didn't respond, Jeff answered the question. "Vic's a little OCD. Hence, the gloves and Ziploc bag," Jeff said to Ted.

Victoria closed up the bag and then put it in her purse before she turned around. Ted and Jeff stood there as they held hands, looking a bit baffled.

"It's disrespectful to leave a gay pride flag on the ground. At least, to me, I find that incredibly disrespectful. Since the previous owner abandoned it, I'm going to give it a good home. Maybe I'll hang it up in the cottage guest room—after I wash it, of course," Victoria said. "We can make the guest room more colorful—if you'd like, Jeff. I consider that your room, so if it needs more color, you just let me know, and I'll make it happen. I thought the flag would be a nice addition in there. At least, for now, until I'm able to get an interior designer over to spice it up how you like."

Jeff wiped away a few tears, fanned his face, and said, "The guest room will look so beautiful with that flag and more color. Sorry, just give me a second guys. I'm feeling a little emotional today. Vic made such a good point—that flag would have just blown away, or probably been thrown in the trash or something by some asshole. Like, we were just going to walk by and leave the flag there without doing anything. That's what we would have done if Vic wasn't here. And that breaks my heart."

Victoria walked over to her brother and gave him a big hug. "I didn't mean to make you cry, buddy."

"I love you, Vic," Jeff said. He squeezed her tight for what felt like a long time before he released his grip. "Vic's a big advocate for gay rights," Jeff informed his fiancé. "Last summer, for Gay Pride Month, she donated one hundred percent of all her book sales to LGBTQ+ charities."

They all continued with the walk back to the parking lots. While they paced along the sidewalks, Victoria checked her personal phone; the limo driver sent her a text with his exact coordinates. "This way," Victoria directed. Ted and Jeff followed. "Stay close," Victoria called back as she gently held onto her brother's arm to ensure they all stayed together in the sea of colorful people. Not only that, but Jeff and Ted were slow walkers, so it was critical that Victoria set the pace if they wanted to get out of here without the holdup from traffic.

As they walked the rest of the way to the vehicle, Ted and Jeff conversed more about Victoria's contributions to the gay community, which was, in fact, very accurate. Victoria was a significant financial contributor, and she loved to support organizations that meant a great deal to her brother. She'd do anything for her family, especially her brother. From a young age, Victoria had done everything possible to protect him, and she didn't ever plan to stop.

14

Larry

On the what appeared to be a 1980s television set, Larry watched and listened again as the same pharmaceutical company discussed the benefits of this new drug for erectile dysfunction. Before the commercial could get to the part about all the adverse effects, he thought to turn off the TV already, but then looked around the motel, realizing there wasn't much else to do, so he left it on.

The motel room had green carpet with some weird dingy curtains that looked like they belonged at a grandmother's house or a funeral home. The old, worn-out bed was the worst part about the place. It creaked and wobbled whenever he tried to adjust his position, which was mostly a useless activity, considering the mattress was the lowest possible quality. As Larry pulled up the covers closer to his bare chest, he noticed what looked like a booger. Upon closer inspection, he realized it was a bed bug. He shot out of his bed and shook himself off. This place sucked.

If Victoria had paid him more than a grand, he wouldn't be in this predicament. Larry sighed loudly and checked his regular phone. A message from that unknown number was displayed on the screen:

You have until next week to get me more money. You know the consequences if you don't.

Larry swallowed and shoved the phone back in the front pocket of his jeans. The man he owed money to was a dangerous dude.

Behind Larry on the side table was his burner phone. He reached for it. The screen was empty. He sighed loudly and threw the stupid phone across the room, which was right when it finally buzzed. He ran over to where it landed and grabbed it in the same way a person stranded at sea would clasp onto a torpedo buoy. It was a message from Victoria:

Please go to the right address today and figure out a plan for how you're going to get inside. Don't forget to wear the disguise.

Larry rejoiced. Finally, things were back in action. He had no clue as to why Victoria had this convoluted plan to kidnap her dad. Although Victoria never talked about it, he knew her biological dad had abandoned her family at a young age, and clearly she still had some resentment over it. Larry figured she'd tried every other way to get in touch with the guy, and this was her last resort.

Regardless of the extreme measures she was resorting to, Larry didn't care. In fact, it wasn't even that big of a deal. Mic was Victoria's father. In the grand scheme of it all, this wasn't actually kidnapping. Instead, he was helping Victoria reconnect with her dad, shorten that gap between them a bit. That was all. This method was the only way for Larry to get the money he needed in such a short timeframe. Larry was an ex-prisoner. He didn't have an eight hundred credit score or a track record of success, and he desperately needed that money to pay off his gambling debts and get on with his life. Finish the job, get the money, and move on. That was all the mattered.

15

Larry

Present Day

Larry drove in his truck toward the correct address this time. The vehicle rumbled as if it might break down any second. It had been a while since his last oil change. He couldn't even remember when he'd brought it in for that. The car's inspection sticker had a date from four years ago, so it was likely around then. Back when he'd gone to jail, no one had driven his car. He'd left it at his parents' in the driveway. They only had a two-car garage, so his truck had weathered the rain, snow, wind, sun, animals, tornadoes, and whatever else came its way. The once pristine leather seats had cracked long ago. The seats were like calloused feet, rough enough to scratch your skin if you didn't sit on them just right.

When he'd finally gotten out of jail, he started the truck up again, and after a jump start to get the engine rolling, the car, at first, seemed good as new. Then, dirt and leaves had spat out in his face from the air vents before those gave out. He was no mechanic and figured this was, unfortunately, what happened without the regular upkeep. The worst part though had been the smell. The car had a dead animal smell to it, which hadn't changed to this day. His mom had even let him borrow one of those car air freshener things, which hadn't done the job, but it didn't matter much. He'd gotten used to that rotten smell by now. For now, the wheels still turned. Whenever the truck gave out, if he couldn't fix it cheaply himself, he'd bring it by that local auto repair shop again.

Larry clicked on the right blinker, which surprisingly still worked fine, and took the final turn into the neighborhood. This was the same place he'd gone to last time. Victoria's messy handwriting created some confusion, and he still didn't see how that had been his fault. Victoria should have written those numbers so there could be no ambiguity. However, like always, he was the one who messed up. Again. Everyone always pointed the finger at him. He was used to it.

Like last time, Larry parked his rusty ole truck in the neighborhood park. As he got out, sweat trickled down into every crevice of his body. From a short distance ahead, he heard the sound of a mother call her young daughter over, saying something about how it was time to head home. The kid clearly didn't have the same agenda as the mother, and she threw a fit over it.

Wearing the disguise Victoria had given him, Larry gave a friendly smile, trying to pretend like he was harmless. A friendly lad. Unfortunately, it was the truck that often gave off the wrong impression. His was the kind of truck a kidnapper drove, which in a way made sense. That was exactly what he'd been using it for lately. However, Larry knew he wasn't a creep. His car maybe made him look like that, but deep down, he knew he had a big heart. He was a good guy. He wouldn't even hurt a fly, that was what his mom often said about him—all those times she'd bailed him out of trouble.

He put some headphones in his ears, turned on that one song that came free with the phone—he couldn't afford cellular data or music subscription services—and began a walk-jog toward the correct address where Victoria's father lived. In addition to the headphones, he wore a red headband, a pair of basketball shorts, a workout tank, and knee-high socks with a pair of sneakers. Victoria had said to blend in, so he was doing his best to do that now as he jogged through the affluent neighborhood as if he lived around here. Naturally, Larry had a lanky body type. He probably looked just like the typical long-distance runner that pounded the pavements around these parts.

After about the distance from one house to the next—the front yards were bigger than most—he slowed down his jog to a walk. His heart was in overdrive. Out of shape. Fitness had never been Larry's thing. Instead, his hobbies included weed and eating bags of Fritos in front of a television set. Most people wanted a big house, with a clean-cut yard, and a big, loving family. If Larry could just pay off his debts, finally upgrade to that big screen television, and afford his regular supply of weed and junk foods, that would be the life. Once he had the money, he could do all that and more. He had other goals, too, obviously. A curvy, thick woman with an average-looking face to cook him a home-made meal every now and then. The woman would be the cherry on top of his delicious sundae.

He was a man of few wants, and he wasn't picky when it came to women. In the past, he'd woken up to his fair share of what most would classify as monstrous faces. Many of the women at the bars he'd frequented were—on the one to ten scale—between a one and four, but then once that makeup came off the next day, they'd be at about a solid one or lower. Completely unrecognizable. He was used to that. But looks didn't matter much to Larry anyway. He had a mirror. It would be completely hypocritical for a guy like him to think he could score a ten at the bar. He wasn't in any way upset about it either. From his experience, pretty women were often snobby and high-maintenance. He'd take ugly and nice over a beautiful snob any day of the week. In fact, he preferred them uglier. They stuck around longer that way.

Finally, after about a mile of walking and jogging, mostly walking though, Larry reached Mic Henderson's home. Based on what little Larry knew about Victoria's dad, it appeared as if he lived a very comfortable life. Hefty mortgages and strict HOAs were the hallmarks of this high-end part of town. Highland Park. That was the name of this area. At least, that was what he thought the neighborhood sign had said. He didn't even want to think about the sizes of the TVs people around here had. It would probably sicken him to the core. Larry didn't even own a television anymore. He'd sold just about every last item to his name. All in an effort to pay off those damn, past-due gambling debts. At one point, he'd considered asking Victoria for a loan. With her family, Victoria always helped out. She paid every bill that came their way. *Those lucky bastards.* He often thought that. Jokingly, of course. His Aunt Cindy and cousin, Jeff, had it made though. How come he didn't get a sister like Victoria? That would have been nice. If he didn't have to work again for the rest of his life, he'd take that deal.

Although he had an inclination Victoria would possibly lend him the money—they were family—it was also highly possible there'd be some strings attached with it. Larry had enough people on his back. He just wanted to finish up this here task, get the money, and take it easy for a bit. Lay low.

Larry pretended to do some stretches in front of Mic Henderson's house as he double-checked the address. The numbers on the mailbox read 3459 and the street said Dickerman Drive. This was definitely the correct address. From where he did his stretches on the sidewalk, it wasn't clear if anyone was home. The garage door was shut. From his view of the exterior windows, he could tell that all the lights had been turned off. However, it was a bright and sunny day, so it was possible that Mic didn't have a need to switch the lights on with all the natural light available.

From the distance, Larry watched as a UPS delivery truck pulled up. Larry continued with his stretches. *Don't look suspicious*, he reminded himself. The delivery man held a box and walked right over to Larry.

"Here you go," the delivery man said, holding the package out for Larry to grab. "I just need your signature. On that line there." He pointed to a line on the piece of paper, which was attached to a clipboard. Then, he handed Larry a pen.

Larry took the pen and signed for the package. "Thank you," he said, giving the guy a friendly nod. Then, Larry walked over to Mic's front patio and set the package down on top of the welcome mat. As he did so, he looked around. Upon closer inspection, Larry noted what looked like one of those fancy security systems. He was sure Victoria had a similar type of set up at her place. If Mic had an alarm system, then Larry wouldn't be able to break in undetected.

Larry sent Victoria a quick text to inform her of what he found out. In the meantime, he continued with his walk jog around the neighborhood. He'd give it at least another thirty minutes to see if Victoria responded to his message before he finished up with this assignment.

Ten minutes into Larry's walk, his burner phone vibrated in the front pocket of his basketball shorts. It was a message from Victoria:

That's fine. I'll get you a new disguise. Give me some time to figure out where we go from here. Leave now. If you're out of money, you can stay at my house for a bit in the downstairs guest room. Will text again soon with more plans.

16

Larry

As Victoria had suggested, Larry drove to her mansion. He was glad that Victoria was letting him stay there, because that guy he owed money would never find him at a place like his cousin's. In the past, Victoria had allowed him to stay at her house. Well, Aunt Cindy had first proposed the idea, and then Victoria had agreed to it. His aunt knew that Larry's parents didn't let him in their house anymore. Of course, the alcohol, drugs, jail, and gambling addiction all played a part in why his parents didn't want him around. They'd given him enough chances to change. Although Larry had already made some changes to his lifestyle—he hadn't smoked in over a week—he still wanted to make more progress and have some kind of success to show his parents the next time he showed up on their doorstep. Larry wasn't all that ambitious. Unlike Victoria, he didn't have big goals. The simple life was what Larry savored. Still, he wanted to stay out of jail and maybe cut back on the weed. He planned to start small first and see how it went.

When Larry arrived at Victoria's mansion, his Aunt Cindy ushered him inside. She wore pajamas and slippers. His aunt didn't look how most aunts looked. She looked just as young and beautiful as Victoria, which Larry supposed was due to those expensive surgeries she'd had done.

Larry followed his Aunt Cindy into the movie room. "You want some popcorn?" she asked.

"Sure," he said as he took a seat. The room was cool and dark, but he grabbed a throw blanket, leaned back, and then settled into the soft chair.

His Aunt Cindy came back with a big bowl of popcorn for him and a large water bottle. The movie theatre room had a mini bar station, where Cindy quickly poured herself a glass of wine.

"They just released the new season; I'm so excited!" His Aunt Cindy pressed play. The introductory credits began to roll. "Hold on, we're almost to my favorite part—look, look. There it is!" His Aunt Cindy pointed to the ginormous screen. On the screen it said:

Based on the best-selling book series by Victoria Henderson

Larry smiled. He sometimes wished he'd achieved something that made his parents jump for joy like that. Despite the wishful thinking, he didn't have any resentment toward Victoria. She deserved all the success she'd earned and more.

17

Rex Mason

Present Day

After a long day of work, Rex was exhausted and worn out. He suddenly regretted making the extra stop at the local pharmacy that evening. The line had been long, but at least he now had the prescription refills for the medicines his mother needed.

Rex left the pharmacy and turned onto the main road to begin the drive over to his mother's place. As he drove, he thought about how much he disliked working for Victoria Henderson and her family. Over the years, he'd blamed and disliked her more and more. Rex wasn't sure if he could ever forgive her for how she'd destroyed his family. However, before he could even begin to think about all that, he needed to find the proof of what she'd done all those years ago. As he'd planned since his first day of employment with her, he'd find the evidence he needed to confront her. No one could stop him from finding the evidence of the truth. Not even her.

In his rusty 1973 Chevrolet truck, he made the last turn onto the gravel road that led to his family's mobile home. He lived within a reasonable distance from Victoria's mansion, only about a twenty-minute drive. Such a short distance separated people like him from wealthy folks like her.

After Rex parked his vehicle, he grabbed the bag with his mother's prescriptions. The rusted old truck door squeaked when he opened it. Dust and dirt kicked up beneath his worn boots as he walked along the small gravel path that led to his mom's mobile home.

From the exterior, the mobile home looked like the rest of the mobile homes in this trailer park. Rectangular, white-paneled, and fitted with a couple of small windows, but the inside couldn't even compare to how other penurious people lived. Poor folks, like him, always had more hardships to overcome, but even though his family was on the lower end of the income bracket, he knew that poor didn't have to mean filthy. In fact, a small home should be simpler to maintain—especially compared to mansions like Victoria's.

He took the wooden steps up to the front entrance and pushed the door hard to get inside. Sky-high piles of unopened mail, cardboard boxes, dirty laundry, broken lamps, rat shit, old food, broken electronics, and a lot of other garbage greeted him. The piles seemed to grow more and more each time he stopped by her place. A smell like a moldy sewer permeated the air. Even though he frequently visited his mother's home, his nostrils still stung every time he went inside. His mother's hoarding had started twelve years ago, shortly after his brother, Drew, died tragically. Despite Rex's efforts to help her clean up, the hoarding had only gotten much worse as the years passed.

Rex navigated through the cluttered and unkempt space to his mom's bedroom. As he walked toward her room, he heard voices of past memories. It was her favorite video tape to watch—the one of him and his brother playing outside in the backyard when Drew had been just seven years old. At that time, he would have been four. He didn't have many memories from his childhood, but he remembered that particular day very well because it was his mom's fondest memory. She watched this video tape all the time.

He shifted some heavy boxes filled with old books out of the way so he could clear the entrance to get inside his mom's bedroom. When he finally made his way in, he observed his mom, laying on a stacked-up pile of clothes—her usual spot—which she used as her bed. The bed was somewhere beneath the sea of laundry. When he flipped on the bedroom lights, roaches scurried across the room. His mom paused the video recording, looked up from the television, and greeted him with red-rimmed, teary eyes. "How was work, son?" Her thin, gray hair looked as if it hadn't been washed in years. The baggy white t-shirt she wore had huge holes, and a cluster of stains. Roles of blubber seeped out, entirely unconstrained by the threadbare garment.

"Good. Here. I was able to swing by after work to pick this up," he said, handing his mom her bag of prescription pills.

"The pharmacy was still open this late?"

"Yep."

"Thank you, Rex. Can you hand me my purse? I should have a little bit of cash left in there. Food stamps, too, if you need more for when you do the groceries. It's right there," she said, pointing. The purse was buried like a treasure chest in another stack of dirty clothes.

"Don't worry about it, Ma," he said. Rex knew she didn't have much money in that purse. His mom used to work at the local grocery store, but after Drew died, the depression had settled in, and she stopped the job and just about everything else. Without his help, his mom would have already died a long time ago. Rex sometimes wondered if the way he cared for his mom only made her suffer more. Perhaps she'd be better off dead.

After he visited with his mom for a bit, Rex got in his truck and drove to the local bar. He had plenty of time to kill before his girlfriend, Lacey Nicholls, finished her shift at the hospital.

The bar, Billy Joe's, was the highlight of the small town where Rex lived. Billy Joel's had a huge area dedicated solely to two-stepping to the best country tunes, and people drove from all over the Dallas-Fort Worth metroplex to enjoy the live concerts and dancing.

On this particular week-day evening, the bar wasn't nearly as crowded as it was on the weekends. Once inside, Rex made his way toward the big neon blue *Bud Light Here We Go* sign where a tall, long-haired brunette woman in a tank top and cut-off jean shorts stood behind the counter, ready to serve him a beer.

Rex paid for the beer and then walked toward an empty table overlooking the dance floor. He pulled back the leather stool and took a seat. Directly in front of him, a serious two-stepping couple was showing off their skills. The man lifted the woman in the air, her sparkly cowgirl boots flickering in the bright neon lights. From there, the man guided the woman down as she performed a split in her tight jeans, before pulling her back up into a standing position and into a series of twirls. Eventually, the advanced level two-steppers proceeded further down the dance floor and out of view.

As Rex sat on the stool, he allowed his entire body to relax. His job was strenuous, and with all the heavy lifting, he often felt sore at the end of the day.

After Rex drank a few beers, the soreness he had felt earlier lessened. He was relaxed, listening to the greatest country tunes and watching the beautiful women two-step on the dance floor. Dark skin, light skin, big or small, it didn't matter; Rex found all women beautiful. He believed women were the most divine creation. Still, he'd only ever admire them from a distance; his girlfriend Lacey was the woman he loved more than anything.

Many men preferred strip clubs when they wanted to look at women. In the past, Rex had been to his fair share of those. But as Rex became older, and once he became a more regular church-goer, he stopped going to those kinds of places. Even though Rex knew that he wasn't perfect, he did his best to treat people how he wanted to be treated. The church taught him to view women as sacred, not objects. He constantly tried to sacrifice his needs to meet Lacey's. Although Rex tried, he didn't live by the Bible religiously. Rex and Lacey had pre-marital sex. Not only that, but Rex still hoarded hate in his heart toward Victoria. He sought the truth, and, at times, revenge. As much as Rex wanted to forgive and move on, he wasn't ready for that yet.

"Rex Mason, is that you?" a familiar voice called.

Rex turned around. His brother's old buddy, Nick, from high school gave him a friendly squeeze on the shoulder before taking a seat on the stool beside him. "Well, I'll be damned. It's been a while. What have you been up to, man?"

"It sure has. How have you been?"

"Working, you know how it is."

Rex took a swig from his beer and nodded his head in agreement. "Sure do. Where you working at these days?" he asked as his eyes spotted two attractive blondes swirling around on the dance floor, clearly drunk.

His friend Nick nudged him on the shoulder. "I'd love to get those two in a room together, if you know what I mean."

"Yeah, they're cute."

Nick moved the stool in closer proximity to Rex. "So, this guy I went to college with—he was my roommate freshmen year—me and his dad really hit it off one day I went over there. He got me hooked up with this incredible job, man."

"That's great, dude. Happy for you."

"Dude, listen to this, I basically sit on my ass all day, do a few sales calls, and bam—ten grand every month. That's the base."

"Sounds like you got yourself a nice setup."

"It's technology sales. You should really get into this field, man. The moment you finish that degree, you call me and I'll hook you up. You'd love it— I'm sure Lacey would love it, too. Shoot, she probably wouldn't even have to work anymore. You come home after a long day, she'll have dinner ready, the house cleaned. You'd be living the dream."

Rex stayed silent and stared in the direction of the dance floor. Colorful neon lights shone like a spotlight on all the dancers. Boisterous laughs and joyful conversations took place all around him. Everyone was living their best lives.

"What—don't tell me y'all broke up?"

"We're still together." Rex looked down at his watch. "Listen, man, it was great seeing you, but I gotta go. It's been a long day, and I'm wiped. You have yourself a good night. Tell Jen and the kids I said hi."

"Alright—well, listen, if you need anything, let me know. I know it's been a while, but I'm here if you need anything. Money, food, a place to stay," Nick paused for a moment, clearly thinking about what he planned to say next. "You know I'd had done anything for Drew back then. He was my boy. God, I hate to even think about it. It was so tough. I had to get out of this town for a bit. You understand. But Drew was a brother to me, and so are you. You need me, I'm there."

"Thanks, man. That means a lot."

"I mean it. We got a place not too far from your mom's place. Join us for dinner soon—Jen and the kids would be thrilled to see you."

"I'll think about it." Rex navigated through the crowds of drunk people and made his way outside to where he'd parked his truck. He was sick of the sympathy and bumping into the same old people who only wanted to have the same old conversations.

He wouldn't be going to no dinner. The only reason people invited him places anymore was because they felt sorry for him. He was sick and tired of being everyone's charity case. Soon, he'd finish up what he needed to do here, and him and Lacey would be out of this town for good.

18

Rex

Present Day

Following Billy Joe's, Rex took a short drive to clear his head before he finally arrived back at his girlfriend's house. The small home didn't look like much. It was a two-bedroom, one-bath that had a green roof and tan siding. Lacey liked to remind Rex that the inherited home was a good starting point for them, but one day, they'd save up to buy a home where they could raise a family. Lacey had a motherly nature about her; she'd make a wonderful mother and wife one day.

Rex parked his truck in the driveway and walked toward the front entry. The dim front porch lights had attracted a swarm of moths. As Rex pulled open the screen door, he remembered how he still needed to install more exterior lights on the property. Although they didn't live in a high crime area or have much for criminals to steal, Lacey's safety was of utmost importance to him. He made a mental note to swing by Home Depot sometime this week.

Once inside, Rex kicked off his boots and walked toward the kitchen. Lacey had her back to him and stood by the sink as she vigorously scrubbed a pan.

"Dinner's in the fridge," Lacey said. She didn't turn around to hug him like she usually did when he came home.

"You want me to heat you up a plate?" Rex asked as he pulled open the refrigerator.

"I already ate."

Rex plated the leftovers, unsure what to say next.

Lacey switched off the water faucet, and then turned around to face him. "It's not enough for you, is it?" Tears slowly filled her big beautiful brown eyes.

"What are you talking about, baby?" Rex set the plastic container filled with leftovers down and walked over to his girlfriend. He tried to hug her, but she pushed him away.

"You know what I'm talking about, Rex. Don't play dumb with me. You're in love with her, aren't you?"

Rex was taken by surprise. "I'm in love with you."

"Then why are you so obsessed with her. Is that what you want? Those fancy dinners and big houses. You want to wear a suit and have a maid cater to your every last need." Lacey wiped away tears. "What—she offer to buy you one of them fancy fishing boats or somethin'? Has it always been about the money? I don't understand, Rex. I work nine to five every day, been saving up. For us. I want to buy you that big boat you've always dreamed. Get us a nicer home, too. I get this shack ain't much, but it's better than most. I'm doing my best, Rex. It's not enough, is it?"

"You do more than I could ever dream of. Stop this, Lacey. Stop. Come on, now. What's this about?"

"You know what it's about."

"I don't."

"You're obsessed with her."

"Who?" Rex asked.

Lacey gave him a questionable look.

"Who?" Rex repeated.

"Victoria."

This made no sense. "Victoria? Victoria Henderson?"

"Yes, there ain't any other Victoria in this God-forsaken town."

"She's my employer."

"Your search history, Rex. I saw it." Instantly, Rex regretted all the times he'd searched for information about Victoria on Lacey's desktop computer.

He shook his head from left to right. "No. It's not like that."

"Tell me, what's it like then? 'Cause last I checked you get off at three." She turned to look at the digital clock on the oven. The time was slowly approaching eleven thirty at night. "Mr. Jones let me finish up my workday early today. Been waiting for you all afternoon. Thought we could go down to the pond. Go fishing. I got all the rods all ready and everything." Lacey paused for a moment to wipe away more tears. "I may not be rich, but I sure as hell ain't stupid—I'm going to bed. You can sleep on the couch." She threw the kitchen towel on the counter and walked out of the room.

Rex had no idea how to explain himself.

After he ate dinner alone, Rex went into their small living room and took a seat on the couch. He reached for the stack of paperwork on the end table next to where he sat. He'd printed out information pamphlets for the local community college. Unlike most of his peers, Rex never went to college. He barely finished high school. Although he now made a decent income as a handyman for Victoria, it was all very temporary until he found the evidence that she'd killed his brother. That night Drew had been murdered, his brother told him something that should have led the detectives straight to the killer. But no one had listened to him back then.

Even though that case went cold a long time ago, Rex hadn't stopped the search for the truth. He'd work for Victoria for the rest of his life if he had to. The tragic memory reminded him of what that detective told him: 'That sweet young girl had nothing to do with this—giving false statements like that about someone can ruin their life. You better stop with the lies, boy.' Back then, he hadn't made up anything. He'd only spoken the truth—Victoria knew more than what she'd shared.

The only reason he'd listened and let it go was because he'd realized the cards he'd been dealt. A privileged white man like himself shouldn't suggest a nice young lady like Victoria could do anything sinister. Rex never liked to think he was better than anyone else, because he wasn't. He'd always viewed himself at the very bottom of the pecking order. Last place. He realized he had privilege based on the color of skin, and he always did his best to recognize, and be aware of that. However, Rex didn't understand why he'd been told that male privilege existed. He hadn't ever received any special treatment for being a guy. In fact, from his experience, he was treated worse because of it. Unlike Victoria, he never had a sweet and innocent face. He looked like the type of guy that could keep a straight poker face while making up an endless string of lies.

Back then, the detectives faced a challenge. They had to determine who'd told the truth and who didn't. It was between him and Victoria. And they didn't even have to think much about it either. They took one look at him and one look at her, and they'd made up their minds. Most of the time, that probably had worked for them. Most of the time, men like him were the guilty, lying ones. But not this time.

As much as he didn't want to, Rex would work for Victoria until he had what he needed to prove that she'd killed his brother. Until then, he'd have to figure out what to tell Lacey. It seemed like everyone else in this small town thought he was a deceitful man, but he couldn't let the one woman who loved him unconditionally come to those conclusions about him. Because he wasn't a liar. He just had to figure out the truth.

Part 2

19

Victoria

August 13, 2007

Victoria stormed into her mother's bedroom. "Are you ready?" she asked as she watched her mom stroke black mascara onto her eyes.

"Almost," her mom replied, still looking in the bathroom mirror.

"I'm going to be late for my first day of school."

"No you're not. We have plenty of time. You're not the only one with a big day. I start a new job today, you know. Have you checked to make sure your brother's ready?"

Victoria sighed. "Yes. He's in the living room watching a show. We're just waiting on you." She hated being late. Tardiness always made a scene, and she didn't want to give her teachers the wrong impression.

After another minute passed, Cindy placed the mascara wand back into the tube and then turned to face her daughter. "How does my makeup look?"

"Good. Can we go now?"

Her mom stroked red lipstick across her lips. "Go get the keys and start the car. I'll be right there."

* * *

After a long morning of classes, it was finally lunchtime. Victoria walked to the cafeteria holding her brown paper lunch bag. She hoped to find the basketball girls so she wouldn't have to sit by herself.

The boisterous noise of high school students filled the air. Victoria glanced around the lunchroom to see if she could find anyone from the team. She'd met some of the girls already at the pre-season practices but had completely forgot to ask them what period they had lunch. It hadn't crossed her mind that she'd need someone to sit with until today.

A stocky girl with short brown hair, glasses, and freckles approached her. She held her lunch tray close to her body. "I noticed you were looking around for someone to sit with. You're in my English class—um, you asked to borrow a pen from me. Do you maybe want to sit together? I'm Rebecca, by the way," she said in a soft voice, fumbling nervously over her words.

Victoria studied her for a moment before responding. This girl was clearly a nerd, and Victoria did not want to be associated with the unpopular crowd. However, it looked like it was either Rebecca or eating lunch alone. She figured it'd look better if she at least had someone to sit with during lunch. "Sure. Where do you want to sit?"

"You want to go outside on the benches? It's kind of loud in here."

Victoria let her new friend lead the way. The moment they stepped outside, beads of sweat began to form on Victoria's forehead. Once they found an open space, Victoria placed her cardigan down on the bench before sitting down so that the hot metal didn't burn the back of her legs.

"So, how do you like it here so far?" her new friend asked as she poked into her Caesar salad.

"It's alright. I mainly just came here to play basketball."

Rebecca looked up at her in shock. "You play sports? That's awesome. I wish I was athletic."

Victoria didn't know what to say to that, so she just continued to eat her turkey and cheese sandwich. From the corner of her eye, she noticed a tall, attractive, and athletic-looking guy walking past them. His springy stride exhibited poise and ambition. This was the type of guy who was going places. In that same moment, time seemed to wane as his mystical eyes met hers. He smiled at her with the kind of smile that could make even the most pessimistic person want to smile right back. Smiles like his were regularly used.

"Oh my gosh, you know Drew?" Rebecca whispered.

"Who?"

"Drew," she replied, discreetly pointing at his back as he walked through the set of double doors which led back into the school.

"I don't know him; I don't know anyone. It's my first day." Victoria laughed.

"Well, he's the quarterback of the football team. Basically the most popular guy in the entire junior class—I think he likes you. He was smiling at you!"

"Really?"

"Um, yeah. He doesn't smile at me like that. I don't even think he knows my name and we went to the same middle school; he lives on the same street as me, too."

"That's cool." Victoria made a mental note to plan a study session at Rebecca's house soon.

Since her new friend lived on the same street as this guy Drew, that meant Victoria could potentially bump into him and perhaps get to know him. Out of all the new faces she'd seen so far that day, Drew's was the only one that she cared to think about.

Rebecca and Victoria finished eating and agreed to meet at the same spot again tomorrow for lunch. Once the bell sounded, Victoria walked to her sixth-period class, thinking only about Drew.

She couldn't stop thinking about him.

20

Coach Nichelle

August 13, 2007

Coach Nichelle Whitlock clicked pause on the recording she had been watching of her team's biggest competitor, The Golden Stars. Out of everyone else in her division, The Golden Stars posed the biggest threat.

Although she scouted the competition religiously every pre-season, this had been the only year she'd dedicated every spare second of her time to it. She had even given up her twice-weekly bowling club meetups. Her bowling buds had thankfully understood; they knew she'd be back at the alley come springtime. As of lately, all her free time had gone toward studying the competition.

In the past, she'd been realistic. She'd put all the pieces together and realized she didn't have the team to get past the playoffs. However, this year, the team was solidly better than average, and better than ever before. Not only that, but they had Victoria now. In all her years of coaching, Nichelle had never coached a girl with such natural athletic talent. Victoria was going to be their ticket to the playoffs and would lead them to a state championship victory.

Now, Nichelle just had to do her part to prepare the entire team, because Victoria's skill alone wouldn't help them defeat The Golden Stars. Victoria could only get them so far. The right strategy was what her team needed to come out on top, which was why Nichelle was dedicating all of her energy into developing the best strategies early on. Everything she did now, would pay off later. The thorough approach and information that she'd gathered from watching all those tapes would help her devise ways to improve her team's defense. Most people thought offense was the most critical aspect of a team's ability to win, but in truth, defense was key.

It was her seventh year as the girls' basketball coach at Oakwood High, and although she'd always taken her job seriously and put great dedication and passion into grooming her athletes for the collegiate level, this was the most excited and serious she'd ever been for the start of a new season. The first day of practice was finally here, and she couldn't wait to get started.

Nichelle stood up from her desk and did some stretches to combat the back pain from sitting down for far too long. After she finished with a few yoga poses, she grabbed her 'Coach of the Year' coffee mug and took a swig of the lukewarm drink. The mug had been a gift from one of the senior players last year, Arianna. With all her work, Arianna, was now playing Division 3 basketball at Dallas College. If it wasn't for Nichelle's relationship with the Dallas College coach, Arianna never would have gotten that opportunity.

With her other hand, Nichelle picked up the Baby Yoda stress ball on her desk—another gift from a player who graduated already—and gave it a few squeezes. It was such a thoughtful gift. As most of the girls on the team knew, she was a huge *Star Wars* fan. At present, Nichelle didn't feel much stress at all, just energized, but she stilled loved to mess around with this thing.

In addition to her job as basketball coach, Nichelle was also the PE coach. On Fridays, she'd let the students just chill and take it easy, work on homework—whatever they wanted to do during that period. Meanwhile, on those days of the week, Nichelle and her assistant would hang out in her office with the door closed and take turns shooting the Yoda doll into the mini basketball hoop that hung on her door. The stress ball was mostly used for that purpose.

Nichelle finished the last sip of her coffee and then checked her Garmin watch. The time read 2:29 pm. The nifty watch had cost her about a grand, but with all the cool features, it had been totally worth it. Any second now, the girls would be heading into the locker rooms. Practice started at three, but her team liked to get in the gym early to start warming up.

"Hi Coach Nichelle, can I get the balls out?" a voice from outside her office called. She recognized it was Jordan, the extroverted, sometimes bossy team captain. If it had been up to Coach Nichelle, she would have gone with the calmer and more introverted Sarah for team captain. But as usual, she'd let the team vote, and Jordan had that gregarious personality that was hard to overlook when it came time to cast the ballots.

Before stepping out of her office into the gymnasium, Nichelle checked to make sure her collared Nike T-shirt was tucked into her matching Nike sweats. She adjusted the whistle that hung around her neck. Next, she licked her fingertips and slicked down her short brown hair on each side, making her middle part more pronounced and less poofy. She liked to think her hair was still mostly a brown color, but she knew that some gray streaks had started to creep in already—even at the relatively young age of thirty-nine. Although her hair probably had a few end wisps sticking up uncontrollably in the front, as it often did, for the most part she felt that she looked nice and put together. Ready for the first day of practice. She felt that even minimal efforts like this helped her to look more professional. Professionalism was something she liked to instill in her girls. She knew they'd look back one day and thank her for all the reminders to tuck in their uniforms.

"Yes, please do. Thank you!" she yelled, although Jordan had already begun to get the basketballs from the storage cabinet. "Oh, hey, Jordan, when you get a second can you come here? I need to talk to you about something."

"Yeah, one sec!"

Jordan jogged over.

Nichelle stuck her hands in the pockets of her sweats and looked down toward the gymnasium floors for a second to think of how to word what she planned to say next.

"So, as team captain, you know I expect more from you than I would from everyone else. With great power, comes great responsibility." She paused, letting Jordan absorb that insightful quote from *Spiderman*. It was one of her favorite quotes, and it wasn't the first time she'd used it.

Jordan looked puzzled, so Coach Nichelle explained further. "Well, we have a new girl on the team, as you know, Victoria. I need you to make Victoria feel at home here. A part of the team. I know we don't know Victoria too well yet. She seems a little shy, but I hope you can make her feel like she belongs here."

"Okay, I will."

"Good, thank you."

Once Nichelle had said what needed to be said, she let Jordan head off to the locker rooms to get ready along with the other girls. She returned to her office momentarily just to grab her dry erase basketball board and get her better pair of shoes on.

Occasionally, when the girls needed an extra person on the court, she liked to sub in. She had never been the all-star athlete back in the day when she played ball, but she had always been the solid sixth man. Consistent. Reliable. When one of the starters had been injured or having an off game, there she had been to consistently save the day. The memories made her smile.

As she waited for the team to gather in the gym and start the practice, she gazed up at all the awards that hung on the wall. Football State Champions: 1972, 1986, 1992, 1998, 2001, 2004. Cross country had a similar track record of state championship wins. Similarly, volleyball, tennis, swimming, and every other sport had a state championship triumph—except for the girls' basketball team.

Goosebumps prickled her skin. This was going to be their year.

21

Victoria

August 13, 2007

After an exhausting day of school and basketball practice, Victoria was glad to be home. She grabbed her spare key from the side pouch of her backpack and let herself inside. "Jeff?" she called.

"I'm upstairs," her brother yelled back. Victoria set her backpack down and walked up the stairs to where her brother sat in front of their small television watching a show.

"Where's mom?" she asked.

"She's out with Aunt Jenny for dinner. Mom said they'd be out a little late tonight, but Larry's coming over to babysit," her brother answered and then paused the show.

Still sweaty from her basketball practice, Victoria took a seat on their brown, worn-in couch. "Ugh, we don't need Larry to babysit. Does she forget that I'm seventeen?"

Jeff laughed. "Probably."

"Is there anything to eat for dinner?"

"She left us money for pizza. It's on the kitchen counter."

"Okay, I'm starving. I'll go ahead and order it."

"Okay." Her brother stared down toward the carpet.

"What's wrong?"

"Nothing."

Victoria pressed him for more details. "I didn't see you at all today. Did you have a good first day? I still can't believe you're a freshman already."

"It was alright."

Victoria noticed the tears in his eyes and moved closer to her brother to comfort him. She placed her hand on his shoulder. "Something's wrong. What happened? Tell me right now."

A few tears slid down Jeff's cheeks, but he quickly wiped them away. "Just these stupid bullies. During my second period class today, we all had to go around the room and share something exciting about our summer. Some jerks next to me were laughing because they said I talk like a girl. I mean, it's not a big deal. I don't really care what they think."

Victoria clenched her fists tightly. "What guys? What were their names?"

"Um, Joel and Stephen, I think. But it's not a big deal. Other than that, everything went pretty good. I met this girl named Sally, and she was so sweet. She's in drama classes and thinks I should sign up, too. I think maybe I'll give it a try; I'll see what Mom thinks. So yeah, Sally was in my lunch and invited me to sit at her table with all her friends. They're so nice! And then, the rest of the day went well. Oh, and I signed up for band, too. I'm going to play the trumpet!"

Victoria leaned over closer to her brother and gave him a big hug. "I'm sorry those stupid idiot guys in your class made fun of you. Guys like that are just jerks and that's all they'll ever be."

"I know."

"Well, so you're going to sign up for drama classes? That's cool. Should we do some roleplaying tonight!?"

"Yeah!"

Victoria took a quick shower, ordered the pizzas, and then her and Jeff pretended to act as characters from *Peter Pan*, since that was the play their school performed during the fall season. Just as they were getting tired of all the acting practice, she and Jeff heard the doorbell ring. They walked to the front door and peeked outside the window. Larry waved at them.

"Finally," Victoria said, opening the door. "You do realize our moms will be back soon right?"

Larry looked at Victoria with wide pupils. "Duh, why do you think I'm here?"

"Hi Larry!" Jeff exclaimed. He was always excited to see their cousin for reasons Victoria didn't understand. Larry seemed a bit out of it whenever he came over, which Victoria knew was from all the recreational drugs he consumed.

"Hey, little man! I missed ya," Larry said, giving Jeff a friendly pat on the head. They made their way into the kitchen and all sat at the table together as Larry vacuumed down what was left of their pizza.

After enough time had passed, Victoria checked her fitness watch. "It's so late. Jeff, why don't you head to bed. I'll be up there soon."

Her brother yawned, gave Larry a hug, and then said goodbye before walking up the stairs to his bedroom.

Once Victoria knew Jeff was in his room with the door shut, Victoria turned to face Larry. "I need you to get me some weed."

He laughed. "What? Why? I thought you didn't smoke."

"It's not for me. It's for someone else."

"Mm, I see. Okay, fifty bucks."

"Fifty dollars? No way." Victoria shook her head. "I'll pay twenty."

"Thirty-five?"

Victoria sighed. "Deal."

They shook hands, and Larry agreed to get her the weed by tomorrow. They planned to meet by the bleachers near the football field at 3:00 pm. At that time, no one would be using the field and they could perform the exchange discreetly. Victoria was going to make sure those guys who bullied her brother would get a little taste of what real bullying felt like.

22

Victoria

August 14, 2007

"Rise and shine," Cindy called as she entered Victoria's room and slid open the curtains.

Victoria rubbed her eyes. "What time is it?"

"Time for you to get up." Her mom pulled open her closet door and threw her school uniform on the bed.

Victoria looked over to her alarm clock. The time read 6:03 am. "I don't need a whole hour to get ready! I'm going back to bed."

"We need to discuss your college applications, and this is the only time we have to do it. You're going to be busy with practice later, and then homework, and this is extremely important for your future."

"Ugh," Victoria said as she rolled out of bed.

After Victoria pulled on her uniform and brushed her teeth, she walked downstairs and met her mom in the kitchen. Various college applications and informational packets covered the entire kitchen table. Her mom turned around with a plate of bacon, eggs, and toast. She handed the plate to Victoria. "We need to get your SAT scores up. You

23

Victoria

August 21, 2007

Even though it was just a week into the new school year, Victoria had begun to feel at ease. Not only was she already the star of the girl's basketball team, but she also had a friend, and she'd been invited to a party usually reserved for the popular, more outgoing crowd.

Victoria had been counting down the days until the party date approached. She even had purchased a new outfit for the special occasion: a cute plaid, button-down summer dress with matching sandals. The dress hadn't been cheap, but thankfully she'd been able to steal some cash from her mother's wallet without getting caught. Fortunately, her mom had never been great with money management and so she hadn't even noticed it was gone.

Saturday night finally arrived. It was the big day, the back-to-school bash. Victoria could always count on her mom and Aunt Jenny to be out on a Saturday night. Her mom would tug Aunt Jenny along almost every weekend until her mom found a new guy to date. Then, her mom would date the new guy for a few weeks, at most, and then he'd mysteriously disappear. Once that happened, her mom and Aunt Jenny would religiously spend Saturday nights back at the same country bar. The same process had gone on and on for as long as Victoria could remember.

"Jeff," Victoria called to her brother. She knocked on his bedroom door.

"Yeah, it's open." Her brother had their mom's makeup spread across his bedroom floor. He wore a mountain of blush on his cheeks, and lipstick was applied well past the lines of his lips.

"You look nice. I love the makeup."

Jeff laughed. "You're lying! It's hard to do it how mom does. I'm trying to get better. Just for fun. I wish we could wear makeup to school."

"Yeah, that'd be cool. Anyway, I'm going to head out."

"Where are you going?"

"It's a party. Only juniors and seniors are invited—unless you're on the football team. They get invited to everything."

Her brother looked disappointed. "Oh, that sounds fun. I wish I could go."

"Me too, buddy. But hey, Larry should be here any second. And mom left money for pizza."

As soon as Larry finally showed up, stoned and ten minutes late, Victoria gave her brother a hug goodbye and then was on her way. She hopped on her bike and rode through the neighborhood until she arrived at Drew's place.

24

Victoria

Present Day

On this day, Victoria took a short drive to a Wawa gas station about thirty minutes away from her cottage. When she'd first purchased her cottage outside Philadelphia, she had no idea what the fuss was about with these Wawa places, because the Buc-ee's gas stations in Texas were way bigger and better.

Victoria clicked on her blinker and then turned into the Wawa parking lot. Once in park, she turned on one of the stolen iPhones she'd brought with her. This particular iPhone had the phone number she'd given to Karl. Cell phone towers could detect locations whenever the phone was turned on and in use, so Victoria always took precautions to never be at any of her properties or anywhere that could trace the phone conversations back to her.

Shortly after she'd turned on the phone, a string of messages from an unknown number popped up. It was Karl. He had sent her a message saying that he was available tomorrow afternoon if she wanted to look at some homes. She sent a message back to confirm the plans, and as he'd requested, she also sent specifications, such as budget, square footage, and location, for the kind of home she pretended to want.

After a quick Google search to confirm what kind of homes average people could afford, she responded back with the details. Karl texted back immediately and suggested they should meet at his place so they could drive together. Victoria confirmed the plans and even went as far as to include a smiley emoji to reiterate her excitement.

Now that the plans had been confirmed, Victoria turned off that phone and then grabbed another stolen iPhone from her purse. She had a whole stockpile of them in there. She clicked the button to turn it on and then typed in the address he had given her into a search engine. It suddenly made sense why he wanted to meet there. The home was quite extraordinary, although it didn't even come close to Victoria's houses. However, he clearly wanted to win Victoria, or Sammie, as he knew her, over with the extravagant place. What woman wouldn't take her clothes off at the potential hope of a relationship with a man who looked like Karl and lived in a home like that? He was the full package.

Next, Victoria put on the pest control uniform with the name badge. After that, she slipped on a short-haired brown and gray wig. Finally, she pulled up YouTube and watched the "How to Fake Wrinkles with Makeup" tutorial and followed all the necessary steps. As she hoped, she looked like an old hag. The uniform was as generic as they came. Nothing special. She'd bought everything with cash at a Dollar General on the other side of town. She stuck on the name badge: Sandra Mc-Corna—some random name that had come to mind when she'd initially made it. Then she put on a hat with a logo which looked legit and could pass as an actual pest control company. Finally, she put Karl's address into her car's GPS, pulled out of the gas station parking lot, and pressed down on the gas pedal. It was showtime.

Victoria, now dressed as Sandra McCorna from Grove Pest Control, parked her car a few houses away from Karl's. In her hands, she carried a pest control starter kit spray—she'd bought it off Amazon a while back—and then made her way toward the front entry. She rang the doorbell.

An attractive, dark-skinned woman answered the door. She looked confused. "Can I help you?" she asked.

Victoria responded with a sense of authority. "Just here for your seasonal spray." She held up the pest control solution higher in her hands.

"Oh, hold on a second, my boyfriend didn't tell me anyone was coming today. Let me go give him a call real quick—"

"No need. I'm just here to spray outside." Victoria now had the information she needed. Karl had a girlfriend.

Karl's girlfriend looked at her name tag and then said, "Okay, Sandra. That should be fine then. The gate's open for you to go round back. Do we owe you anything?"

"We'll mail the invoice like we always do." Victoria gave a professional nod.

As Victoria sprayed the pest control substance all around the yard, she thought about how easy it was for her to assume a role of another character. Not just in fiction, but also in real life. In a way, she could be whoever it was that she wanted to be.

It occurred to her that she'd always been quite adept at making shit up. Perhaps that was why her fiction novels sold so well. The lies came easily. Almost too easily sometimes.

Trust. Victoria supposed that was the downfall of humanity. The amount of trust they gave to those around them. The belief that another person had their best interest at heart. No one ever did. Everyone wore a mask. Some just wore it better than others. At the end of the day, even those who looked like they had good intentions at heart, didn't. Those good intentions always had selfish strings attached. Victoria knew this well. She was playing the very same game as everyone else. Victoria was doing good, eliminating these serial cheaters, but it wasn't just for them. Everything she did was for her own benefit, too. It made her feel powerful and like the master of her fate. No one could hurt her. She wouldn't let that happen. Not now, or ever again.

Once she finished at Karl's, Victoria returned back to where she'd parked the car earlier. She was proud of her progress and how smoothly today went. Now, she was a step closer to the grand finale, the final twist, as she sometimes liked to think. She loved how the cheaters never expected the punishment. That part had always truly astonished her.

On days like this, when everything seemed to fall into place perfectly, she was reminded of how much Karl's girlfriend would benefit.

With Dave, Victoria, too, had helped in a big way. All Victoria's previous research about Dave had proven that his wife had been hurt tremendously by her husband's cheating behavior. Dave had been one of the worst serial cheaters Victoria ever killed, which was why she'd sent that note to his wife, Holly. It wasn't something Victoria usually did after she murdered a serial cheater. But she'd wanted Holly to know that someone had been looking out for her and understood the pain she'd experienced. All the pain that Dave had caused her. Now, Holly would be able to move on and start fresh with someone who wouldn't betray or hurt her like Dave had. Like all the other women Victoria had helped, Holly was safe now.

Victoria was just about finished with the final errand for the day, her doctor's appointment. This time she'd come in for a blood test. She'd made up some symptoms—something about experiencing extreme levels of exhaustion lately—and so the doctor thought it would be a good idea to run a blood test. Although the doctor said he'd call her with those results soon, Victoria didn't care about them in the slightest bit.

Victoria held out her credit card for the front desk attendant. "Here you go." Then, she reached in her purse for the check. "For my past due bill."

The guy, Jimmy Sheldon, understood the code words.

"Thank you, ma'am. Here you go. Have a nice day, we'll see you next time," he said as he handed her the receipt. At the bottom, in black ink he'd written: *row 2, bush 5*

Victoria thanked him. She would schedule another appointment again in around three months, which was when Jimmy would have more propofol injections stolen and ready for pickup.

When Victoria had first started murdering serial cheaters, she eventually realized that she needed something to weaken these men. At first, she'd used sleeping pills, but she didn't like how long they took to kick in. Then one day, during research for a novel, she'd discovered a powerful anesthesia—propofol injections. It wasn't long before she came to the conclusion that she needed a regular supply of them.

That was when she decided to look into Jimmy at the front desk. Here was a guy who got paid pennies to sit at an uncomfortable desk, deal with high-maintenance and demanding patients, and take orders like a little bitch from doctors, nurses, managers, and pretty much everyone else above him. Like many people did, Jimmy had a look about him that said life had been nothing but getting kicked in the balls, day in and day out. Victoria had taken one look at this guy's vehicle, a busted up 1994 Honda Accord, and then followed him home to the shitty apartment where he still lived with his mother and determined that he didn't have much. A little online research showed Victoria that Jimmy's mom had been diagnosed with cancer recently. The GoFundMe Jimmy had set up for her months ago had only received three hundred and thirty-nine dollars in donations—hardly enough to cover the travel expense for cancer treatment in a third-world country. Based on the minuscule amount of donations Jimmy had received for his mom, they'd never be able to afford the cost of cancer treatment in the United States. So, after a long, probably ball-busting, hell of a Monday, Victoria had approached Jimmy in the parking lot after he'd finished his shift. She asked him how much twenty-five grand could change his life, and then asked how much twenty-five grand every three months would change his life, and based on the tears and hope in Jimmy's eyes that day, Victoria came to the conclusion that money could buy happiness.

Victoria got what she needed, and Jimmy got the money to cover his mom's cancer treatment, and then some. So far, so good. However, Victoria knew there would come a day when some over-achiever, got-nothing-better-to-do medical staffer started to take notice. When that day came, Victoria would pivot their strategy, and she and Jimmy would find another way to achieve their goals. For now though, Victoria and Jimmy would be just fine.

Victoria took the elevator down to the first floor of the building and then walked outside to the parking lot. She walked to the second row, and then counted down until she reached the fifth bush. Quickly, she looked around and once she knew that no one was watching, she used her hand to dig up the soil. Before long, her hand hit a plastic bag. She snatched it out of the dirt and immediately shoved it in her purse. Then, she got inside her car, checked to make sure it was the number of injections they'd discussed—it was—and finally drove home.

25

Rex

Present Day

On a sunny Texas afternoon, Rex rode, Shadow, the eight-year-old, black stallion. The horse stood tall and strong at sixteen hands. Faster and faster he went down the long stretches of pasture. For a short moment, Rex imagined himself free. Free of the shackles that had kept him chained to the dirt. Free of the devastation that had torn his family a part. Free of the mystery and horror of his brother's unsolved murder. Free from it all.

He leaned forward as Shadow climbed the final hill. Once they reached the top, Rex pulled back on the reins. The horse slowed down to a jog and then a walk. He walked the horse the rest of the way to the stables. Riding the horses was Rex's favorite part of this job.

After Rex was finished riding, he unsaddled the horse and then did his regular feeding rounds. He scooped large bucketsful of oats to each of the horses and threw hay in the pastures for them to graze on later. He tugged the hose into the water bowls and let those fill up all the way.

Just when he had about finished up, he saw Cindy walking toward him. Victoria's mom was what most men would refer to as a MILF. This afternoon she had on a see-through bikini cover. Underneath, she wore a bikini that highlighted and emphasized every last curve. He wasn't sure the purpose of a bikini cover like the one she wore; Rex could clearly see her big, likely fake but still really nice to look at breasts, which had stretched that tiny pink bikini top as far as it would go. Rex sometimes wondered what her intentions were. In the past, Rex had been teased by women every now and then—he was no stranger to that . He sometimes wondered if that was what Cindy's plan was. Regardless, Rex loved Lacey and would never cheat, emotionally or physically. Rex was not that kind of guy. However, he wasn't opposed to a quick look. It wasn't like he had any other choice.

"Rex," she said, pulling up her sunglasses on top of her head. "Before you go, there's a new chandelier I need you to install in Victoria's room. Whenever you're finished up out here, meet me by the pool and I'll show you what I need you to do."

Rex turned off the water hose, made sure all the fences were shut properly, and then walked toward the pool. Occasionally, Victoria's mom would ask him to do random jobs around the house in addition to his usual work. However, this was the first time he'd ever been asked to work in Victoria's room. It was exactly the kind of job he'd been hoping for.

Eventually, Rex made his way toward the lounge chair where Victoria's mom had been sun-bathing.

"Come on, follow me. I'll show you where—it was too heavy for me to move it up the stairs, so it's in the hallway still," Cindy said. As Rex followed her, he noticed she didn't even bother to put on the cover-up this time, and the bikini bottom she wore was actually a thong. He tried not to stare at her ass as she walked in front of him.

"There it is," she said, pointing to the big box on the marble floors in the front entryway. "Can you carry that up here, and I'll show you which part of Victoria's room that I need it in. It's actually going in one of her closets."

"Sure," Rex replied. He hoisted the heavy box on his shoulders and then followed Victoria's mom. The temptation not to stare at her ass only increased as she walked above him up the stairs.

A part of him thought she was purposely trying to test him or something. He wasn't sure. But this definitely wasn't entirely appropriate employer behavior. That he knew.

After Cindy finished with the directions and what seemed like flirtatious small talk, Rex was finally left alone in Victoria's room. Once he heard the sound of the back door open and close from downstairs, he knew it was safe to look around. He stepped out of the closet, which was much larger than any closet he'd ever seen before. His and Lacey's master bedroom closet looked miniature compared to this closet. Completely unlike his mother's house, the room—well, and the entire mansion for that matter—was devoid of clutter.

Next to the king-size bed was a large desk that contained a closed Mac laptop and nothing else. Rex supposed this was probably where Victoria did most of her writing. He checked the drawers. They were all empty except a few blank notebooks and a handful of pens. Next, he checked the end table near the bed. A coaster was on top, and inside the drawer was a phone charger. No sort of incriminating evidence existed in this room as far as he could tell. The way Victoria kept her room made it appear as if she hardly lived in it. He knew that she wasn't here all the time. During those times she was away, he often wondered where she went. He hadn't a clue.

Just when Rex was about to give up, he checked one final spot. Underneath the bed, he found a cardboard box. It was filled with copies of the latest book in Victoria's best-selling series. The label said that box had been shipped from an address in Philadelphia. He walked over to Victoria's desk, ripped a sheet of blank notebook paper out of the spiral, grabbed a pen, and then wrote down the address from the box. He wasn't sure if it meant anything, but maybe it could lead him to something useful.

26

Victoria

Present Day

Victoria, now disguised as Sammie, rang the doorbell to Karl's house. He gave her a quick greeting and hug. Then he placed his phone and keys on the table in the entryway and said, "Let me use the restroom real quick, and then we'll head out. How does that sound?"

Once Karl was out of sight, Victoria pulled a pair of latex gloves and an iPhone-compatible stylus from her purse—she always went overkill with the protective measures—and began installing the Grindr app. Karl had many apps on his phone, and she positioned this app so that it easily blended in with the other ones around it. She was sure he wouldn't even notice it was there.

From there, she set up the Grindr account for him with the email account listed on his business card. She clicked next and continued with the rest of the profile setup. The app asked for her to add a profile photo and description. She'd get to that part later. Then, for extra verification, it asked for a phone number. Victoria entered Karl's cell phone number and then input the verification code. After inputting the code, she deleted the verification text message that the app had sent to his phone.

Next, she clicked on the app for Karl's email and swiped down to re-fresh. Like she'd expected, the app didn't send anything there. She knew apps updated and changed procedures all the time, though, and she al-ways liked to confirm that the process worked exactly as she remem-bered.

Next, she found a user located three miles away. The user had a pic-ture of his bare chest as his profile photo and listed his name as Big Daddy D. The description on his profile was relatively bare, too, all it said was: *no face, no chat. Damn it,* Victoria thought. She'd seen other users include that in their descriptions before. Oh well, she'd have to get to this step eventually anyway.

Momentarily, she glanced up from Karl's phone. He still wasn't back yet, and she didn't hear any motion nearby, so she figured there was still time. Quickly, she navigated back to the profile settings section of the app and clicked to add a photo. Thankfully, Karl enjoyed taking pho-tos of himself. He had a series of selfies readily available in his photo gallery. She added the most recent photo to his profile, then navigated back to Big Daddy D's profile to start the first thread of conversation. Finally, she went to the settings section on Karl's phone to make sure all Grindr app notifications had been turned off. They had been. To play it safe on time, Victoria decided that would be it for now. She'd accom-plish more later.

"Alright. Sorry about that. Had a bit of an upset stomach. Must have been something I ate. You ready?" he asked as soon as he returned.

By then Victoria had put the phone back exactly like how he'd left it and stripped off her gloves.

"I'm ready when you are." She followed him out the back door to his garage. Together, they got in his Corvette and were on their way.

Karl took her to see several homes, well outside of the price range she provided to him earlier. He made up some excuse about how two hundred grand over the budget was nothing to worry about. "It's pen-nies on a mortgage," he'd informed her. "And I work with the best lenders. I'll get you all taken care of. Don't even worry about it."

After the exhausting day of looking at homes Victoria never planned to buy, they returned to Karl's house. He poured her a glass of wine.

"So, which was your favorite?" he asked, handing her the glass.

"Probably the first one," Victoria replied. She truly had hated them all and felt a bit sorry for the poor folks who had to budget to afford their minimal lifestyle. Victoria had grown up poor, so she was familiar with a budgeted lifestyle, but she didn't ever want to live a reality in any other way than how she lived now.

"That's a good pick—especially if you plan on having kids one day. It's a great school district. Some families move there just for that."

Victoria allowed Karl to drone on about random facts she didn't care the slightest bit about. The guy loved to hear his own voice, clearly. Then, he took her on a tour, obviously intending to show off his lavish home. "I tore out all these cheap carpets the previous owners had in the bedrooms. If it's cheap, I want nothing to do with it. Top of the line is the way to go. You pay more in the long run if you cheap out."

Victoria nodded her head as if he'd taught her something enlightening. "That's a nice light fixture," she complimented, pointing to the chandelier in the room where they stood.

Karl nodded his head in agreement. "My girlfriend—I mean ex-girlfriend picked that out."

"Oh. When did you and your ex breakup?"

Karl looked up and to the right—which liars often did when they were accessing the creative side of their brain—as he clearly formulated a lie. "A couple months ago," he said, and then continued, "I'm in no place, emotionally, to move on with someone new. At least not yet. I need to give it some time. But I like you, Sammie. I've enjoyed our time together. A lot." He walked closer to Victoria and tried to run his fingers through her wig. She couldn't have him accidentally tugging it off. That would ruin everything. So, she backed away from him.

"Sorry. It's just—my ex. He used to hit me. And sometimes when the fights got really bad, he'd drag me by the hair. I'm not quite ready to be touched like that by another man. At least, not yet. We can kiss and do all the rest. But the hair is off limits. I'm so sorry. I hope you can understand and it's not a deal-breaker for you." Victoria sniffled and wiped her eyes. A guy like Karl was attracted to the damsel in distress personality type. It probably made him feel like a superhero.

"Oh Sammie, that is heart-wrenching. I tell you what, we'll take things slow. Move at whatever pace you feel comfortable with. There's no rush. I'm not going anywhere."

"You're such a gentleman. Thank you for understanding. Most men don't—so it really means something, to me, that you do," she lied, again emphasizing how much better he was in comparison to other men. This kind of message would speak straight to his ego. Deep down, Karl was insecure. Most cheaters were.

Karl continued on with his own bullshit. "You're such a special woman. I'm so glad we met. It must have been fate that brought us together." This was his attempt to make her feel a false sense of security.

It was her move now. Victoria reached for his hand and clasped onto it gently to show that she believed what he'd just said. Trust had been established between them. "Should we finish the tour?" she asked.

"Yes, but first I've been dying to kiss those beautiful lips all day." Karl pulled her close and kissed her. Victoria allowed him to feel up and down her body.

After the sloppy make-out session, more superficial small-talk, and, of course, additional alcoholic beverages, Victoria figured the time was right to slip the sleeping pills in his drink.

"Your drink's empty." Victoria held up Karl's empty glass. "I'll go make us some more," she insisted. Karl gave her a peck on the lips before she got up to drug him.

In the kitchen, Victoria crushed up the sleeping pills and stirred them into Karl's glass. Then, she returned to the living room and handed it to him. "Here you go, babe. Oh whoops, I forgot mine. Be right back."

Victoria returned to the kitchen and watched from the distance as Karl took a few more sips. She hoped that the pills would kick in sooner rather than later, because she was sick of their mundane conversations.

"Babe, my sister's calling. I better get this. Hold on," Victoria called.

"Okay, take your time," Karl said with a slight slur to his tone.

While pretending to talk to her pretend sister, Victoria grabbed a pen and notebook from her purse, and then walked to the patio. She kept up with the faux conversation on the back porch where she took out the notebook and pen and began to work on a few scenes from her novel. The next book wouldn't write itself, and Victoria knew it was critical to squeeze in as much writing time as she could—whenever and wherever possible. That was what the best writers did.

Twenty minutes later, Victoria had completed at least a couple of paragraphs, which she considered sufficient, considering the distractions. She returned inside. As planned, Karl had passed out from the pills, and it looked like he had been right about what he'd said earlier: he wasn't going anywhere.

As soon as Victoria was sure that Karl was completely incoherent, she grabbed his phone. The first time she'd gotten into his phone, he'd left the screen unlocked. But, upon this second attempt, she learned he had a passcode. His fingerprint. So, Victoria maneuvered his thumb onto the scanning pad and unlocked it. Then, she looked over at him one more time—still passed out. She was careful with where she sat and what she did in his home, because she'd have to do a full clean of the place after she killed him. Not a trace of DNA could be left behind.

Next, she took a seat on the adjacent chair and pulled up the Facebook app on his phone. Karl had a very active Facebook page. He posted constantly. Mostly related to real estate. On his profile, it said he was in a relationship, but he'd restricted the settings so it was only visible to his Facebook friends, which meant he had full control. Undoubtedly, he didn't accept friend requests from the women he slept with on the side. Karl was a secret cheater. He covered his tracks, which was good for her purposes, considering the last guy Victoria killed was a known cheater. It was critical that Victoria didn't kill too many open cheaters. It was always easier when they were more on the down low, or else the detectives could uncover a pattern that could potentially lead back to her. But this definitely wasn't Karl's first rodeo, she thought. He knew how to cheat and not get caught.

The next task was to pull up the Grindr app and see if Big Daddy

D had messaged Karl back. He had. And there was a green circle on his profile, meaning he was currently online. *Perfect*, Victoria thought. Right away, Big Daddy D made it clear that he didn't want a pen pal. He cut right to the chase. So, they planned a meetup for Friday night.

Victoria returned Karl's phone and then began the next phase of the plan. In the master bedroom, she pulled open the closet and examined his clothes. Like her brother and the previous cheater, Karl also dressed nice. Unlike most straight men, he had a sense of style. With that in mind, Victoria realized she wouldn't have to stage any stylish clothes. That checked off a task from the murder to-do list. Following the closet inspection, Victoria walked over to his bathroom. In the bathroom drawers, she discovered a grooming kit, hair gel, shavers, body wash, and soap. Karl took care of himself—which would further support the narrative she was creating for him—since many gay men and in-the-closet gay men did the same.

"Karl," a recognizable woman's voice called from the front part of the house. *Why couldn't things ever go according to the plan?* Victoria wondered. Quickly, Victoria scanned the bathroom. In the back corner, behind the toilet she discovered a toilet scrubber and Lysol. She looked down at the gloves she had on. *This could work*, she thought.

"Mr. Lawrence," Victoria, still disguised as Sammie, called out in her best Russian accent. That was the last name Karl had on his business card, and it was critical that Victoria behaved professionally in this improvised character disguise. Victoria held the cleaning supplies and walked toward the front of the house.

"Who are you?" Karl's girlfriend asked in a state of confusion.

"Oh, I see, the Mr. Lawrence did not inform the Mrs. Lawrence. I'm the cleaner lady. New. So sorry. English. Very limited. I finish the guest bathroom. Then, Mr. Lawrence say I good to go."

Karl's girlfriend hung up her coat and her shoulders now looked more relaxed than they did before the explanation.

"Finally. I've been telling him we need a lady to come by and clean. We stay too busy with our clients. We're both in real estate."

"I see. I see. Very well then, Mrs. Lawrence. I very happy to know you. I see you next time. Thank you."

"I'll be in the office. Down the hall to the left if you need me. I have a few offers I need to write up. But something vegan for dinner would be nice—before you go."

When Victoria was about to remind the woman that she was the cleaner, not the cook, she recalled all the wine glasses and the plates from her and Karl's dinner.

"Of course. I do the meals. Then I go."

"Thanks—I'm Ebony, by the way. But you can call me Mrs. Lawrence if you want. That's fine."

"Great to meet you, Ebony. Mrs. Lawrence. I remember the next time," Victoria said. She strolled in the opposite direction of Ebony into the living room and kitchen. She tidied up the area and made it look as if Karl was passed out taking a nap. Speedily, she cleaned all their dishes. Finally, she grabbed her purse and discreetly went out the back door of the house, through the side yard, and hurried to her car.

Victoria drove to a grocery store parking lot, still far enough away from her cottage, and wrote out a message:

Those drinks really hit you hard tonight. Hope you feel okay tomorrow. I really had a great time with you, Karl :) Night! P.S. Your girlfriend thought I was the new maid ;) don't blow our cover! You should save my contact name in your phone as Maid lol, see you again soon I hope!

She carefully re-examined the text. It had to sound sweet and playful enough, which it did, thanks to the smiley, wink face, and exclamations, so she pressed send. Then, she turned the phone off and began the drive back to her place. It had been an eventful day, and she was exhausted.

27

Amy

Present Day

Amy arrived to the office early to get a head start on the day. She made a plan for where she and Brad needed to go today and then looked over some important paperwork related to the case. The first paperwork she looked at was related to the fingerprint analysis. Dave Anderson's fingerprints had been found on the sex toys. Several prints had also been lifted from the condo. But when they ran a search for those, nothing came up in their system, which meant that whoever they belonged to wasn't a criminal or registered sex offender.

"Someone's up early this morning. How long have you been here?" Brad asked as he pulled up a chair to sit down next to Amy at her desk.

"Don't sit. We should probably head out. I was just waiting on you."

"Well, that's a first. Usually it's the other way around isn't it?"

Amy grabbed what she needed from her desk and then she and Brad proceeded to the parking lots. Once they were in Amy's car, Brad turned to her. "I got you this," he said, handing her a GPS stand.

"I thought you didn't like my GPS."

"I don't. But I figure you'll still be using it whenever we both go back to working with our usual partners. It's safer to have it up on your dash-board like this. Here, I'll show you." Brad retrieved the stand and got it set up on the dashboard for her.

"See how much easier this will be for you now?" Brad said, pointing to the GPS on the stand.

"Thank you," Amy said.

Although Amy wanted to use the GPS with the new stand, Brad still insisted they use the map on his phone. So, that was what they did. Brad input the address from the driver's license they'd found in the condo, and that was where they drove to next.

The address on the driver's license ID took them to an apartment building in Philadelphia. The place didn't appear hospitable. In a few of the floor units, some of the windows were boarded up. Other windows had bars over them. It was definitely not the kind of place that most people would want to call home. Amy knocked on the door of the cor-rect unit, and she and Brad waited for someone to answer.

After a couple of minutes passed, a woman with yellow, coffee-stained teeth that matched her bright blonde hair answered the door. She had a skinny frame and wore sweats and a T-shirt that literally said: 'I may be wrong but I doubt it.' Based on her appearance, Amy was sure this was the woman's ID.

"Can I help you?"

"Yes, we're with the Philadelphia Homicide Unit. We're investigat-ing a case. We found an ID at the crime scene that we believe belongs to you." Amy held up the driver's license. "Is this yours?"

The woman snatched it. "Yes, I've been looking for that. Where'd you say it was?"

"Why don't you tell us? How do you know Dr. Dave Anderson?" Brad asked.

The woman gave them both a questioning look. "I don't know any-one with that name."

Brad and Amy looked at each other briefly and then Amy focused her attention back on the woman. "So you were not seeing Dave, not having an affair or a friendship? Nothing like that?"

"Like I said, I don't know him, and I don't know how my ID got there—it's been lost. You think I'd be living in a dump like this if I was dating some big shot doctor?"

"Do you remember where you lost it?" Amy asked.

"The last place I had it was at the club. I had a lot to drink that night. Misplaced it. Like everyone else who has a few drinks every now and then." The yelps and cries of a baby echoed in the background. The woman turned around and yelled, "Philip, can you feed him that damn bottle? It's on the kitchen counter—next to the McDonald's bag!"

The cries continued, louder this time. "Is that all you need from me? I gotta get back to my baby now since my boyfriend isn't doing nothing to help."

"That's all for now," Amy said. "Thank you for your time."

The woman slammed the door in their faces without saying a good-bye, and Brad and Amy walked down the cement stairs back to where they'd parked.

"I think she's telling the truth," Amy said as she started up the car.

Brad buckled his seatbelt. "Same. I don't know what to make of that. Did the victim own the condo or rent it?"

"The records indicate that he owned it. An investment property turned convenient affair spot, it seems."

"Strange."

"You don't think it was staged, do you?" Amy asked.

"I'm not sure. It's possible. Or that woman could be lying. She could know more than she's telling us. Let's finish up today's tasks and go from there. If we need to, we can always come back."

28

Amy

Present Day

Amy and Brad returned to the office after they finished up in the field and agreed to meet up later at Brad's place to work on the investigation over some dinner. Brad suggested that a change of scenery could help clear their heads and offer new insights.

Amy stifled a yawn and started to pack up her stuff. "Bye, Wes," she called to the Chief. It was just the two of them left in the office tonight.

"Wait, Amy, can you come here? I need to talk to you," the Chief called.

After Amy had what she needed, she met him in his office. "Yeah?"

"How's everything going?" the Chief asked.

"Good. I sent you the updates the other day," Amy replied.

"Right. I haven't had a chance to read it yet. What's the progress look like?"

"Good. Something that stuck out to me recently that I thought you might want to hear about is the Grindr messages. The timeframes."

The Chief stood up tall with his hands in his pockets. "What about them?"

"I reviewed the files of the past victims. The timeframes are similar for some. For Dave, the records show a two-month time period between when he downloaded the app and when he last sent a message on his phone. I noticed a similar occurrence with other victims."

"That is an interesting observation. Good work."

"I thought so. Also, the driver's license that was left behind at the crime scene."

"What about it?"

"I think it was staged," Amy said.

"Really?"

"Or coincidence. I can't see how it ties in with the other evidence. The owner said she lost it. I'm wondering if it was stolen and staged at the scene to throw us off."

"That's possible."

Amy's laptop was starting to feel heavy in her hands, so she set it down on an open chair in the Chief's office and then said, "I also have a wild card for you."

"What's that?"

"Are we sure we profiled this serial killer correctly? I know this would send the case in an entirely new direction, but what if our killer's a woman?"

"Not possible."

"Why?"

"Amy, there's a violence to these murders that isn't consistent with how women commit crimes. These homicides are executed in a sophisticated manner with a high level of proficiency. Not only that, but in terms of strength, a woman wouldn't be capable of it. I'm sure of it. I hope you have more conclusive findings to share at tomorrow's meeting. Members from the FBI team will be in attendance, and they need to see that we've put in the necessary work."

"There'll be plenty of updates to share with everyone."

"Good," Wes said and then walked closer to where Amy stood. He ran his fingers through her hair and tried to kiss her.

Amy pulled away. "No, it can't happen again. It was a mistake. You and I both know that."

The Chief looked disappointed. "You're right. I'm sorry."

They said their goodbyes and then Amy exited the building. As she drove to Brad's she thought about the Chief. The main reason she didn't want to sleep with him again was because she knew that he was in a rebound phase. He wasn't looking for a serious relationship. Not only that, but Amy didn't want sexual relations to define how far she climbed the ladder at her job. If she wasn't good enough to make a name for herself in this industry on her own, then she'd accept it. However, she refused to sleep her way to the top. They'd only hooked up once. Amy had been heartbroken from her breakup, and the Chief had been dealing with the aftermath of his divorce. They were both emotional over their losses and caved into each other's emotional and physical needs that night. It was well after she'd been promoted to Homicide Detective, so she knew her current position had nothing to do with what happened between them. Regardless, though, she didn't want any special treatment from the Chief. She needed to earn his respect—just like everyone else did.

A fifteen-minute drive took Amy to Brad's place. The apartment building was new and modern, much nicer than her's, which made sense. Amy had observed that men often made more money than women, even if they had the same qualifications and abilities. She wasn't sure how much more of a salary that Brad made than her, or if he made more, but she figured that he probably did. The only comparison point in terms of salary that Amy had to go off was the internet, and what her dad had made when he was alive and working. As of right now, Amy wasn't even close to the national average salary, but she figured after a few more years, she'd be within that range.

Amy knocked on Brad's apartment door. Brad answered. "Come in," he said as he pulled open the door.

"Nice place," Amy complimented.

In addition to modern elements, Brad's place also had an industrial vibe. A brick backsplash covered a part of the kitchen wall, and a black iron stair rail guided the way up the couple of steps that led into the open-concept living and kitchen areas.

"Thanks. You can take a seat at one of the bar stools. Dinner's almost ready."

"You cooked?"

"Yeah. I'm on a health kick, remember?"

"That's right." Once seated, Amy pulled out her laptop and the case files and set them on the countertop.

"What are those?" Amy asked, pointing to the light-colored squares in the pan.

"Tofu," Brad replied.

"Oh, I don't think I've ever had it before."

"It's a plant-based protein. Much better for you than those chicken nuggets you had the other day."

"It smells good—are you vegan nowadays?"

"I'm not; I still eat meat, but it's good to incorporate vegan meals a couple of times a week," Brad informed her.

"I bet. Well, I'm excited to try it." Amy looked over the files related to the ongoing investigation while Brad finished up sautéing the tofu.

A short while later, Amy started up the conversation again. "So, we have that meeting tomorrow morning."

"And?"

"Well, I just want to be prepared," Amy replied. She disliked meetings like the one planned for tomorrow morning. Although Amy considered herself confident and extroverted, she preferred to meet one-on-one instead of in a group. She never got nervous except when she presented to a large group of mostly critical men.

Brad was now cooking what looked like a stir fry in the pan. "This isn't a valedictorian speech. Pretty sure we'll be fine."

"I know, but I still would like to have a few notes typed up. Stage fright's a real thing for some people."

Brad laughed. "What? You get nervous for these meetings?"

"Sometimes."

The food sizzled on the stove. "You'd be good undercover then—I would have never guessed that. You always seem calm."

"I handle my emotions well. For the most part."

Amy refocused her attention on the file that contained the typed-up transcript of an interview with a witness. Brad spoke next. "When you interviewed the condo residents that first day, what did you find out?" he asked.

"Nothing, basically. The neighbor directly to the right of the victim's condo, Sharon—she's an older woman—said she was getting back from the grocery store when she noticed a redhead in brown wedges and daisy dukes leave Dave's at about the same time she got back from the store. Sharon stated that she didn't recognize the woman; I think that redhead was Mary—the woman the victim had a history of text messages with."

"Could be." Brad plated the food and handed Amy her dish.

"Thanks," Amy said. "Since we didn't have much to go off for Mary, I had our task team contact the telephone company to see if we could get an address for her that way, but the phone wasn't registered to Mary."

Brad finished a bite of his food and then asked, "Who was it registered to?"

"Someone else. I can't remember the name off the top of my head, but it's in my notes. Tomorrow, I'd like us to interview the owner of that cell phone—I think it's likely that Mary used a stolen device. If that's what we find out, then I think our original direction could be totally wrong."

Brad looked like he was considering the possibility. "You think how the FBI profiled the serial killer is wrong?"

"Right now, with everything we've learned, and what my gut's telling me, yes."

"How would you profile the killer then?"

"I think the killer's a woman. A woman serial killer."

Brad laughed.

"Forget it. I knew I shouldn't have said anything yet. The Chief, at least, didn't laugh when I brought up that possibility."

Brad looked amused. "What'd the Chief say?"

"He said it wasn't possible, but he didn't give me much time to discuss how I came to those conclusions. If you'd give me a second to explain, I think you'd maybe understand why I think it's a very real possibility."

Brad scooped up a bite of the food and then said, "Go ahead. I'm all ears."

Amy continued, "The only unfamiliar visitor our witness observed was this redheaded woman. Not one resident, and there's quite a few that live there, noticed any unfamiliar men in or out of the condo building around the time of the murder. Based on the autopsy report, the time of death likely occurred sometime in the morning hours, which lines up with when the redhead left the apartment. Based on that evidence alone, it's possible the unidentified woman could have killed him. That's reason number one. Reason number two is the staged ID. If the ID was staged, then it's possible other items at the crime scene, like the sex toys, for example, could have been staged."

Brad tried to speak. "Let me finish," Amy said. "Reason number three relates to the Grindr messages. I analyzed the timeframe of Dave's messages. They took place over a period of two months, which reminds me, we need to interview those men he messaged from that app still. But we'll get to that."

"Wait, what about the timeframe? Can you go back to what you were saying?"

"Right. Sorry. Let me just take down this note." Amy wrote down a reminder to interview all the men that Dave had messaged on the Grindr app.

"You say sorry a lot," Brad noted.

"Sorry—ugh. What would you prefer me to say? Fuck off?" Amy asked. She couldn't help that, unlike many of the men she worked with, she had a kind-hearted nature. Brad laughed and then coughed to prevent choking on his food. "Are you okay?"

Brad smiled. "Yeah, thanks."

"Anyway, so back to what I was saying. The timeframes. I noticed it with two of the previous victims. The murder that took place in New Jersey. And also the one in Maryland. The Grindr messages from those victims also had a similar timeframe of about two months."

"Did you notice any other similarities or patterns between them?" Brad asked.

"I'm not finished with the analysis, but I did. Dave had a history of cheating, and so did the victim in New Jersey. The rest of the victims did not though, so I'm not sure what to make of that yet."

"If all the victims had a history of cheating, then you'd possibly have me sold on this woman serial killer proposition." Brad stood up and walked over toward where Amy sat. He held out his hand as if he were about to grab her plate. "You done?" he asked.

Amy looked down at her mostly empty plate. "Yeah, thanks. It was horrible by the way. I'm sure you can tell how much I hated it," Amy said sarcastically.

Brad smiled. "You clearly liked it more than Chick-fil-A. You didn't finish all of your nuggets the other day."

Amy couldn't even remember if that was true. She remembered she ate all the fries, but it was possible that she'd had a few nuggets left over. "I don't know about that. It was good though. Way better than I expected, that's for sure."

On her laptop, Amy jotted down a note about what Brad mentioned. If they could dig deeper into some of the previous investigations, perhaps they could unveil that more of the victims had histories of cheating behavior. That could make the possibility of a woman serial killer more likely.

Brad stood by the sink and hand-washed the dishes. "You need help with that?" Amy asked.

"Nah, I got it," he replied.

"Don't you think we should at least mention it tomorrow at the meeting?"

"Mention what?" Brad asked. He switched off the water and began to dry the clean dishes with a towel.

"The possibility that our serial killer could be a woman. I mean, I know it would cause quite a stir—especially since the media's already convinced the public that we have a 'homophobic killer' on our hands, but my gut's telling me that I'm right. I really think it could be a woman serial killer."

Brad took a seat on the stool next to Amy. "Does your intuition determine all your decisions?"

Amy thought about it for a second. "No, I use intuition and logic. It's like a combo meal; I use both."

"If you don't mind undermining the Chief, then I say let's bring it up. It wouldn't be the first time the Chief's been wrong," Brad added.

"We've all been wrong. We're human," Amy reminded him.

"I've never been wrong." He smirked.

"I don't know about that."

For the next hour and a half, Amy and Brad looked over more case-related material. Amy took down additional notes and put together a plan for tomorrow.

Amy stifled a yawn. "It's getting late. I better get going." Amy pushed back her bar stool and stood up. When she tried to turn around, her shoe caught onto one of the stool's legs, and she fell backward. Brad reached out his arm and caught her. His forearm and hand gripped the lower part of her back tightly. Amy blew pieces of hair out of her face. Their eyes locked. For a fraction of a second, Amy considered what it would be like to kiss Brad. With both hands, he pulled her up and closer to him; she grabbed onto his strong shoulders to steady herself. Their faces were closer than they'd ever been before. "Be careful next time," he said.

Brad's hands gripped onto Amy's lower back for what Amy thought was longer than needed. However, in that moment, it didn't bother her. Amy pulled away and steadied herself. "Sorry. Thanks for that."

"It was either that or I let you fall. I considered the latter."

"Well, I'm glad you stuck your arm out."

Brad shrugged his shoulders. "Reflexes, I guess."

"I'm going to head out. I'll email you the notes I write up before the meeting tomorrow morning," Amy said.

"I don't need notes. Everything I need to know is right up here." Brad pointed to the side of his forehead.

Brad walked Amy to the door. As he leaned against the door frame, Amy glanced at the muscles in his bicep. "Thanks for dinner," she said.

"Anytime—I'll walk with you down to the parking garages."

"That's okay. I can handle it; I've dealt with my fair share of bad guys. And my dad taught me jiu-jitsu."

"Your dad was a great guy. I don't think I ever told you that."

Amy smiled at that. "Thanks, Brad. Bye now, I'll see you tomorrow."

As Amy walked the rest of the way to the parking garage, she thought about how Brad held onto her after he prevented that fall, and the way he stood in the doorway, with his strong biceps on full display. It wasn't that she didn't realize Brad was physically attractive, because she'd already known that. But something felt different about him tonight. Although she'd worked with Brad in the past, there'd been different chemistry between them this time around. She wasn't quite sure what it was, but she liked it.

29

Amy

Present Day

The following day, Amy stood at the front of the large meeting room as she provided an update to the Chief and special agents from the FBI Investigative Support Unit. Brad stood next to her, but right then, everyone's eyes were on Amy. She clutched onto her notes a little tighter as she spoke. "So, any questions about anything I just went over?" She looked across the room.

"Thank you for the updates, Amy. Good work, you two," the Chief said to her and Brad.

After the Chief spoke, the agents in the room seemed to assume the meeting was finished and began preparing to leave. For a moment, Amy considered saving the more controversial updates for their next meeting. However, if Amy wanted to solve this case, she'd need to step out of her comfort zone. The best homicide detectives, like her father, didn't make assumptions about any piece of evidence. They questioned and proposed possibilities.

Her dad never took the easy way out. He went above and beyond to ensure every piece of evidence was examined and analyzed fully. The

Chief had assigned Amy to this case for a reason. He believed she could solve it, but it would be impossible to solve anything if the entire investigative team wasn't on the same page. The only way to make that happen was for Amy to share her findings and propositions with them. All of them. Even if those propositions said that men with more experience, more accomplishments, and more status were wrong. Although Amy had several years of experience as a Homicide Detective, the men in this room had much more. These agents were the best of the best. Many of the guys in this room looked as if they could be her father; that was how much older they were. Even though it was intimidating, Amy reminded herself that she belonged in this room, too.

"Wait. I'm not finished," Amy said. It appeared as if Amy hadn't spoken loud enough, so she said it again, this time louder. It wasn't until the Chief spoke up that everyone gave their full attention to Amy.

The Chief looked down at his watch. "We're already running over our designated meeting time. So, let's make this quick. Go ahead, Amy," he said.

"Right. Thank you, Chief," Amy said. She held up her notes to recall how she planned to start this phase of the meeting. The second it took her to find that note felt like the longest second of her life. She swallowed and then stood as tall as she could. She cleared her throat and began with what she had to say: "So, as you all already know, we've been hit with several curve balls as we've worked our way through this case." In her peripheral vision, Amy could see Brad nod his head in agreement. She looked across the room as she spoke. "I went back through several of the case files, which we all believe are connected to the ongoing investigation. So far, we've determined that our killer targets gay men. For the most part, all these men are in the closet. Although, when the previous victims' family members and friends were interviewed, some of them were not shocked or surprised to find out their loved one was gay. Many suspected it. However, not all said that. In the case of many of the previous victims—the victim killed in New Jersey, for example—family members and friends were in disbelief and denial that their loved one had relations with other men."

Amy took a quick sip of water, and then turned to the next page in her notes before she continued. "This is a quote from Victim #4's father—the homicide which occurred in New Jersey. The father stated that in no way whatsoever was his son gay. He even went as far as to swear his life on the fact that his son was not gay. He was certain that the items found at that crime scene had been staged. That was the first time any suggestion of staged evidence had occurred."

"How does this all relate to the ongoing investigation? Can you focus more on that, please?" one of the agents asked.

"I'm getting there," Amy said. She took another sip of water and then continued, "At the crime scene of our current investigation, we found a driver's license. We interviewed the woman who it belonged to, and she informed us that it had been stolen. She had no relations with the victim whatsoever. I believe that was a staged item."

"She could have also been lying," Brad added. "We haven't determined that part yet, and we plan to interview the woman again—if needed."

"That's true. Yes, we considered that possibility as well. Now, we know that it's possible some evidence was staged. We know that some family members of the Homophobic Killer victims disagreed with the direction of the case."

"Amy, time please. Five more minutes, and then we have to wrap it up. Please get to the main points. You can pick back up next week, but we need to stay on schedule," the Chief interrupted.

"Right. Okay, I'll wrap this all up in a nutshell," Amy said and then continued, "I found the timeframe of the Grindr messages unusual. Several of the victims used the Grindr app within similar timeframes—specifically, they used the app over a period of two months. Not only that, but with our ongoing investigation, we discovered the victim in our current case had a history of cheating. Victim #4 also had a similar history. When we examined the phone records of Mr. and Mrs. Anderson, we noted the wife exhibited some anger over her husband's affairs. She even went as far as to say that she could kill him. Now, based on what we know so far about Mrs. Anderson, I don't believe she had anything to do with her husband's murder. However, her messages made me realize a new possibility. In consideration of all the evidence, and as a woman myself, the question that came to mind was, could our serial killer be a woman?"

The room went silent.

"Amy, we already discussed how that was not a possibility," the Chief spoke first.

"I never agreed with that conclusion. I still think it could be a very real possibility, and I wouldn't be doing my job if I didn't share those insights with the entire team."

One of the FBI agents spoke next. "These crimes are along the lines of the most violent crimes many of us have ever seen in our entire careers. We have FBI agents that comprise the most highly trained and skilled profilers in the nation, and you think they're wrong, and that a woman, a woman serial killer, committed these crimes?"

Some of the men whispered and had smiles on their faces as if they were laughing at such a ludicrous possibility. Amy looked over to the Chief. He looked pissed. She'd embarrassed him.

"I stand behind that reasoning. Yes," Amy replied.

The same agent spoke again. "The level of sophistication behind these crimes far exceeds that of what most women are capable of. No offense to you, Detective."

"I couldn't agree more," the Chief said to the FBI agent.

"Well, I don't. Amy's right," Brad said. "Amy's onto something, and it wouldn't be appropriate to dismiss those findings at this time. The pressure's high. The media wants a killer, and the stakes are only going to increase the longer we take to find him—or her. " Brad looked the FBI agent directly in the eye. "With all due respect, Agent Berkshire, we all want to get this killer behind bars as much you do, but we'll do it the right way, which means taking the time to consider every piece of evidence and every possibility. You don't want to put another innocent man behind bars now, do you?" Brad asked. Agent Berkshire stayed quiet. "I didn't think so," Brad said.

"I agree with Brad and Ashley," another agent in the room spoke up.

Amy was about to correct the agent, but Brad beat her to it. "Amy. Her name's Amy."

"Amy, of course. I agree with you two. We know our killer's highly sophisticated. With a level of skill that could possibly suggest a background in the military or the police force. For all we know, the killer could even be someone internal. In this very department."

"What's your point?" Brad asked. His tone was sharp and direct.

"My point, Detective, is that with that level of skill comes a certain knowledge. This killer understands the logistics of how we solve crimes like this one. So, they take extra measures to not get caught. It's possible, like Amy suggested, we have a man disguised as a woman. If that's the case, we need to go back and review all witness testimonials. Reevaluate the evidence with a fresh lens. A new perspective."

"That's not—" Amy was about to correct this agent before the Chief spoke over her.

"I'm on board with that," the Chief said.

"We'll consider all possibilities until we have more evidence for further conclusions. Now, we've already run over time. See everyone next week," Brad said. He looked over to Amy, tilting his head toward the door as if telling her 'let's go'.

Amy packed up her things. She gave the Chief a look that said 'screw you' before she left. Although she and the Chief had a good relationship, she was pissed at him right now and wanted him to know that.

"Amy," the Chief called after her. "Let's talk in my office, please." That statement upset Amy even more. He didn't have the balls to apologize for the way he talked down to her in front of everyone. Like that one time they hooked up, he preferred to do it in private.

"Not now," Amy replied.

"I didn't mean—"

"Yes, you did, Wes. You did," Amy said before she shut the door on his face. Although it wasn't the way Amy normally would treat a superior at work, she and Wes went way back. Wes had been her father's best friend and a big part of their family back when her dad was still alive. They were also comfortable with each other, or else Amy would have never slept with him that one and only time. She'd forgive him about the way he handled the meeting, eventually, but she wanted him to know that, right now, she was still upset. Amy's father would have been upset at Wes, too. Her dad had always believed that women detectives were just as good, if not better, than men. Before he died, he'd told her that women had a much better intuition than men did. He'd often reminded her to pay attention to her own. Not only that, but her father told her that women were often able to make witnesses feel more comfortable during interrogations, and as a result, women had a better chance of acquiring more useful data from witness testimonials.

Amy caught up with Brad and walked with him to the parking lot. "Thanks for that," she said once they reached her car.

"I was standing up for the evidence. Not you," Brad said once they got inside the vehicle.

"I know. That's what I was thanking you for," Amy replied.

30

Victoria

Present Day

It was the morning of Victoria's first date with Henry. Since she had some time to kill, she decided to grab her guns and practice her shooting.

Victoria grabbed what she needed and then went around back to where she had cleared out a big section of her backyard to function as a gun range. Tall trees surrounded and shaded the long strip of land.

From a considerable distance, Victoria already had multiple targets set up. After each practice, once the targets had become blasted with bullets, she always exchanged the used targets with new ones so she could get right to the shooting and didn't have to worry much about set up.

In a way, the gun range was like her peaceful haven. She loved to practice just for the sake of making improvements, but it also provided her with much fun and relieved any built-up stress.

The targets had been specially made. They looked like men. Between the legs of each target was a red X, which was where Victoria liked to aim. She also had a red X labeled on the top of the target's head, right between the eyeballs. Those were her two favorite places to practice with the shots.

Victoria spent that entire morning at her gun range. Whenever she was shooting, it was as if nothing else existed. Just her, the gun, and the target. The sounds of the shots and bullets when they hit the target were like the sounds of ocean waves crashing into the shoreline.

She shot several rounds of bullets and was proud of all the times she'd hit the targets dead center. After the fun-filled hours passed, the time finally came when she had to pack it up so she could get ready for her date with Henry. It was the first time she'd ever gone on a date mostly as herself. The only parts that would be different from her real self were her backstory and name. This date with Henry was a big step in the right direction for Victoria, and she couldn't wait to find out if he could be everything she'd ever hoped and dreamed for in a man. Only time would tell.

As Victoria got ready for her date, her personal cell phone rang. It was her mom. Victoria answered. "Yes?" This was a huge interruption to her getting-ready routine, and whatever her mom had to say better be worth it.

"Vic, you got a new one-star review. I'm pissed. The reviewer said the book was too violent. With way too many triggers. And then it was a long rant about how your main character wasn't likable or relatable—your books are about serial killers, what were they expecting? A feel-good story? It makes no sense whatsoever."

"Mom, how many times do I have to tell you? Every single author gets those kinds of reviews. It's not a big deal," Victoria assured her. At first, when she'd started out in her writing career, the one-star reviews had upset Victoria, and her mom had gotten even more upset over them. However, now Victoria understood that compared to the other mainstream authors, her books hardly had any one-star reviews. In terms of one-star review accumulation, she was winning in that she hardly had any compared to everyone else. Once she'd realized that, those negative reviews didn't bother her anymore.

"I know. You hardly get any bad reviews, but it still upsets me to see them. You know how much I love your books. You work so hard on them. I wish we could just prevent those one-star reviews from showing up on Goodreads. Is there a way to block or hide them?"

"No, it's fine. Like I said so many times before, don't worry about them. I could write an absolute piece of garbage, throw my name on it, and it would still hit the top of the New York Time's Bestseller list. Probably mostly get five-star reviews, too. It's like if LeBron James has a bad game. It doesn't matter. He's still LeBron James. We've reached the level in the game where we've already won, Mom. There's no need for us to freak out over the reviews. It doesn't matter. Now I need to go. I have a lot of writing to get done."

"Alright. I guess if you say so. So, I shouldn't try to delete the one-star review?"

"No," Victoria said and then hung up the phone. Victoria checked the time and furiously hurried. She didn't have much time to spare now thanks to the major interruption. However, it would be fine. She'd make adjustments to her routine and still arrive at least five minutes early.

* * *

Victoria and her date, Henry, sat side by side in a booth at the fancy restaurant. As they glanced over the menu, Henry turned to face her and said, "This food is to die for. My mom and I come here all the time."

Victoria absorbed the information. Every word and every sentence had to be analyzed. In the past, she'd made the mistake of being too naïve. Trust wasn't like unsolicited advice. She didn't give it away for free. Not ever again. That had gone terribly wrong. Right now, she viewed Henry as the enemy. Everyone always started off as the enemy. As soon as a weakness was observed, she could plan the attack, and then move in for full domination. That was the current strategy with Henry.

"That's nice. What's good then?" she asked, purposely trying to keep the conversation flowing. That was what people did on dates. Plus, she needed him to talk more so she could continue to analyze the hidden messages behind what he said.

"The filet mignon dish is excellent. It's a little on the pricey side—but don't worry, dinner's on me." He gave her a friendly nudge.

The waiter came by to get their orders: two filet mignon. Then, Henry started up again with the conversation. "So, tell me about yourself, Daisy. What do you like to do in your spare time?"

Murder cheating men, she thought, but then said, "I like vacations. Shopping. Anything that involves spending money." If he could fall in love with the worst kind of woman, then he could fall in love with her.

Henry smiled. "You sound just like my mom. I think you'd both hit it off. She can be a bit critical of the women I date. But you know how that goes. She only wants the best for me."

Interesting, Victoria thought. The last guy she dated, Drew, never mentioned anything about his mother. In the family, the mother nurtured, cared, and loved. Since Henry and his mother seemed close, that surely had to be a good sign.

"Do you have a father?" Victoria asked. She hadn't heard Henry speak about him yet.

"Yes. I know this sounds cheesy, but my mom and dad's relationship is why I think I'm still single. I look at them, the love they have, and naturally, I can't help but compare. My parents are the embodiment of a healthy relationship. Most people these days, prefer the hookup culture over commitment. But not me. I want a strong and healthy relationship to last a lifetime. When I propose, it will be a one and done. Till death do us part."

"What do you mean by that?" Victoria inquired.

"Marriage is sacred. My mother taught me that. When you commit to someone, it's forever. Even if my future wife became crazy, obese, or ugly, it wouldn't matter. I'd love her regardless. Unconditional love. That's what it's called. I guess you could call me a man of character. I do what I say, and I say what I mean. If I say I love you, it's a one-hundred-percent guarantee."

As Victoria listened to Henry speak, she still hadn't deciphered what the hidden message was. It was highly possible his words were intended to lure her into bed.

"If marriage is so important to you, and your mom, then I assume you wait until marriage for sex."

"Absolutely."

"Me too," Victoria lied.

Henry held her hands gently and looked at her in the eyes. "I'm so glad I met you, Daisy. I genuinely mean that. You're special."

Victoria looked back at him into those deep brown eyes. It was like no one else in the restaurant existed. Just the two of them. Perhaps, Henry was the one. He could love her just as she was. That was what he'd said. However, only time could tell if he meant it. As always, she'd have to be patient with the process.

After more light-hearted conversation, Henry stood up to use the restroom. When he was out of sight, Victoria picked up his phone. Earlier, she'd watched him enter the code, and she had it memorized now. She input the necessary numbers and then swiped it open. A man's phone held his deepest, darkest secrets. The browser history was Victoria's favorite information to gather. But she'd get there. Right now, while he was off-guard and entirely unprepared, she needed to check his messages. Observe those conversations closely. The most recent conversation was with his mom. He had his mother saved under the contact name 'Mommy' with a red heart next to it. The moment Victoria clicked on that conversation thread, she realized that she'd need much longer to read through the conversation. They had enough chats to match the word count requirements of an entire novel.

She didn't have much time, so she clicked back over to the rest of his messages. So far, she didn't see any names of other women. However, Victoria wasn't unintelligent. She knew that a contact saved under the name Dominoes Pizza could just as easily be a secret lover.

Before he returned, Victoria returned the phone to the exact position. It had been tilted to about what Victoria estimated as a thirty-two-degree angle, and he'd left it a measurement of two knuckles away from the end of the table. So, that was precisely where Victoria repositioned it.

The dinner date with Henry went better than Victoria could have ever anticipated. Based on the easy flow of conversation, it seemed like a strong connection could potentially exist between them. Overall, Victoria was very satisfied with how everything went.

After Henry paid for their meals and left the waiter a generous tip, he walked Victoria to where she'd parked. "Those are great on gas," he said, gesturing at her Toyota. Victoria nodded in agreement. *There isn't much else to compliment about the vehicle*, Victoria thought.

"I'd love to see you again. Are you free next week for dinner? At my place," Henry asked.

Victoria clicked the unlock button on the car keychain. "I'm not sure. I'll need to check my schedule, but I'll let you know. Thanks again for dinner, Henry," Victoria said. The response was one that she'd practiced and formulated beforehand. From her evaluation of Henry thus far, he seemed like the type to enjoy the chase. He preferred to work for it, so that was precisely what Victoria planned for him to do. She'd wait until he reached out again with a text or a call before she confirmed that next week worked for her. That approach would keep him on the edge of his seat, for a little while, at least.

"It was my pleasure. Take care now," Henry said. He waved at Victoria as she drove away.

31

Victoria

Present Day

Victoria was reminded of how overbooked her schedule was lately as she drove to the scheduled meet up with Big Daddy D. Well ahead of the agreed upon meet up time, Victoria sat at a small booth that overlooked the entire restaurant. She was disguised in a blue summer dress, a long brunette wig, and oversized sunglasses.

After several lemonades, the guy she suspected was Big Daddy D finally arrived. He sat at a table for two near the back corner of the restaurant. From her peripheral vision, Victoria observed as Big Daddy D impatiently checked his phone for a message from Karl. The Grindr app notifications on Karl's phone had been set to silent. All the messages that he was probably sending to Karl would go unread—well, until Victoria was able to get back to Karl's phone and respond for him.

Thirty minutes passed, and it looked like Big Daddy D had accepted the fact that he'd been stood up. That didn't prevent him from ordering a barbecue sandwich, though. Victoria kept a close watch on his movements while she finished eating her French fries.

After Big Daddy D finished his meal, he looked around the restaurant and then he got up from his table and exited the restaurant. A dine and dash. *Such a jerk*, Victoria thought. Swiftly, she gathered her stuff, and walked over to his table. She left a huge wad of cash—enough to cover his food and provide a generous tip to the waitress—and then she hurried out the door to follow him.

Victoria followed Big Daddy D's blue Ford Escape until they arrived at an apartment building in downtown Philadelphia. From the distance, and still in full disguise, Victoria followed him. "Coming, please hold the door," Victoria called. Big Daddy D did as she said, probably assuming she lived here, too, and then they got in the elevator together.

"What floor?" he asked.

Victoria looked at the lit-up floor number. "I'm floor eight, too. Thanks."

As the elevator rose up, Victoria gripped a propofol injection inside her purse.

They exited the same floor together, and Victoria walked in the same direction as Big Daddy D. When he got to the correct apartment, Big Daddy D put his key in the door to unlock it. That was when Victoria penetrated his neck with the injection needle. After a short moment, he fell over. Victoria grabbed the key and opened the door and then rolled him inside.

"Greg, is that you?" a voice called.

Victoria remained calm. "It's Claire. I'm an old friend of Greg's. Good ol' Greg here overdid it at the bar. He hasn't changed a bit—I tell you."

A lanky guy in sweatpants and a sweatshirt walked over to where Greg was comatose in the hallway. Although the situation wasn't ideal, Victoria remained calm. The guy laughed when he saw Greg passed out. "I gotta say I haven't seen Greg this drunk. Ever. This is great, though. I'm glad he had some fun. Hopefully he'll remember some of it. I'm his roommate, Ethan."

"Nice to meet you. It was so great to finally catch up with him. We go way back. Childhood friends. Neighbors. I missed him like crazy. Where's his room?"

"Straight back and to the left. It's the only room on that side. I'm heading out for some food. Do you want anything?"

"Oh, I won't be staying. But thanks. I'm just dropping him off, and then I gotta run. Sadly."

"Alright. Well, the door will lock on your way out, so don't forget anything."

"I won't. Thanks!"

Victoria dragged Greg the rest of the way to his bedroom and then with as much strength as she could muster, got him positioned up on the bed. Big Daddy D was a bigger guy, much bigger than the cheaters she usually killed. Like his Grindr profile photo and description, his room was also bare. The only color came from the dark blue comforter on his bed.

Victoria pulled out the tools she needed from her purse: the plucker, Ziploc bag, and gloves. Then, she unzipped his pants and lowered his boxers enough so she could pluck some pubic hair from him. Eventually, she would disperse the coarse and curly pieces of hair throughout Karl's bed. It'd be difficult for Big Daddy D to explain to the detectives how his pubic hair ended up there. Additionally, pubic hair—according to Victoria's extensive research about it—had more complexities than head hair, meaning it could better display individual-specific markers during a forensics analysis. This critical step would surely throw the detectives for another loop when they, in the near future, investigated Karl's murder.

Once Victoria was done, she positioned Greg in bed with the comforter pulled up so at least he'd be comfy and stay warm. Then, she hurried out of there, got in her car, and drove home.

Later that night, when Victoria was in bed, her phone buzzed. It was a text from Henry.

Can you meet next Wednesday for dinner? I'd love to see you again. :)

Victoria smiled.

32

Victoria

Present Day

It was the day Victoria had planned to see Henry again, and she now stood outside of his house, ready to embark on another date together. The house was what she'd expect of a physician. Manicured lawn, large square footage, centered in a nice, safe neighborhood, and overall great location. Although it looked like a doll house compared to Victoria's home in Texas, it was well-maintained and what most people would consider pretty, she supposed.

Victoria rang the doorbell, and a short moment later Henry swung open the door to greet her.

"Daisy, you look beautiful. I'm so glad you're here. Come on in," he ushered her inside. Like the exterior, the interior of the home was immaculately maintained. Henry gave her a peck on the cheek and then led her down the marble hallway into a glorious living room. The most noticeable feature in the room was the photograph above the fireplace.

"Wow. I love that," Victoria lied as she pointed to the enormous picture of him and the woman from his Facebook profile photo.

Henry smiled. "My mom thought it would be a nice center piece for the room."

"She was so right about that," Victoria lied again.

Victoria clutched onto Henry's hand as he showed her around. "I want you to feel at home here, so we can change whatever you want."

"That's so sweet of you," Victoria replied, thinking about how she couldn't wait to get that eyesore of a photo in the living room taken down. Eventually, Victoria would replace that photograph with one of herself and Henry. That would fit much better up there.

Now in the kitchen, Henry popped open a bottle of wine. It didn't look as high-end as the wine Victoria usually bought for herself, but she supposed it would suffice for tonight.

Henry poured the wine into the glass and then handed it to her. "I've actually been thinking that I want to sell this place. Get a new home. The commute's been taking a toll on me. The hospital where I work is about forty minutes away. In traffic. Ideally, I'd like to be within a ten-minute drive. It's important to me that you love the home. I want it to feel just as much your home as it is mine. Would you want to go with my mom on the house hunt—what do you say?"

Victoria smiled. "Why can't just me and you go?"

"I'd love that, and prefer it actually, but it's tough right now for me to get away from my job. Mom and I went on a few vacations this year, and I about used up all my PTO. So, Mom offered to help with the house hunt."

"Well, that was incredibly kind of your mom to step up to the plate like that."

"She's the best. It will give you time to get to know Mom, too. I know you two will hit it off when we go over there for dinner—when I officially introduce you—but the more time you two spend together, the better. I know she's going to adore you, Daisy."

"I can't wait to meet her!" Victoria lied. His mother sounded like a nightmare, but surely she'd step down once she realized that Victoria—well Daisy—was the new woman in Henry's life.

A short while later, Victoria and Henry made their way to the backyard patio. Henry stood by the grill as he flipped chicken breasts for dinner. "I hope you like home-cooked meals, because I love to cook."

"It smells delicious," she replied. Victoria took a sip of wine.

"Can you do me a favor?"

"Sure."

"Can you get us some plates, and bring out the side dishes? Green beans and sweet potatoes—I pulled them out already. On the counter. The plates are in the first cabinet when you walk in the back door. On the left."

Victoria agreed to the task. She set her wine glass down and then made her way inside. On the kitchen island, Henry's phone lit up. Victoria looked to see who or what was causing the activity. Mommy with the red heart emoji had sent him a message. She sure texted him excessively, Victoria thought.

Before she retrieved the plates and side dishes, Victoria decided to look around. Next to the pantry was a small built-in desk area. On top of the desk was a Mac computer and desk organizer, which contained pens, pencils, scissors, sticky notes, paper clips, and highlighters. Victoria pulled open the first drawer. Stacked receipts and blank printer paper. The first receipt was from a gas station. She shifted through them. They were mostly related to everyday purchases. Toward the bottom of the stack was a receipt from a flower shop. On that receipt, in sloppy handwriting, which Victoria presumed was Henry's, there was a note that said: *Mom Valentine's Day*. Interesting, Victoria thought. She'd have to look into that. Make sure that wasn't a cover for another woman. Although the time period was well before Victoria had even met Henry, she didn't want to take any chances. If he was the type of guy to cheat, well then, she'd have to find a way to kill him. Eventually. However, she hoped that wasn't the case with Henry. Punishing him would present several risks for Victoria—especially since she wasn't in a physical disguise.

Victoria closed the top drawer and then opened the one underneath it. This drawer was full of clipped coupons. Between the photograph of his mother above the fireplace and the excessive clipped coupons in the drawer, it now made sense to Victoria why Henry was single. From what Victoria gathered so far, the mother was a woman deterrent. In a way, that could potentially be viewed as a huge bonus, because the parasitic relationship with his mother combined with all the time he'd need to spend with Victoria meant Henry wouldn't have time to cheat. Plus, Victoria wasn't like most women. She'd barrel through these minor flaws—the overbearing mother and extreme coupon addiction—to get to the final prize, which was Henry. The additional information she gathered tonight put together a few missing puzzle pieces, but there was still much more about him for Victoria to uncover. Victoria closed the drawer and then returned to the original task. After she located the plates, she brought them outside to the table. Then she went back in for the side dishes and silverware.

"I got forks and knives, too. It took me a second to find everything," Victoria said once she was back outside on the patio.

"Fantastic. Thank you, " Henry said. He used the thongs to put the grilled chicken on a plate.

"This looks fantastic," Victoria said. The use of the same word established a similarity between them. People had a tendency to like other people who they viewed as similar. Victoria wanted Henry to view this Daisy character as similar. It would bring them closer.

Henry served the food onto their plates and took a seat. "So, I was thinking about it the other day. We talked so much, and it was such a lovely conversation, but I don't think I ever asked—what do you do for work?"

"I'm an aspiring writer. Working on my first book." Victoria regretted the lie almost instantaneously. It was too close to her true identity. "I'd love to open a bookstore one day. That's my true dream. The writing is more like a side hobby."

Henry finished a bite of his grilled chicken. "So, you're a reader. That's great. What kind of books do you enjoy?"

"History and memoirs, mainly. Those are my favorites." Victoria hated those genres. College was the last time she had cracked open a history book. Memoirs seemed to be mostly about celebrities, which she had zero interest in reading. She was a celebrity, and the only celebrity that interested her was herself.

"Fantastic. What about fiction, do you read any of that?" Henry asked.

"I love the romance genre. I'm a sucker for that." Again, another lie. Victoria couldn't stand the bore that came along with that genre.

Henry smiled. "I've read a few of Nicholas Sparks's novels—you know, if you're serious about the bookstore, I'd love to help you. I want to see all your dreams come true."

Victoria smiled at that. She didn't need any kind of financial assistance, but it was nice to have a man like Henry care about her needs and wants.

The conversation flowed the rest of the night. They talked more about work, hobbies, and what they both sought in a relationship. After dinner, Victoria helped Henry clean up, and then they took a seat on the leather couch in the living room. "That's such a cute photograph of you and your mom. I've never seen anyone use a photo like that as the focal point of their living room. I guess she had it made for you?" The only reason Victoria kept bringing up the photo was because she hoped that eventually Henry would come to realize he should replace it. Immediately.

"Yeah. Mom likes to surprise me with gifts like that. I'm her only son, so she spoils me a bit." Henry put his arm around Victoria. "I need to ask you something, Daisy."

"Sure, what is it?"

"I would like to date you. Exclusively."

"As in, just me, no one else?" Victoria asked.

"Yes. Can I call you my girlfriend?" Henry asked.

Victoria smiled and agreed to the title. Then Henry pulled her in for a hug with those strong arms. She hadn't been hugged like this in a very long time, and it felt intoxicating, almost like the way she felt when she killed and castrated cheaters. Just like she was meant to kill cheating men, right then, it felt like she was meant to be in Henry's arms. *Her boyfriend.* She loved what this meant for them.

33

∞∞∞

Bill Thompson

Present Day

"Hmm, this is strange—Henry updated his Facebook status to 'in a relationship.' Did he tell you about this?" Bill's wife, Marilyn, turned to face him. At this hour of the night, they were both lounging in their respective sections of the bed.

Prior to the interruption from his wife, Bill had been diligently crunching the numbers related to an RV purchase. In the Excel spreadsheet pulled up on his laptop, he had put together side by side cost comparisons of various used and new RVs. The latest RV he'd discovered, the 2020 Coachmen RV Apex Nano 185BH, checked off everything he desired out of this new investment. However, he still had to weigh the cost of a new vs. used RV to see what made the most financial sense. Several variables, such as depreciation and the miles he planned to put on it would play a significant factor in his decision.

"Ugh—what now, Marilyn?" he asked as he navigated back to the RV Value Mart website so he could recall what that price was for the newer RV model.

"Oh, forget about it. You don't care—get back to whatever it is you were doing over there," his wife said, waving him away. Then she picked up her cell phone to dial their son's number.

Bill ground his teeth together and refocused his attention back on his laptop screen. He knew what was coming next and patiently waited for Marilyn to leave a voicemail so that he could get back to his spreadsheet without any more distractions. "Hi. It's Mom. I need to talk to you. Please give me a call back first thing tomorrow. I know you're probably already asleep. I love you, Hens. Muah. Night-night."

Bill cringed at the way his wife talked to their thirty-four-year-old son. "He's a grown man, Marilyn. You need to stop calling our son fifty times a day. He has real responsibilities and obligations outside of our family. You really need to start respecting his space. If he wants to date a nice woman without telling us about it, then that's his choice. He shouldn't have to update you before he makes that decision—you've about ruined every single healthy relationship he's ever had."

Marilyn placed her index finger over her lips. "Shh."

Bill reached for his heartburn pills on the end table to combat the acidic sensation he was beginning to feel again in the middle of his chest. "No, it's getting ridiculous. You know how important your opinion is to him, but instead of finding something nice to say about the girlfriends he brings home, you only point out what you don't like. "

"That's not true. Our son's a doctor, Bill. I'm only looking out for him—I'm no fool. Women chase after men with money. Lock them in. And Henry's got such a big, caring heart. He wouldn't even see it coming. I'm only looking out for his best interest. I don't want these women taking advantage of him or messing up his financial stability."

Bill grunted and then washed his heartburn pill down with a sip of water. "It sounds like you're describing yourself."

His wife adjusted her reading glasses and turned to face him. "What's that supposed to mean?"

"That's why you married me. For money."

His wife smiled. "Darling, you were an engineer. Not a doctor. Even with the consideration of inflation, our son's making double what you did in your career. I can't believe you even think there's any kind of comparison to be made." Marilyn chuckled as she flicked through the newsfeed on her Facebook page.

"Oh, cut the shit, Marilyn. I may not have had the highest paying job, but I was making a very comfortable income, and you knew how much I had saved up back when we first met. I didn't keep that a secret from you. You're trying to protect our son from the exact same thing you did to me."

"Save the sob story, Bill. You didn't start making any kind of real money until you were promoted to Senior Engineer, and you wouldn't have been able to accomplish all that if it weren't for me. Working's a luxury, especially when there's a woman at home to tend to everyone else's needs, but her own. Who—for all those twenty-three years of marriage—was the one putting a hot meal on the table when you came home after a long day's work? Who was cleaning and maintaining the home, washing and ironing your clothes, and waking up in the middle of the night to tend to a crying toddler?"

Bill stayed silent.

"I would have loved to indulge in the luxury of a career, darling. You got to bask in the honor and glory that came with being the breadwinner. Meanwhile, I sacrificed my dreams of becoming an actress—for you. I would have made it big in Hollywood had I held onto my dreams, but I gave all that up for you. All the dreams you ever wished for came true. Mine didn't. So, don't you dare try to make me out to be the monster here when I sacrificed so much for this family. How dare you?" His wife pointed her finger at him.

Bill stared straight ahead and continued to remain silent, while his wife continued talking.

"You're the delusional one, with this jealous insecurity over the fact that our son makes more money, in the first year of his career, than what you ever made at the peak of yours. It's so absurd! You better thank your lucky stars that I'm looking out for our son's finances, because boy do I tell you what, at this rate, with all your medical expenses, that savings account of ours won't last us very long." His wife rolled her eyes. "Marrying you for money—give me a break. What money?"

Bill's heart was racing rapidly, and he wiped away the prickles of sweat that had formed on his forehead and took a deep breath. He didn't need the added stress that came with reflecting upon the outlook of their shaky financial situation. Back when the stock market crashed in 2008, they'd lost most of their savings and never fully recovered. It had been his fault. He'd made a risky decision at the worst possible time, and it turned into one of the biggest mistakes and regrets of his entire life. Since that unfortunate circumstance, they'd lived a comfortable, middle-class life. However, if Bill had never taken that risk, he could have provided for his family in the way that he'd originally intended. He blamed himself every single day over the setbacks they'd faced from that single mistake.

"Our savings won't last us through retirement. I give it ten years. Max. After that, when our accounts run dry and you're in a wheelchair, shitting yourself, you'll be thanking me for protecting our son's finances to ensure he has the financial means to take time off work to wipe your ass and buy you a new pack of diapers—well, that is, if you don't get Alzheimer's like your father did and you still have the cognitive capability left to thank me. Because I tell you right now, we won't have the money for full-time care, unless Henry's able to step in and provide that for us."

"I get it. Can we stop this nonsense now?" Bill yelled.

Marilyn laughed. "You're the only one getting upset. I'm fine." His wife slowly stood up and yawned. "I'm going to brush my teeth and then we better get to bed."

Bill's heart was pounding, his sympathetic nervous system on full alert, like he'd just run a marathon. He wasn't going to be able to sleep tonight. He'd end up doing what he always did after an argument with Marilyn: lay on his back as he stared up at the ceiling, regretting the other huge mistake he'd made in his life. A prenup. When he'd first fallen in love with Marilyn, she'd swept him off his feet. He'd been so blind-sided in love that the possibility of a divorce hadn't even occurred to him. By now, however, divorce had crossed his mind countless times. But he knew how that battle would play out. Marilyn would fight him for all that remained. She'd do everything within her power to steal as much as she could from him, and then after all the attorney fees and stress, he'd end up alive with hardly a penny to his name or dead from a heart attack.

Once his wife was in the bathroom with the door closed, he took his fist and punched it into her pillow, while mumbling profanities under his breath. Every now and then, on occasions like this one, he wished a miracle would happen and his wife would just fall off a cliff or get hit by a car. He hated himself after, of course, for allowing such dark and evil thoughts to seep into his conscience. But it was the only viable solution. His only way out.

Bill took a few final moments to cool down his temper. *In and out, in and out*, he reminded himself as he took deep breaths to slow down his heart rate. He didn't want to fight any more with Marilyn, because he knew what she'd bring up next. The RV. Regardless of their financial uncertainties, he was getting that RV, and Marilyn wasn't going to get in his way about it either.

Marilyn returned from the bathroom. "Why don't you close up your laptop and turn off that lamp? It's already so late, and you've exhausted me now."

Bill followed Marilyn's instructions and tumbled back into bed. His wife slept peacefully as he tossed and turned all night.

34

Victoria

August 21, 2007

Victoria rode her bike to Drew's house. Earlier, she'd written down the address on a piece of paper, but she didn't need to confirm it. Empty red solo cups littered the lawn, loud hip-hop music played, and groups of students stood outside in the front yard. Most were holding a red cup, filled with what Victoria assumed was alcohol.

After Victoria parked her bike, a tan, skinny girl with light blonde hair and emerald green eyes walked toward her. Victoria recognized her as Emma, a senior member of the cheerleading team.

"What are you doing here?" Emma interrogated. The rest of her pretty cheerleader friends stood behind her.

"I was invited," Victoria said.

Emma put her hands on her hips. "By who?"

"Stephen."

"Stephen who?"

"I'm not sure his last name. He's on the football team. A freshman."

Emma and her crew laughed. "Yeah—freshmen don't give out the invites. I do."

"Oh, I didn't know."

"Well, now you do. Go on now. Get back on your bike and get out of here." Emma swatted her away like a fly.

Just when Victoria turned around to leave, a guy with a deep voice said, "I invited her, too." It was Drew. The guy she hadn't stopped thinking about since when they'd smiled at each other that first day of school.

"Stop being a bitch, Emma," Drew said, and then he looked at Victoria. "Come on in. You want a beer or something?"

Victoria smiled at Emma as she walked past with Drew. "Sure," she said before she followed him inside.

Drew made Victoria a drink and then led her outside to the backyard. A bunch of guys lounged on patio chairs and smoked. Next to them were several couples making out. Another cluster of students was circled around a bonfire, roasting hot dogs and s'mores.

"It's crazy in there," Drew said, referring to the house party. "You're the new girl. On the basketball team, right?"

Victoria nodded. "Yeah."

"How's that going?"

"Good." Victoria took a small sip of her beer. This was her first time drinking, and she didn't like the taste.

"You don't drink or party much, do you?"

"No, not really. This is the first time I've been invited out."

"Well, I'm sorry to hear that. I'll make sure you get an invite to all our parties, how's that sound?"

Victoria liked the sound of that.

"Do you want to get out of here for a bit? There's a neat pond right behind my parents' house. We can hang out more over there. It's quiet and we can get away from the drama. Emma, she's my ex. She doesn't like it when I talk to other girls."

Victoria thought about it for a second. She still didn't know much about guys and dating. But she liked this guy and figured this would be the best way to get to know him more. Plus, Victoria wanted to get as far away from Emma as possible. As Drew had said earlier, that girl was such a bitch.

The sounds from the party eventually faded as they walked along the dirt path. Before long, the only audible noises were the chirps of crickets and other insects in the night.

Victoria and Drew talked about a variety of topics—football, school, plans for college. The woodsy trail eventually led to other smaller trails; they took a small path that led to the pond Drew told Victoria about earlier. The Texas stars glimmered overhead, reflecting off the calm body of water. It was a surreal sight.

"This is my secret spot. I come out here a lot. To think. You're the first girl I've ever taken here, you know."

Victoria smiled and looked in the direction of the pond. "It's lovely," Victoria complimented.

"You're lovely," Drew countered. No guy had ever called Victoria lovely before. They took a seat on a fallen tree trunk and absorbed the beauty of the night together.

"I hope I'm not making you uncomfortable or saying too much too soon, but I've seen you around. You're beautiful. I haven't been able to stop thinking about you—I'm glad you came tonight."

"Me too." Everything about this night felt so right. These were the kinds of moments girls Victoria's age dreamed of. She was alone with a handsome guy beneath the beautiful starry night.

Drew wrapped his arm around her and pulled her closer to him. A man had never touched Victoria in such a loving way before. Most girls grew up with dads who hugged them all the time. But Victoria's dad had left a long time ago. She had never known what the touch of a man felt like until right then and there. Drew's gentle and secure touch made her feel things that she'd never experienced before. Almost instantaneously, she could see herself in love with this guy. Actually, she was sure that she loved him from the first time they'd locked eyes at school that one day. She'd replayed that moment over and over in her mind already.

Drew kissed her and made love to her. He was her prince, she his princess. This was the love story Victoria had always dreamed of. Everyone in this school would kill to be with a guy like Drew, and here she was with him. Victoria gave Drew full control of her body as she lost her virginity to him.

"What if you're my secret girlfriend?" he whispered in her ear.

Victoria wrapped her arms around him tighter and rested her head on his shoulder until it was over. Afterward, he zipped his pants back up and told her to wait by the pond. He'd refill their drinks and be right back. Victoria did as he said and waited patiently. Her heart fluttered, and her cheeks hurt from smiling so much.

The night rolled on, and Drew still hadn't made his way back to their spot, so Victoria got up to check on him. In the dead of the night, she followed that same path back and eventually made her way toward his fenced back yard. Just when she was about to open the gate, she heard someone say Drew's name. Long strands of grass rubbed against her calves as she listened. From where she stood, she could easily hear someone calling Drew's name. She smiled, realizing he'd just been sharing their wonderful love story with his friends.

"Drew fucked the weird girl," an unrecognizable deep voice said. *Who were they talking about?* Victoria wondered. They couldn't be referring to her as the weird girl.

"You better watch out, Bradley. Drew's catching up to you," someone said.

"Hey—actually that weird girl should count as two points. Come on." That couldn't be Drew who'd said that. Victoria quietly crept closer to the fence so she could make out their voices better.

"Who are y'all talking about?" another male voice asked.

"Victoria. Henderson. You know, the new girl." Victoria's heart sank to the ground at the realization. This had to be a mistake.

"I don't even know who that is." This voice she recognized. It was Drew's good friend, Charlie.

"She's in our history class. She sits right next to you!" that same unfamiliar voice said.

"Well, how was it, Drew?"

"I suffered through it. Obviously," Drew said before raucous laughs filled the night sky.

There wasn't a flicker of doubt in Drew's voice. He'd meant what he just said. Somehow, those five words had the capability to inflict a wound unlike Victoria had ever experienced before.

Silent tears gushed down Victoria's face. She let them fall. Everything froze around her as she absorbed the words as if they were water, and she, a sponge. Her feet felt cemented into the depths of hell. *Suffered.* The other day, Mrs. McFriar, Victoria's English teacher, had given a lecture to the class about the power of strong verbs; Victoria, all of a sudden, realized her teacher hadn't been wrong about their impact.

'Suffered' was such a strong verb to describe an experience that, to Victoria, had been butterflies and bliss. It had been like the clouds above had finally opened. Heaven, gods, and angels had existed. But that bubble of happiness and love had blinded her to the truth.

He'd suffered; that was the word he used. Victoria's love had caused Drew to suffer. *How could that be?* He'd made Victoria feel so special, called her beautiful, and said that he wanted her to be his girlfriend. *How could he change his mind so soon? What had gone wrong between now and when he'd forgotten he'd left her by the lake?*

Then, the realization suddenly hit her like a splash of cold water on the face. He'd betrayed her. Lied. Just like the condom he wrapped around his dick when he shoved it inside her, he'd used her and then threw her away. Victoria gasped for air, but it was as though all the oxygen on Earth had suddenly been depleted.

With all the energy she had left, Victoria turned around and ran as fast as she could through the field. The weeds slapped her shins, and dirt penetrated into the soles of her shoes. When she reached the sidewalk, she kept running. As her sandals pounded the pavement, more tears flew off her face. Right then and there, she didn't care about her bike. She didn't care about school. She didn't care about the dangers that young girls encountered alone in the middle of the night. In that moment, nothing else mattered.

Victoria ran home faster than she'd ever run before. Usually, when the lactic acid built up to this level in her body, she'd slow her pace or take a break, but tonight the heavy breathing and sore muscles didn't bother her. She hardly noticed. The only palpable pain was the one caused by Drew's hurtful words. It was like something she'd never experienced before.

Back when Victoria was a kid, she'd broken her leg on the trampoline, which had some similarities to tonight's torment. At the time, her mom hadn't realized Victoria's leg was broken until almost a week later. However, the painful events of this evening were, by far, much worse. She'd have to do everything in her power to ignore the agony. Be strong. And get through it. That was the only way.

35

Victoria

August 22, 2007

The next day Victoria filed away the heartache Drew had caused so that she could deal with a new and major problem. Usually, on Sundays Victoria's mom would spend most of the day sleeping off a hangover. However, this Sunday was not like most.

At around ten in the morning, Victoria walked downstairs for breakfast. Unexpectedly, her mother was awake. Her mom sat on the couch in the living room. Next to her was an unfamiliar man with a shiny, bald head. Her mom invited Victoria to take a seat in the chair across from him.

That was when her mother smiled and made the introduction. "This is my wonderful daughter, Victoria."

The man smiled like he cared, but those sharp, cold eyes told Victoria that he didn't.

"Wow, she's a spitting image of you, Cindy. So beautiful," this man said. The man grabbed her mother's hand and gave her a big kiss before he whispered something in her ear. It seemed like they'd forgotten she was still in the room. Her mom never kissed men in front of her, so this was weird. However, the weirdness of the situation suddenly made sense when her mom said, "Vic, this is Tony, my serious boyfriend. He's going to move in with us."

Tony looked at Victoria. "Don't worry. You don't have to call me, Dad—well, unless you want to of course."

Victoria stayed silent.

"Why don't you go wake your brother up, please?" the man said.

"Why?" she asked.

Tony clearly wasn't used to that question. "Because I said so," he replied, his voice smooth and calm. "We have church at noon. And I want to make sure you kiddos have plenty of time to get ready."

Victoria didn't want to go to church. The pain of Drew's betrayal was still crushing down on her. The only plans she had today were to stay in her room in case she needed to cry more about what happened. Just when she was about to tell Tony that she wouldn't be going to church, she looked over to her mom. Her mom had the biggest smile on her face. It was the biggest smile she'd seen her mom wear in a long, long time.

"Okay," Victoria agreed as she stood up to walk up the stairs.

"It's yes sir. You say yes sir when speaking to me, please."

Tony looked at Victoria, waiting for her to say it. Again Victoria looked at her mom's big smile. Her mom needed this man and wanted this man. Her mom was clearly, for reasons Victoria still had yet to understand, in love with this man. "Yes sir," she said. Then, she walked the rest of the way up the stairs.

36

Victoria

September 23, 2007

A month passed, and Tony had begun to assert his presence, acting like the head of the household. With Tony as the king of this castle, as he liked to remind them, family life began to look much different. They no longer went to bed with a dirty kitchen. Clothes hung in a particular way on the hangers. Grocery store errands always involved a list. The worst part was that Victoria and Jeff now had assigned chores on the weekends.

It was another lovely Sunday afternoon. Victoria's seemingly functional family had just returned from church. During church, the preacher had discussed how important it was to not overindulge oneself, quoting the Bible verse from Proverbs: 'If you find honey, eat just what you need, lest you have too much and vomit it up.' Victoria interpreted this to mean that it was important to practice self-restraint and not overindulge in life's pleasure.

Now, at this hour in the afternoon, the king of the castle comfortably grazed out of a pizza box, stuffing his fat face like a pig as he lounged on the couch and watched the Cowboy's game. Victoria found

Tony's behavior odd since the preacher from church had just spoken about how they shouldn't stuff their faces with temptations. *Shouldn't he eat the pizza more mindfully?* she wondered.

"Victoria, napkin. Hurry," he ordered.

"Can't you get it yourself?"

Tony gave her a cold stare. "Excuse me, what did you just say, miss?"

"I said, you do it. Get up off your lazy, fat ass and get your own napkin. I'm not your servant."

Tony threw his pizza box aside and stood up. Pizza grease stains covered his white cut-off T-shirt. "Get to your room. Now," he demanded, pointing his finger toward the stairs.

Victoria darted toward her mom's room, but he chased after her and pulled her by the hair. She screeched out in agony, and then he quickly released his grip. Moments later, her mom rushed out from the master bedroom. "What in God's name is going on out here?" she demanded.

Tony spoke first. "I kindly asked your daughter to get me a napkin; she was within arm's reach. She threw a tantrum over it—called me a lazy, fat asshole."

Victoria squinted her eyes and looked at him in disbelief. "No, I didn't. I was way over there, about to be busy with homework, and so, I jokingly suggested that he get off his lazy, fat ass and get his own napkin. It was a joke."

Victoria's mom gave her a look of disappointment. "You know we don't cuss in this house, young lady. Please apologize to Tony right now, and go to your room."

Victoria sighed and walked away.

"Victoria Marie Henderson," her mom called.

The full name was never a good sign, so Victoria turned around. "Sorry," she mumbled. She walked the rest of the way up to her room and then slammed her door. As a way to relieve some anger she wrote some notes in her diary about how much she hated Tony, who she now started to refer to as the Mean Man.

Victoria's Diary When Mad and Needs Something Friendly to Talk To (it does not contain many bad words, don't worry)

Dear Diary,

I am using this old diary to write right now because I am really mad at the Mean Man. I always get mad at him 24/7. We just don't get along. I can't explain it. I just don't ever look forward to being around him. I wonder if I'm the only one who feels this way. I can so tell he doesn't like me. I'm not his real child. He pretends to treat me and Jeff like his kids, but he's mean to us. He pretends to be our dad, but my mom was married and divorced a long time ago. The guy who left us with no money, and we don't even know where he is, so my mom started dating this Mean Man. I don't know. I think it's bullshit out of all honesty!

Okay, well I am extremely tired, so goodnight!

Love with all my heart,
Victoria

P.S. I'll try to write tomorrow!

37

Victoria

September 29, 2007

Victoria sat at the desk in her room as she worked on homework. She heard Tony call her name several times but chose to ignore it. He could walk his lazy ass up the stairs if he needed to speak to her.

A few moments later, he barged into her room.

"Your brother and I are waiting for you downstairs. We have lots of chores to get done today. Your mom's at work, and she'll want to come back to a clean house—so we need to get started. Now." He stood over her as she sat at her desk.

Still seated, she turned around. "You can't just barge in my room like that. I could have been changing. I'm telling Mom."

He laughed at that, but his laugh didn't sound friendly at all.

"I already called your mom. I told her you weren't listening. She gave me permission to come up here and get you."

"I don't have time for chores today." Victoria turned away from him and pretended to read from her science textbook.

Tony slammed her book shut. "Listen here, little lady. Let me teach you a valuable life lesson that my father taught me. The guy who pays the bills, puts food on the table, and keeps a roof over your head—he's in charge. And right now, that guy is me. So, you're going to get up, walk down these stairs, and meet me in the living room. Right now," he ordered.

Victoria looked at him and rolled her eyes. Then she pushed her rolling desk chair back, purposely trying to run the wheel over his bare foot. She barely missed. She stood up to head downstairs, but before she could exit her room, he grabbed her by the shoulder with one hand and whipped her around. She was now face to face with him. With his dominant hand, he squeezed her cheeks together and tried to look her straight in the eye. "Don't you roll your eyes at me, you little bitch." Victoria avoided the eye contact with him. "You understand me?"

Victoria stayed silent. But the longer she stayed silent, the tighter he gripped her face.

His hot, tuna-fish breath repulsed her. "Yes, sir," she mumbled eventually, only so he'd get his disgusting self away from her.

The first chore that Tony assigned Victoria and her brother to work on was the refrigerator. After Tony complained about how messy of a fridge her mom kept and explained the process for how they were to fix it, he left Victoria and Jeff alone to complete the task.

"Vic, I thought Tony said we have to take everything out first before we scrub the inside," Jeff whispered. They both knew Tony was in the other room and could easily hear whatever they said.

"This way will be faster," Victoria said. They'd already cleaned the entire kitchen, which took a while before it passed Tony's inspection. After that Victoria had asked if they could take a break for lunch, but Tony said no. Not until they finished the refrigerator. Victoria's stomach felt empty, and she knew her brother was hungry, too.

A few minutes later, Tony walked in to check on their progress. "Why hasn't everything been taken out of the fridge?"

"We already did that part," Victoria lied.

"Is that true, Jeff?" Tony asked her brother.

Jeff looked between Victoria and Tony; he didn't know what to say, so Victoria spoke up for them both. "It was more efficient to do it without taking everything out. We didn't need to. We can still clean the shelves just as well this way."

Tony stood there in silence, grinding his teeth together. Meanwhile, Victoria sprayed the cleaner on the top refrigerator shelf and used the rag to wipe it down. "You can go back in the other room now and finish watching your show. We don't need your help. We'd rather do it ourselves—without you in here," she told Tony.

"Jeff, you're done for today. You can go play, watch a show—do whatever you want. Your sister needs to practice doing the chores correctly. Go on," Tony said, directing Jeff out of the room.

Jeff placed his cleaning rag on the kitchen counter, and then looked at Victoria with sorrowful eyes.

"It's fine, buddy. You go play. I'll come join you soon," Victoria reassured him.

"No, she won't. But you go have fun in your room now, Jeff. No playing with your mom's makeup, though. You understand me?"

"He can play with whatever he wants. You're not our father."

"We do not commit sins in this house," Tony yelled. "Your brother's a boy. Boys do not play with makeup."

"I'm telling Mom," Victoria said as she walked off to try to get the phone.

"Jeff, upstairs please. Now. I need to speak with your sister. In private," Tony said as he blocked off Victoria's pathway.

Jeff did as he was told, and then it was just Victoria and Tony together in the kitchen. Tony pulled his belt from his pants and gripped it tightly in his hands as he stared at Victoria with those evil eyes.

"Put your hands on the counter and turn around."

Victoria backed as far away from him as she could. "I'm seventeen—I've been too old for whippings since middle school. I'll tell Mom you're a pervert if you do that. And Mom listens to me."

"You're right, Victoria. You're too old for a whipping. But young adults who act like children need to be taught a lesson. Now, turn around and put your hands on the counter."

"I'll call the police if I have to."

"And how do you suppose you're going to do that? No one's going to save you, Victoria. No one cares about you. You're baggage—do you know what that is?"

Victoria hadn't heard the term before.

"It's like trash, basically. Your dad didn't want you. Your mom got stuck with you. It's an unfortunate circumstance, really."

Victoria knew that wasn't true. "Shut up. You're just a mean man. A mean, mean man. Get away from me!" Victoria tried to run away, but he pushed her up against the counter and held her down. His hands gripped hers, and he tried to hold them down so he could whip her backside, but she rolled her body around so they were face to face again. She felt his disgusting hot, tuna breath against the side of her cheek. Victoria extended her hands out to try and find something to protect herself. Her left hand hit the knife block. She pulled a knife out and slashed his thigh. Tony pulled away in agony but then chased after her. Still holding the knife, she took a sharp turn and tried to dodge out the back door, but within seconds he caught up to her. His strong hands pulled her to the ground, and he stood up over her, then kicked her out the backdoor. She rolled down the cement stairs; the little bit of grass in their backyard softened the fall. In shock, Victoria gasped for air and waited for the pain to subside. It hurt to move.

Tony left her there but came back moments later. He threw her school backpack at her. "You want to do homework instead of chores? Well, there you go," he said before he slammed the door shut. Victoria stood up to open the back door and let herself inside to go to her room, but it was locked.

Victoria licked her dry lips, put the knife in her backpack, and then hoisted it on her back. Tony had locked her out of the house. It occurred to her that she could take her bike to the local gas station and buy a snack and a water bottle; she had five dollars in her backpack.

As she walked toward the garage to get her bike, she remembered that she'd left it at Drew's house. With nothing else to do and nowhere else to go, she started to head in that direction.

38

Drew

September 29, 2007

Drew was home alone with his brother Rex, and he'd gone to get a soda from the kitchen. That was when he saw Victoria. She was looking around his yard, as if she was in search of something. He hadn't spoken to Victoria since the party.

When he'd returned to where they had sex at the pond, she had left. Then, earlier that week, when he'd tried to talk to her at school, she'd ignored him. He wasn't sure what he did wrong.

"Rex," Drew said as he walked into their living room. His brother held the controller in his hands and had started to set up their Halo X-box game. "Huh?" Rex asked, distracted by the game.

"Victoria's here."

"Who's that?" Rex asked.

"Victoria Henderson. She's in one of my classes. She likes me—probably here for round two."

Rex laughed. "Does she have big tits?"

"No, not as big as Emma's—but she has a tight ass. And a nice face."

Rex laughed again. "Alright. I'll play without you then."

"Good idea."

39

Victoria

September 29, 2007

After searching all over Drew's property, Victoria finally found her bike. It had been moved and hidden behind some bush.

"Victoria." She heard a screen door shut and then Drew walked in her direction.

What he'd said about her replayed over and over again in her mind. She hated Drew and needed to get away from him.

Victoria hopped on her bike and started to ride it down the path, which she hoped at some point would intersect with a main road. It didn't matter where the path led as long as it took her away from Drew.

She pedaled as hard as she could. After a short while, she heard the sound of heavy breathing. She turned her head. Drew had followed her on his own bike.

"What do you want?" she yelled.

"I want to talk to you. Let's go to the pond."

Although she didn't want to, Victoria listened. She was furious that he'd followed her, but figured this was an opportunity to finally say all those mean words to his face. Everything she'd written in her diary about him. Drew was just like Tony. They were both mean men. And Victoria hated them so much.

Victoria threw down her bike and ran the rest of the way to that same spot they'd gone to before. She set her heavy backpack down next to her and waited for Drew. Once he was within view, she finally spoke. "What—does the weird girl embarrass you? Is that why you hid my bike behind that bush?" Victoria confronted him.

"My brother did that. We had to hide it so our parents didn't know about the party."

"No—you're a liar, Drew. A liar."

"What's wrong with you?"

"You lied about Emma; she's still your girlfriend. You cheated on her. With me." Shortly after Victoria and Drew had hooked up, Victoria had watched tearfully as Emma and Drew kissed each other in the hallway at school.

Drew stayed silent.

Victoria fumed, and her heart raced. The memory of Tony calling her baggage replayed in her mind, and the pain she'd experienced when he kicked her down the cement stairs. He knew he was more powerful than her, and he'd used that to control and hurt her. And then she looked around and recalled what Drew had said to his friends that night. *He suffered through it.* That was what he'd said to them. *How could he say such mean things?* He'd pretended to love her and then he discarded her. That shouldn't be okay. Even though she hated them both, the pain Drew had caused her was much worse than anything Tony had ever done to her. Drew loved her and then betrayed her, and he deserved to pay for that crime. Victoria was going to show him what it was really like to suffer. Because what he'd said wasn't true. He hadn't suffered at all from anything he did to her that night. Only Victoria had.

"Take your clothes off. Let's have sex," Victoria ordered.

Drew smiled and did what she said. As they held each other close, Victoria battled decisions inside her head. Drew's touch made her want to forget everything and start over. In many ways, she longed to love him, but she couldn't, not after what had happened. *He used me,* she reminded herself as she reached for the knife in her backpack. Once she had a firm grip on the blade's handle, she stabbed it into his back as hard as she could and didn't stop until he was dead.

Victoria felt the way she did when she'd killed those animals for her dissections. She didn't want to hurt them, but she couldn't stop herself from killing them. She needed them for her projects. It was as if another being had taken over her body the entire time. Nothing in that moment could have stopped her. The sensation was all-consuming.

Now that Drew was dead, Victoria took a step back and observed the damage. Drew now lay naked, his body encompassed within the tall weeds and covered in blood. Flies buzzed all around, quickly beginning to feast on his remains.

In her hand, Victoria gripped tightly onto the knife. She looked down. Her entire right hand looked like it had been dipped into a pool of blood. Little droplets of blood slowly trickled down to the grass below.

As she stood there and observed the situation, Victoria didn't feel bad for what she did. She'd told Drew to go away. She'd warned him, but he didn't listen. Although she didn't want to hurt him, he'd hurt her first. What she did only made them even.

Quickly, Victoria put Drew's clothes back on. As she rolled his jeans up his legs, she felt something in his pocket. It was his wallet. Victoria grabbed it and put it in her backpack. Once Drew was clothed, she dragged him into the water. Then she swam into the pond to clean off all the blood from her body.

A mean man robbed and killed Drew. That was the lie Victoria told herself as she hopped on her bike and rode until she arrived home.

Before she could knock on the front door, Tony answered. "Hurry up and get inside," he said, grabbing the top of her head. "Why are you all wet?"

Tears formed in Victoria's eyes. She looked up at him. "I'm so sorry. I didn't mean to do it. I—"

"You can show me that you're sorry tomorrow. When you do the chores right. Until then, go upstairs, shower, then come back down here with your brother and get the dinner table set. Your mom will be home from work soon."

As Victoria started to walk up the stairs, Tony grabbed her by the shoulder. Victoria turned around to face him.

"You were never locked out of the house today. You understand me? As far as your brother and I know, you were working on chores. Downstairs. All day. When your mom asks about your day, that's what happened. Is that clear?"

More tears fell down Victoria's cheeks. "Yes, sir."

As Victoria walked into her room, she heard the sound of thunder and then heavy rain. The lights in her bedroom flickered for a short moment but stayed on. She looked out the window. The sky was dark. A bad storm brewed overhead.

In the bathroom, Victoria switched on the shower. She grabbed the knife from her backpack and looked at herself in the mirror. *What have I done?* She tried to remind herself that this was all Drew's fault. However, she knew that murder was a crime that resulted in punishment. She didn't want to go to jail. More tears trickled down her face. The shower blasted out water in the background, covering the sounds of her sobs. She grabbed the knife and prepared to stab herself in the heart with it. Just when she was about to do it, her brother called out from the other side of the door. "Vic, you wanna do some acting practice with me after dinner?! Please, pretty please?"

The knob turned, but the door was locked. Victoria gathered herself together before she spoke. "Yeah, buddy. Let me just shower real quick. I'll be right out." There wasn't a hint of sadness or guilt in her voice. Victoria put the knife away in the bathroom drawer, and then made her way into the shower.

40

Victoria

September 30, 2007

The following day, there was a loud knock on their front door. Victoria was in the kitchen, washing the dishes. Tony had gone to work. Victoria's mom answered it.

"Victoria," her mom called.

Victoria switched off the water, dried her hands on a towel, and then met her mom in the front entry.

Two tall and unrecognizable men stood in their doorway.

"These men are with the local police department, Victoria. Please tell them where you were yesterday."

"I was home. All day."

"Thank you, Victoria. Now get back into the kitchen please."

From the distance, Victoria heard her mom say, "Exactly as I told you. My daughter doesn't know anything about that boy. She does her studies and sports. That's it. It's so sad what happened. But I can assure you, my daughter had nothing to do with it."

After a few more exchanges of conversation, her mom closed the front door, and everything went back to normal. That was the last and only time the detectives ever came by with questions.

41

Victoria

November 5, 2007

After things had slowly started to return to normal after Drew's murder, Victoria's mom called her into the living room. Victoria expected a serious conversation about something—it always seemed like the living room was where her mom liked to have those kinds of talks.

"Victoria, please sit," her mom said, directing her to the chair across from the couch. Tony and her mom sat across from her.

Victoria crossed her arms and waited for her mom to lead the discussion.

"So," her mom started, "I got to thinking recently. I think you and Tony could use some bonding time. One-on-one. Tony had this great idea—he's going to take you to his gun range—"

"What, so he can kill me?" Victoria interrupted.

"No, Victoria. If you let me finish, you'll come to see how fun it's gonna be."

Her mom finished talking and explained how Tony and Victoria would head down to Tony's hunting property. Apparently, he owned lots of land in West Texas. He'd teach Victoria how to shoot a gun, and then they'd hunt some deer and stay at his cabin for the weekend. Her mom said the trip would be fun. However, Victoria wasn't so sure that the word 'fun' and 'Tony' could exist together in the same sentence. But it didn't seem like she had a say in the matter, and when the time came to head to Tony's hunting property, Victoria obliged.

* * *

The next day, the weekend hunting trip began. After they settled in, Tony took Victoria to the part of the property where he'd set up a gun range. The Texas sun beat down brutally overhead. Besides the shooting targets, there wasn't much else to look at. Sandy dirt with bits of weeds here and there spread out for miles and miles. It definitely wasn't a spot that most people would consider vacation-worthy.

"Have you ever shot a gun before, Victoria?" Tony asked.

"No."

"Well, before we get started then, let's go over a few ground rules. First, always make sure to keep the gun's safety on when you're not using it. The second you put it down and it's no longer in use, the safety goes on. Do you understand?"

"Yes sir. Seems basic enough."

"Good. Now, the next thing you need to know is that the only time you ever point a gun at another person is either when an intruder's on your property or you're defending yourself. Is that clear?"

"What about if—"

"Those are the only times. Guns are not a joke, Victoria. When you have a weapon in your hand, you're in control. The moment you let that gun control you, you put yourself at the greatest possible risk. You must always be in control of the gun. Now, come over here so we can go over the basics."

Tony showed her how to hold the gun. Then he handed her some pink earmuffs. "Here, I got these for you. The gun's loud. These will protect your ears."

Pink wasn't Victoria's favorite color, but she took them from him and put them on. After he explained how the gun would have kick back and what to expect, he showed her the proper stance and way to pull the trigger. After the brief instruction, Victoria looked ahead at the target and did exactly as Tony said. The gun kicked back hard and bam—she hit the target dead in the center.

"Great job, Victoria. I'm impressed," Tony praised her. A big smile spread across Victoria's face. Maybe her mom wasn't so wrong after all.

Most of the morning, Tony and Victoria spent shooting the guns at the targets. Tomorrow, they'd do the deer hunt.

In the meantime, Tony told her about a surprise. They drove his truck to the other end of the property. On a dirt track, there was an old Mustang.

"It doesn't look like much," Tony said. "But don't judge a book by its cover. That's what my father used to say. Come on now, I'll show you."

As they walked over to the sports car, Tony explained how he'd installed a certain kind of engine in it. This engine made the car fast. Like a race car.

Victoria got inside on the passenger side first, while Tony sat in the driver's seat.

Tony revved the engine. "Hold on," he said. Almost as soon as he'd finished saying it, they had already driven the entire way around the dirt track. It was the fastest Victoria had ever gone in a car. It was like a rollercoaster ride. She smiled and laughed the whole time. He let her have a turn next.

"Now, before we get started. Let me go over some rules," Tony said. He raised his voice over the loud engine.

Tony had rules for everything, Victoria had learned. However, she sat there in the driver's seat and waited patiently for him to go over all of them because she really wanted to drive the car fast like he had. Her heart fluttered with excited energy. At that moment, she felt alive in a way that she'd never experienced before. Tony explained how to switch the gears, grip the wheel, and then he went over a term called rev-matching.

"If you can downshift and not feel the transition between gears, you're doing it right," he said.

Then he looked out at the dirt track. "On the turns, watch out for the infield. There may be some bumps or ridges out there. If your front wheel hits them, it may swerve you, but now that you know, you'll be prepared for that. In case it happens."

"And the final rule. Have fun," Tony said, giving her a friendly pat on the helmet he'd made her wear.

Victoria turned to look ahead. She was in control. The race was hers to win.

The following day, Tony gave Victoria a camo shirt and pants. She assumed the clothes had belonged to Tony at some point, because the sleeves hung way past her hands and the pants dragged along the dirt as they walked together, guns in hand, to where Tony had set up what he called a deer blind.

"When will the deer come?" Victoria asked as soon as they got in.

"You got to have patience when hunting. Sometimes the deer will come. Sometimes they won't. It depends."

They waited patiently in the deer blind for a long while. Nothing happened.

"Is it bad to kill?" Victoria asked.

"No. It's good."

Victoria looked at him for further explanation.

"The deer population would get out of control if we didn't hunt and kill them. We're doing good for the ecosystem."

After another hour passed, a deer finally came across their path.

Tony helped Victoria position her gun and then he whispered, "Whenever you're ready. Make sure to aim for the heart. You don't want to make the deer suffer. It's gotta be a clean kill."

Victoria did what Tony said; she aimed for the heart and pulled the trigger.

"Great shot," Tony said, giving her a pat on the back. "Now, we go find it."

They followed the bloody tracks until it took them to the dead animal. Victoria listened to Tony talk about how they'd get the meat out of it and take it to the taxidermists so that Tony could mount the deer's head on the wall. "It's the prize," he explained.

42

Victoria

November 7, 2007

As soon as Victoria arrived back home, she couldn't wait to tell her mom all about the wonderful hunting trip. She went into her mom's room and was about to share, but her mom spoke first.

"Where's Tony?" her mom asked, her voice sharp and crisp.

"He's unloading everything from the car. Why?"

"I need to talk to him. Tell him I need to speak with him in the bedroom, please."

Victoria did as her mom said. Tony met her mom in the room and closed the door behind him, but Victoria stayed close by so she could listen to the conversation.

From the other side of the wall, she heard her mom yelling. "You have no business emailing these other women. I'm done, Tony. Done."

"It was a mistake, Cindy. I didn't mean no harm. I wasn't going to do anything. It was the devil—tempting me. But I overcame my demons. I'm ready to commit this time. There's no one else. I promise you."

There was a short pause, and then her mom said, "Get your shit and get out." Once she heard the shuffle of feet against the floor, Victoria ran up the stairs and into her room.

From her bedroom window, Victoria watched as Tony packed up his stuff into the truck. After he finished and was about to leave, he looked up at her, holding her gaze for just a moment. He didn't wave, or smile, or speak; he just got in his truck and left.

That was the last time Victoria ever saw him.

Part 3

43

Coach Nichelle

March 1, 2008

Three seconds remained in the championship game. Oakwood High was down by two points. All they needed was a two-pointer to tie or a three-pointer to win the game.

"Time out," Coach Nichelle called to the referee. The whistle blew, and her team gathered around. She knew exactly what to do.

"Girls, circle round." Red-faced and sweaty, her team waited anxiously for what she'd planned to say next. Everything they'd worked toward all year was now on the line.

"We're going to run our Hail Mary." Just when Coach Nichelle was about to draw out the play on her white board, it suddenly occurred to her. The Golden Stars knew this play. They'd expect this.

"Jenna, go sub in for Jordan."

Jordan looked upset. "Coach?" She sounded hesitant, like she was questioning the decision. Some of the girls started to whisper to each other.

"Listen, listen." Coach Nichelle signaled for them to calm down and listen up. They didn't have much time. The referee would blow that whistle any second now.

"They know our play. We ran this against them during pre-season. And they've seen our tapes. We need to throw them off. They won't expect the Hail Mary now that Jenna's in the game. It will throw them off our tracks; it's the only way."

Coach Nichelle looked at them all. Right then and there, she knew this was it. It was the make-it-or-break-it moment. This moment would define these girls for the rest of their lives.

She looked at one of her players. "Kristen, I want you to run out for the Hail Mary like you usually do. They will expect us to pass the ball to you first." She turned to another one of her players. "But—Lauren, you're going to throw it long to Victoria after Jenna sets the pick."

Coach Nichelle then finally turned to Victoria. "Victoria, I want you to run like you've never run before. Lauren's going to throw the ball long once you hit half court. You'll have time for two dribbles, which will get you to the three-point line. And then, I want you to make that winning shot."

Victoria nodded her head. The whistle blew. As the girls ran out to run the play, Coach Nichelle gently grabbed Victoria by the shoulder to say one final thing. Victoria turned to face her with those determined eyes. "Victoria, you've practiced this shot so many times. You do just like you've done in practice, and you're going to win us this game. Go knock 'em dead!"

44

Victoria

March 1, 2008

The referee blew the whistle. The final seconds of the game had begun. Victoria dashed forward to make her defender think she was breaking toward the baseline. The shuffling of gym shoes squeaked against the gym floors. Her teammate set the pick, and Victoria ran as fast as she could toward the half court line. For just a moment, she felt like she was back in that field after what had happened with Drew. Running and running. As fast as her legs would go. Away from the pain. Away from the past. Away from those who'd hurt her the most.

Victoria finally reached half court. She turned around over her shoulder. The ball was in the air and then in her hands. "Go, Victoria. Go. Shoot!" The crowd cheered. It was all up to Victoria now. She took two dribbles and pulled up to the three-point line. Her defender had fallen behind. It seemed like it was just Victoria, the ball, and the hoop. She'd made this same exact shot so many times. All eyes were now on her. She had full control over the game. The win or the loss belonged to her.

The ball left her fingertips. It soared up in the air. A perfect arch.

Swoosh. Nothing but net. She made it. The crowd screamed her name. Coach Nichelle scooped her up and gave her the biggest hug. Then her teammates carried Victoria on their shoulders.

Victoria looked over to the crowd. Her mom was there in the bleachers. "I'm so proud of you," her mom yelled. Although Victoria couldn't hear her mom's words over the uproarious celebration from the crowd, she could tell that was what her mom had said. Everyone was so proud of Victoria.

Victoria Henderson Becomes First Duke University Signee for Upcoming Recruiting Class:

The star of Oakwood High School, Victoria Henderson, signed for a full scholarship to Duke University. Victoria Henderson, a 5 foot 7 inches tall guard from Dallas, Texas signed a national letter of intent to play basketball at Duke University and becomes the first member of the Blue Devils recruiting class. Henderson was named Oakwood High's Offensive Player of the Year and averaged twenty-three points and ten rebounds. Henderson was all-state and all-district. The Blue Devils are expected to announce additional signees in the coming days.

45

Victoria

September 7, 2009

It was Victoria's first week of college at Duke University. Although Victoria and her mom had been shocked when she wasn't accepted at Harvard, Victoria eventually came to the conclusion that the Harvard basketball team consisted of a bunch of nerd wannabe athletes anyway. Duke was a much better fit for her talent anyway. Even the campus was prettier and better than Harvard.

The Gothic style architecture gave the campus an otherworldly and ancient appearance. The most beautiful buildings she'd ever seen were the Dallas skyscrapers, but those didn't even compare in beauty to the arches, finials, gargoyles, parapets, and tracery that so richly defined these unique structures. Duke was where history was made. Leaders were developed. Goals were achieved. It was exactly where Victoria was meant to be. This college was truly lucky to have a brilliant and athletic student like herself.

Unlike Oakwood High School, Duke had an invigorating atmosphere. The students here weren't just going through the motions. They didn't dread class attendance or participation. The way Victoria felt now was similar to how she felt when she received a new pair of shoes. The new unfamiliarity of the place gave her a fresh start. She could be whoever she wanted to be here.

Victoria and her roommate, Kate, walked side by side to their morning class. The freshman-year curriculum consisted mostly of generic courses. According to Victoria's academic advisor, she had plenty of time to choose a major.

"I'm so excited we finally have a class together, roomie," Victoria's roommate, Kate, said as they passed by a cluster of students.

"Me too," Victoria said, trying to mimic Kate's excitement over this.

"I love English! It's my favorite subject—by far. I want to be a famous writer one day," Kate said as she tucked a piece of curly blonde hair behind her ear.

Victoria wasn't sure what to say to that, so she let Kate keep talking.

"Like Stephen King."

"What's so great about him?" Victoria asked. She didn't know much about famous writers.

"You're joking right?"

"I'm not joking, roomie. I've never heard of this guy," Victoria replied. Although the nickname 'roomie' had been Kate's idea, and Victoria found it cringe-worthy, she realized that Kate seemed to like it when Victoria called her that, too.

"Oh, Victoria. I have so much to teach you. You've never seen the show *Friends*, and now you don't know who Stephen King is? These are, like, essentially the same as knowing about the weather. Where are you from again?"

"Texas."

"Were you home-schooled?"

"No, I went to a regular high school."

"Okay, well. I'll tell you what—after class, we're going to the bookstore. You're going to love Stephen King, I promise!"

As promised, Kate took Victoria to the local bookstore after class. They got the books they needed for their creative writing course, and then Kate got Victoria a Stephen King book. Kate insisted on buying it for her.

"It's a gift," Kate told her when they walked over to the checkout counter to pay for their items. It was the first time a friend had ever bought Victoria a gift.

In their shared dorm room, Victoria and Kate worked on homework. They were both working on an upcoming assignment due for their creative writing class.

"Ugh, I'm struggling with my story. Must be writer's block. How's yours going?" Kate asked. She sat cross-legged on the twin-size bed across from Victoria.

"Good. I finished." Victoria replied. She had just a few hours until basketball practice and was now sprawled out on her bed, reading the Stephen King book her roommate had gotten her as a gift.

"Are you serious—you already finished?"

"Yeah."

"Let me see."

Victoria saved her place with a heart-shaped bookmark—another gift from her roomie—and then got up to retrieve the assignment Kate requested.

Victoria handed it to her and then returned to her bed. She picked back up her book and continued where she'd left off. Meanwhile, her roomie was absorbed in the pages of Victoria's short story.

"Victoria," Kate turned to face her, still holding the pages, "this is so good. How did you learn to write like this?"

Victoria shrugged her shoulders. "Class."

"What class? Like a writer's workshop or something?"

"No, our creative writing class."

"Have you ever thought about being a writer?"

"Like Stephen King?" Victoria asked.

"Yes. Like Stephen King. I've read a lot of books, roomie. And I'm pretty critical. I wouldn't just say this if I didn't actually mean it—you're an incredible writer. It's like you've been writing your entire life. Forget pre-med. You could be a famous writer. Make millions of dollars. I mean, it's hard work, and some writers don't ever make anything from their work. But the very best do. If this is your base, I can't even begin to imagine how good you'll be after a couple years of mastering the craft. I have goosebumps right now—I'm not even kidding. Victoria Henderson. Even your name sounds like it would fit perfectly on a best-selling book cover."

Victoria was used to being good at a lot of things. Based on her A+ in the creative writing class so far, she knew she was good at that, too. However, her roommate was making her feel like she wasn't just good at writing, but exceptional at it. The best. Victoria enjoyed all the praise and attention that came with that title. Not only that, but Victoria wanted the status. The power. The money. She desperately craved it all.

46

Victoria

December 27, 2009

Fall turned to winter, and before long, the basketball season was in full gear. Victoria stayed busy with practice and all the travel that came with collegiate athletics. The Duke basketball team was very different from her high school team. The girls on this team were faster, more consistent shooters, and based on all the times she'd gotten her shot blocked in practices— they also had solid defensive skills. Unlike Oakwood High School, Victoria was no longer the star of the show. It wasn't as fun for her if she wasn't the best.

While Victoria stayed busy with basketball practices and games, her roomie kept busy with social activities, like the new sorority she planned to pledge for. Although Kate had begged her to pledge, too, Victoria didn't have time thanks to her insanely busy basketball schedule.

By then, Victoria was beginning to hate basketball so much. Her teammates weren't nice, and on bus rides they hardly spoke to Victoria. The worst part was Victoria couldn't even go home to see her family during the Christmas break. Her mom had insisted she stay on campus so she didn't miss any important practices or games. Soon enough, Victoria decided that she'd be done with this stupid team and sport. It wasn't fun for her anymore. In her spare time, whenever she wasn't at basketball practice or in class, she worked on her first fiction novel.

On this particular blustery winter day, Victoria sat at her dorm room desk, sipping from the mug that said in beautiful cursive writing: 'You are my soul sister'

The mug had been an early Christmas gift from her roomie. While her roomie was still away for the Christmas break, Victoria had become fully immersed in the novel she'd been writing. She filled those blank pages on her laptop with carefully crafted sentences. She couldn't wait for her roomie to come back from break and read this book. She wanted Kate to be the first one to read it. No one had read it yet. No one even knew she was working on this masterpiece.

47

∽∞∽

Victoria

December 30, 2009

A couple of days later, Victoria returned from the dining hall to her dorm room. When she opened the door to her room, all of Kate's stuff was gone, but Kate had returned. Her roomie sat on the bare mattress with teary eyes. She'd lost weight. Victoria had noticed Kate losing weight gradually over the semester, but now her roomie suddenly looked like a bag of bones.

"I'm transferring to be closer to home," Kate informed Victoria.

"Why?" For a moment, Victoria thought it had something to do with her. Perhaps Kate was upset that Victoria didn't buy her any gifts. Victoria suddenly regretted not getting her friend anything for Christmas.

"Um, you know that guy I told you about? Thomas. The one I was dating for a while."

There had been several times when Kate would tell Victoria about guys. Sometimes those conversations would drag out a bit, and Victoria had probably zoned out. The name didn't sound familiar, so Victoria figured that was why she couldn't recall the name. "Yeah, I remember," Victoria lied.

"Well, things ended badly. I've been pretty depressed. And my family's been concerned about my health. They thought a transfer would be the best thing for me. I'm sorry, roomie—I'm going to miss you," Kate said, rushing over to give Victoria a hug. "If you hear any rumors about me, I promise you they aren't true. I didn't know."

48

Victoria

January 27, 2010

Even with her roomie gone, Victoria went to class and carried on with her college curriculum as usual. It was a new semester. She loved the excitement that came with new things. Since Victoria had enjoyed the Intro to Creative Writing class so much, she'd registered for Creative Writing II.

It was the first day of Creative Writing II. Victoria arrived early, and like the other early students, waited for the Professor to arrive and begin the lecture.

"I bet you're glad you don't have a slut as a roommate anymore," the girl seated behind Victoria said.

"Excuse me?" How dare this student say something so cruel about her roomie and best friend?

"I'm surprised you don't know. That slut was sleeping with Thomas. Look, no one in our sorority is supposed to be saying anything about it, but since you're involved now. I mean—she was your roommate. I better fill you in." The girl in Victoria's class scanned the room and then spoke again softly. "The President of Alpha Delta Pi, Becca, well—she's pregnant."

"I'm sorry to hear that," Victoria offered some sympathy. She knew that getting knocked up—especially when still in college—wasn't something people usually celebrated.

The girl looked around the room again, clearly making sure that no one else could hear their conversation. "Yeah. It sucks. Big time. Your old roommate, Kate, she was like the homewrecker, basically. Kind of a slut thing to do. Get involved in a relationship with a man who's on track to become a father. If you ask me anyway."

Victoria stood up for her roomie and best friend. "Kate didn't know. He probably lied to her."

The girl seemed to consider the possibility. "Maybe. Thomas doesn't have a track record of being the most faithful boyfriend. He's kind of a player. But, still, Kate should have known. Everyone knew Thomas and Becca were a thing."

Victoria knew that her roomie and best friend was not a slut. *Why isn't Thomas getting called names? How come he's still able to stay at the university as if nothing happened?*

This wasn't Kate's fault at all. This was Thomas's. Men like Thomas were a problem. Knowing her roomie, Kate would never have slept with Thomas if she'd known that he was in a relationship. Victoria knew her roommate well enough to know the kind of person she was. Thomas was the one to blame here, not Kate. Thomas was the liar. The cheater.

Thanks to Thomas, Victoria no longer had a roomie or friend. He'd taken all that away from her, and now he needed to pay for the damages. Victoria would make sure that he suffered. That part she knew.

Since class was about to begin, Victoria temporarily pushed aside the thoughts related to Thomas. She'd get back to those later. In the meantime, she got out her spiral notebook and a pen, ready to learn and improve her writing skills even more.

Professor Simmons stood at the front of the classroom and began the lecture. "Today's discussion—the antagonist. Who can tell me what makes a memorable antagonist in fiction writing?" Professor Simmons asked the class.

A student seated in the front of the class raised her hand. "Well, they have to be evil."

"Yes, we often find a dark, twisted antagonist in literature. But we need a multi-faceted character. They need to have layers."

Victoria raised her hand to contribute to the lecture discussion. They got graded on class participation, so she figured it was probably best to chime in at some point today. *Might as well get it over with*, she thought.

"Yes, Victoria, go ahead." The professor and entire class looked in Victoria's direction.

"Complexity. The best antagonists are the ones we can also relate to. When their motives make sense."

"Yes, thank you, Victoria. Someone's been doing the readings. That is exactly correct. We need complexity in our antagonists, class. Without it, our antagonist will fall flat. When you, as the writer, have made the reader question the fine line between good and evil, that class, is a memorable antagonist."

After class, Professor Simmons called Victoria over to his desk. "Victoria, your writing is truly mesmerizing. Have you considered a major in English?"

Victoria honestly hadn't considered it yet. "No."

"Well, that's a shame."

"I'm working on a novel though. In my spare time."

The professor's eyes lit up. "No kidding. Well, if you need an extra set of eyes on it, I'd be honored to read it. Give you my honest thoughts and feedback. Have you considered publication?"

"Yes, I want to be published—just like Stephen King."

"Well, there can only be one Stephen King. But that doesn't mean there's not a place for your work in the world. When you're ready, I'd be happy to connect you with my contacts in the publishing industry."

Victoria was delighted the professor recognized her talents. She already knew that she was great at many things, especially writing, but her professor's reiteration of that fact was the validation to spur her forward.

Later that day, in the library, Victoria checked out some books related to dissections. She had a science lab coming up soon and wanted to freshen up her skills so she could show the class how good she was at it. Victoria liked to make those around her feel inferior. Not only that, but she also liked to show off and impress her instructors. She loved all the praise and attention the professors gave her when she was the smartest in the class.

Victoria quickly finished the first chapter from the science book and then kept reading. She was a fast reader, and this topic was so fascinating. In the next chapter, she read over a section related to castrations, and then it finally hit her.

What she planned to do with Thomas was for the good of society. Mean men like Thomas wouldn't make great lovers or fathers, for that matter. They'd probably turn their kids into baggage—forget about them, only care about their own selfish interests. Those were not the kind of men that should walk the face of the earth. And the only way to prevent that from happening was to get rid of them. *Control the population.* It wasn't bad to kill as long as some good came out of it. This was the realization she needed to begin what had to be done.

Later that day, Victoria walked to the dining hall for lunch and thought about how she was meant to be a famous author. In her mind, she envisioned how her book would set the bar for the next level of fiction writing. Forget Stephen King; she would be the author everyone talked about, the very best. Victoria Henderson, the best-selling author. That was precisely who Victoria planned to be.

Soon enough, Victoria wouldn't need the basketball team, the college, or anything else from Duke University. The publishing industry would scoop her up, and before long, she'd be off to much bigger and better things. Her mom would be so incredibly proud.

Before she became a famous author and left this college life behind, though, there was still something she had to take care of: Thomas. Between the final pages of work she had to do on her novel and the punishment she had planned for Thomas, there was plenty enough to keep her occupied.

In the dining hall, Victoria sat alone at a table with her steak and mashed potato lunch. Blood gushed out of the medium-rare meat as Victoria sliced through it. She observed the steak closely as she cut into and ate it.

The way the blood pooled out was truly captivating to watch.

49

Victoria

Present Day

At a club in downtown Philly, Victoria sat at a booth and pretended to sip on a cranberry vodka as she performed tonight's hunting activities. She wore a character disguise, of course. Although she currently had an enormous stockpile of stolen devices and identities, Victoria liked to ensure it stayed stocked to the fullest.

A group of loud and minimally dressed women made their way toward the back of the club. Since that was where the bathrooms were located, Victoria presumed that was where they were heading. Victoria left her drink on the table and a big tip for the waiter and then followed the women inside the bathroom.

Victoria stood in line behind the rowdy group of four women. "I want to dance—let's dance," the woman standing in front of Victoria said to her friend. They started to grind on each other.

"Hi." The same woman who initiated the twerk dancing turned around to face Victoria.

"You're so pretty. Wow." She touched Victoria's wig, and Victoria moved her hands to the top of her head to make sure the drunk lady didn't accidentally pull it off.

"Thanks. So are you," Victoria said, slurring her words to make it appear as if she was drunk too.

"Guys, look at her. Isn't she gorgeous!" The whole group turned to face Victoria.

Victoria gave her friendliest smile.

"You should hang out with us. We should all dance!"

"I want to get fucked tonight," the shortest woman in the group said.

"Yes!" they all agreed.

"Let's find some guys. Okay. We need to go find some guys. After this, we will," the least pretty in the group suggested.

Somehow, after that short conversation in the bathroom Victoria had become part of their group. It suddenly occurred to Victoria that it actually wasn't that difficult to make friends. They just had to be drunk first.

The group invited her onto the dance floor and they all danced wildly to the music. The song "No Hands" by Waka Flocka Flame played loudly from the speakers. Victoria did her best to follow along to the complicated hip-hop, grinding dance moves. After they danced to a couple more songs, Victoria followed the drunkest member of the group back to the table where they had all left their drinks. "I'm Alice," she said with great emphasis on the last letters.

Victoria smiled. "You need to go dance, Alice," Victoria said. "Here, let me hold that for you."

Alice left the wristlet that contained her cell phone, took another big gulp from her martini, and then ran back out on the dance floor to join her friends. Victoria looked over at them. They were all distracted by dance movements and ugly looking men. As soon as Victoria was sure that they weren't looking in her direction, she crept her way through the crowds of people and made her way outside the club. It was too risky to steal more than a single wallet a night, so Victoria planned to head home.

As Victoria made her way along the sidewalk, her personal cell phone buzzed with an alert. Her security system had caught motion at one of the doors to her cottage. She took a look. All she could see was what appeared to be a man in a dark hood. He wore a black face covering, which made it impossible for Victoria to determine the stranger's identity.

Without a second's hesitation, Victoria moved quickly to the secluded space where she'd parked her black Bugatti. She clicked a button on her keys, and the car door automatically swooshed opened. She got in, tore off her wig, set up the radar detector on the dashboard, turned on the engine, and then pushed her foot down on the accelerator. The wheels squeaked against the cement, and then it took off. There wasn't any time for speed limits tonight.

At the exit to get on the tollway, a fancy sports car pulled up beside her. The guy in the driver's seat revved up the engine. He wanted to race.

Better buckle up, buddy, she thought. He probably wasn't aware of how competitive Victoria was, which was fine. She loved to take people by surprise.

As soon as the light turned green, Victoria floored the accelerator. She beat him to the turn that led to the Pennsylvania Turnpike. They both merged through the E-Z Pass Lane and dodged in and out of the slow cars going the regular speed limit.

They drove head-to-head for at least seven miles before the guy in the sports car beeped the horn. Victoria looked over to him, he signaled straight ahead.

In front of them, at least four hundred meters was a deer on the side of the road. The other driver slowed down his vehicle. Meanwhile, Victoria slammed down the accelerator all the way; the deer stayed put as Victoria flew by.

After that, the other car was completely out of sight.

Victoria took Exit 42, which was about a nine-mile drive from her cottage property. She drove fast, but in complete control, along the winding road until she was on the final straightaway. The Bugatti zoomed down the road, almost blending into the darkness of the night.

When she reached her driveway, she slammed down on the breaks.

The car skidded. Dirt and dust flew up into the air. The car door clicked open. She got out. The gravel crunched beneath her boots as she walked over to the trunk of the car. She clicked a button, and it opened. Inside, she grabbed the knife belt and clicked it on. Then she clipped on her holster, reached for the Glock, and shoved it in. Finally, she swung her rifle around her neck and carried the bipod in her left hand. Once she was equipped, she ran to the section of the woods that overlooked the entire property. It was time to hunt.

From atop of a slight hill, she made sure the rifle was loaded before she positioned it in the bipod. After that was taken care of, she grabbed her phone, navigated to the correct app, and with a click of the button, switched on all the exterior lights of her property. The entire place lit up like a football stadium.

She scanned the entire landscape for the intruder. There he was. Frozen. She used the scope and aimed directly between his legs. The temptation to shoot gnawed at her. But she overcame it. That wouldn't look good if she had to explain to the police how a gun expert, like herself, was unable to shoot him in a less damaging spot. When the intruder turned around to run, instead she shot at the ground next to him. Just to scare him a bit. She smiled, and then swung the rifle around her neck and ran after him. She'd come back for the bipod later.

After an eight-hundred-meter sprint, Victoria caught the intruder. She aimed the rifle with the attached flashlight at his back. "Turn around and pull down that face covering," she demanded. "You're lucky I didn't already shoot you. You're an intruder, and in Pennsylvania, I have every right to protect myself on my property."

He did what she said, and Victoria was astounded to discover it was Rex, her handyman. She'd never considered him as a threat before. *What the hell is he doing here?* "Are you trying to get yourself fired?" she asked.

"No. I'm sorry. I know it was wrong to come here. But I know you know, Victoria. About Drew."

Victoria lowered the gun. "I know you're his brother if that's what you're talking about. Look—I felt sorry for you just like everyone else.

You came around looking for a job, so I gave it to you. But now you're trespassing on my property. And I have a problem with that. A big one."

"He went outside to see you that day," Rex continued.

"Come inside. Now," Victoria ordered. She was thirsty and needed water. Not only that, but she preferred to have this conversation on her comfortable couch.

Victoria allowed Rex to come inside and she got them both water bottles. They were now sitting in her living room; he sat on the chair across from where she sat on the sofa.

"I never saw your brother that night, Rex," she started up the conversation again. A long time ago, Victoria decided she'd never come clean about what happened that night. It would destroy all the good she was doing for this world. No one would punish the cheaters if she wasn't around to do it. Not only that, but Drew deserved to die that night. He was a cheater, just like the rest of them. Victoria didn't understand why Rex couldn't just accept that his brother was dead, and that was that. What was the whole point of coming here? He had a great job, and now Victoria would have to fire him. This was unacceptable.

Rex looked down at Victoria's gorgeous silk and wool rug, with what Victoria supposed was admiration, and maybe even a bit of jealousy. It had cost about fifteen thousand and had been totally worth it. The room felt cozy and luxurious all at the same time.

"Drew told me he was going out to see you. I was in the living room. Playing Xbox. I was playing a game and my brother was out there dying. Do you know what that's like? I could have done something. I could have—"

"There was nothing you could have done. It was a mean man. Robbed him. That's what the detectives thought, anyway. I'm sorry you never got a more conclusive answer. I truly am sorry for that, Rex. But don't you think your brother would have wanted you to move on? I'm sure Lacey would."

Rex looked puzzled. "How do you know about Lacey?"

"Background check. I do one on all my employees. The internet's a pretty helpful tool for all that."

"So, you truly don't know anything about what happened to Drew that night?"

"If I did, I'd tell you, Rex. I can't keep secrets like that. Can anyone?"

Rex stood up. "I'm sorry. For this. I saw the address on a cardboard box in your room. And I thought maybe there'd be some answers here. It was wrong. I messed up. It won't ever happen again."

"What were you doing in my room?"

"Your mom wanted me to install some new chandelier. In the closet."

"Oh. Well—I don't know how else to say this, but you're fired."

"I figured."

"You'll get your severance pay though. Should hit your account within an hour."

Rex looked surprise. "Thank you. You didn't have to do that."

"Consider it a gift. Go buy Lacey a ring or something. That's what women want these days. Isn't it?"

Rex stood up. "Thank you for not calling the cops or anything. I'm sorry. Again. I don't know what I was thinking."

They both walked to the front door. "Nothing to be sorry for. Just don't do it again. I don't take intruders lightly."

"I feel horrible over this. I honestly don't know what came over me. I just loved him so much. I'd do anything for him, and it kills me that the case went cold. You have a brother. I hope you can understand." Rex stuck his hands in his pocket. The expression on his face said that he'd blamed himself over this every day of his life since it happened. It wasn't his fault, though. In a way, Victoria wished that she could tell him that.

Victoria would kill anyone who hurt her brother, and she understood in every possible way. "I do. Like I said, stop with the apologies, and get on home now. Bye, Rex. Take care of yourself," Victoria said. She'd heard people use that phrase before and figured it was appropriate.

After she was sure that Rex had left her property, Victoria went into her office and wired him two hundred and fifty thousand dollars for his severance pay. She couldn't have him digging up the past anymore. That amount should keep him busy and away from her property for a while, Victoria supposed.

Rex's surprise visit reminded Victoria that she needed to take a quick trip back home to Texas. She'd finish punishing her father and then fly right back. She really needed to get her dad's punishment out of the way so she could stay focused on the cheaters in Pennsylvania for now.

Victoria went to get her burner phone and called Larry.

"Should I go tonight?" Larry asked as soon as he answered.

"Yes, I'm catching an early flight tomorrow, so I'll need him there by ten in the morning at the latest."

"Alright."

"Use those UberEats props I sent you. You know the drill." Victoria had decided an UberEats disguise would work well for this next kidnapping, since her father had a security system. "After you drop him off, I'll need an hour alone with him. Then, I'll need a same-day return."

"Shit, this ain't Amazon, Victoria."

"I wouldn't ask this of you if I didn't think it was something you could handle," Victoria said.

"Damnit. Fine. Well, I better be getting my money the same day then, too."

"You will. Now, I need to get to bed so I can rest up for my flight. Don't screw this up, Larry," she reminded him. Victoria hung up the phone. Less than twenty-four hours until her father received his punishment. With all the excitement and anticipation, Victoria wasn't sure if she'd even sleep much tonight.

50

Rex

Rex drove his rental car down the long stretch of highway. He'd planned to get a hotel tonight and then take a flight home tomorrow. It took almost the rest of the money in his bank account to take this trip, so he was beyond thankful for the severance pay. Hopefully, it'd be enough for him to purchase some groceries and help with other expenses until he could find another job. The job loss would put more financial stress on Lacey, but he'd do his best to find more work as soon as possible.

As Rex drove, he thought back to what Victoria told him. Although Rex wanted to believe what she said, it just didn't make sense. Why would his brother say that? Had Drew mistaken someone else for Victoria that day? Until Rex discovered the truth, he'd keep doing whatever was needed.

Rex switched on the car blinker and navigated off the toll road. The roads here consisted of mostly potholes and curves, which was very different from the Texas roads he was used to. "Two more miles until you arrive at your destination," his GPS said. As Rex looked down at the map on his phone, a bank notification appeared at the top of the screen. He was almost at the hotel and would check that as soon as he got there.

After the two-mile drive was finished, Rex parked the rental car, and then navigated to the bank app on his phone. He logged in. The numbers in Rex's bank account were like nothing he'd ever seen before. He refreshed the app to make sure his tired eyes weren't tricking him. Was this real? Why would Victoria give him so much severance pay? He knew that for Victoria this was probably nothing in comparison to all the money she had, but still, he'd just intruded on her property and now she was giving him a reward like this? It didn't make sense.

Rex signed out of his bank app and then signed in again. There had to be a mistake. However, when he signed in for the second time, the numbers were the same. Although Rex was genuinely thankful for the money, he wasn't sure how to feel. From a young age, he'd dreamt of a scratch-off win that put tons of money in his hands. Who didn't dream of someday seeing numbers like this in their bank account? As desirable as the money was, it was also a punch to his pride. Why couldn't he earn this himself without Victoria gifting it to him? In all the time he'd worked for Victoria, she'd never gotten him a gift. Why now? And why such an extravagant gift? He'd seen Victoria's pool, though. She had a grandiose nature about her.

This sum of money meant so many things for Rex. He could finally afford community college. He could buy Lacey a big, beautiful ring—the only kind of ring he'd want her to wear. They could get some work done on the home. Fix it up a bit. Make it homier. Or, they could use some of the money for a down payment on a new home. The options seemed endless.

As hope filled Rex's heart, another feeling seeped in. Guilt. He'd completely overlooked the reality of what this meant.

Victoria had paid him off. She didn't want him snooping around. But why? The only logical conclusion that Rex could come to was the same he thought of all the time: she knew what happened to Drew that night.

51

Mic

Present Day

Lounging in bed, Mic Henderson pleasured himself and watched as two naked women caressed one another on his laptop screen. This video was the newest lesbian porn that had been uploaded to the porn site he frequently visited. He'd seen almost all the lesbian porn they offered for free, so this new video was a nice change of scenery. It reminded him that he'd probably need to start paying for the premium version soon. He tired of looking at the same women all the time. Like all men, he craved the new and shiny toys, so to speak.

Just as he was warming up and things were starting to feel really good, his doorbell chimed. He didn't expect anyone and planned to ignore it. Whoever it was would have to come back at a better time. He was extremely turned on and would need to finish up in here before he did anything else today.

Another ring sounded, and then he suddenly recalled how a package he'd ordered was expected to arrive today. It was probably the inventory for his latest endeavor—an online fishing store, which was all operated conveniently from the comfort of his new house. If it was a package he needed to sign off on, then he wasn't going to miss the UPS guy this time. Last time he hadn't been there to sign off on a package, it had taken much longer to get his inventory stocked and caused delays for one of the new fishing pole products he had launched.

With the towel next to him, he cleaned himself up, pulled on his sweatpants, and went to answer the door. A dude with shaggy black hair, a red baseball cap, and sunglasses greeted him.

"Your UberEats order," he said, holding the styrofoam to-go box up higher. "Where would you like me to bring this? The kitchen?"

"I didn't order any UberEats; I've never ordered UberEats before," Mic replied. Surely, this guy had confused his address with the neighbors. That happened a lot.

The UberEats delivery man read off his address and then said, "That's the address I was told to deliver this to. A friend or family member probably wanted to surprise you. It happens all the time."

"Hm. Weird. Okay, you can bring it into the kitchen," Mic said, and then turned around to guide the way. After they were halfway to his kitchen, a sharp, knife-like pain penetrated the side of his neck. The pain stung and caused him to collapse to the ground. The stranger stood above him. Mic tried to speak and get away, but it was too late. That was the last thing he remembered before passing out.

5²

Dr. Hijo

Present Day

Thirty-five years as an ER doctor and Dr. Hijo had thought he'd seen it all. Until today. He waited for one of the nurses to return with the therapist and psychiatrist business referral cards.

"Here you go, Dr. Hijo," one of his nurses said to him as she handed him the cards. Dr. Hijo grabbed them.

"Thank you," he said. This patient would for sure need the referrals after Dr. Hijo told him the news.

Dr. Hijo secured the business cards under his finger as he held the clipboard that contained Mic Henderson's file. In the hallway, Dr. Hijo made preparations to inform the patient of his findings. *What is the best approach here?* he wondered. Quickly deliver the news or slowly get to it.

In all his years, Dr. Hijo never had to inform a male patient that their balls had been surgically removed. His patient, Mic, thought he was coming in for a medical emergency. This was not a medical condition at all. Mic's balls had either been stolen—those body parts sold well on the black market—or perhaps an ex had sought revenge. Dr. Hijo thought those were the only two possibilities. Testicles didn't just disappear. That he knew. Dr. Hijo took a deep breath. He'd left the patient in there long enough. It was time to share the terrifying news.

Dr. Hijo walked into the room. "Well, Mic, I have some good news and some bad news for you. Where should I start?"

"I don't care. I just need to know what the hell is going on. I've never had anything like this happen to me before."

Dr. Hijo took a seat on the stool and turned to face the patient. "I'll start with the good news—there is no emergency, nor are you suffering from an illness. At least, that was not the cause of what you're now experiencing."

"Okay. What's wrong then?" Mic asked.

"It appears that someone stole your testes. An orchiectomy—or in layman's terms, a surgical castration of both testes was performed on you."

The patient's eyes opened fully as if in shock. "How's that possible? Who did this to me?"

"You'll need to speak with the authorities. See what they can do to help. I know this is a traumatic experience for you to deal with, so I suggest following up with a therapist and a psychiatrist. You'll also want to make an appointment with your primary care doctor, right away. They'll be able to help you with a reproductive therapy program or refer you to the best doctor in the area for that. In the meantime, here's a prescription that should help with the pain you're currently experiencing," Dr. Hijo said as he handed Mic the cards and prescription. The patient took them but stayed silent.

"Whoever did this, they stitched you back up, meaning this operation may have been conducted by a medical professional or someone with that kind of experience. When you speak with the police, that information may be helpful for them to know," Dr. Hijo said. He reached in the pocket of his white coat and then continued, "Here's my card. In case they need to speak with me or have any questions."

53

Mic

Present Day

Mic Henderson was in complete shock as he sat in an interview room at the local police station. The last thing he'd remembered was the UberEat delivery guy stabbing him in the shoulder. When he'd woken up again, he had the most excruciating pain between his legs. The pain was like nothing he'd ever felt before. Initially, he didn't know what to make of the situation. It had been made clear to him that he no longer felt the same way down there. But it never occurred to him that someone had actually stolen his balls until the doctor told him that was what had happened. The situation was grislier than he could have ever imagined.

As the ER doctor suggested, he had to report this crime. If someone had told Mic that, one day, he'd be reporting such a crime, he would have fallen out of his chair, laughing. However, on second thought, he'd experienced unbelievable events in the past. He'd won the lottery, which was considered such a rare happenstance these days. Before this, he used to consider himself a lucky guy, but now, he didn't feel lucky at all. It was probably more likely for a man to get struck by lightning or attacked by a shark than to get his balls stolen.

While he waited for the interview to begin, he thought about who could have possibly done this to him. As far as enemies went, Mic didn't have any. Although he had been devastated and in absolute shock about the news, he was happy to know that the most important part of his manhood was, at least, still intact. If that had gone missing, he wasn't sure what kind of state he'd be in right now. But regardless, to wake up like this, with his balls stolen, was still horrific. In all his years, he'd never heard of such a thing until today. After he finished up at the police station, he planned to make appointments with those doctors he was referred to and figure out how to fix this as soon as possible. He didn't want to deal with an issue like this. It was the worst possible time to have his balls stolen.

Finally, after a short wait, a man in business casual clothes walked into the room. "I'm Detective Ansly," the man introduced himself, holding out his hand.

Mic gave him a handshake. "Nice to meet you. I'm Mic. Mic Henderson."

"Great to meet you, Mic. So, when you came in, you spoke with one of our officers. They informed me that you had your balls stolen. Last night. Is that correct?"

"Yes. An UberEats guy came into my house to drop off some food. He put something in my shoulder. It felt like a knife. Maybe a needle. That was the last thing I remember before I passed out. Then I woke up to this unfortunate situation. I have a security system with video. So I know what the guy looks like."

The detective jotted down some notes. "I'll need to see that footage. Do you have any enemies? Anyone who would want to harm you like this?"

Mic thought about it for a long moment. "No. I don't have any enemies. The only person that I can think of who hates me is my daughter, Victoria. Every year for my birthday she sends me a birthday card with a note that says, 'I hate you.' "

"Is she mentally ill or unstable?"

"No. Nothing like that. She's quite successful actually—an author. I don't see either of my kids anymore. But I know that, as much as she hates me, she'd never do something like this. That I'm certain of."

"Of course, I didn't consider that a strong possibility, but I have to cover all the bases. Make sure. Ask the difficult and sometimes obvious questions."

"Right, I understand."

The detective sighed. "Based on everything you've told me so far, I'm very confident that what we have here is a theft."

"The ER doctor I saw earlier said whoever did this to me was probably a medical professional."

"Why's that?" the detective asked.

"The stitches. They sewed me back up."

"I see. Okay, well, I tell you what. Let me take a look at that surveillance camera at your house, and then we'll go from there. How's that sound?"

"Sure. I'm willing to do whatever is needed to find the person who did this to me," Mic replied. As he led the detective back to his place, he began to feel angry over the situation. The shock had consumed him at first, but the longer he thought about it, the more and more upset he became. *Who did this to me?* The question kept replaying over and over again in his mind. That was all he could think about.

54

Victoria

Present Day

After about a month, Victoria had made substantial progress in her affair with Karl. Now, they sat side by side on the couch in his opulent living room.

Victoria, now disguised again as Sammie, turned to face him. "Karl, I need to talk to you."

He put his hand on her thigh. "Of course, what is it, Sammie?"

"What are we?" Victoria asked. She already knew how he'd likely respond, but she had to play the role of Sammie.

"What do you mean?" Karl looked uncertain about the answer, as if he was a contender on the show *Who Wants to Be a Millionaire*.

"Well, we've been seeing each other for a while now, and before we take our relationship further, I just want to make sure we both know what to expect—from our relationship."

"Right." Karl hesitated, clearly thinking of what to say next. "I care for you a lot. I need time still. To get over my ex, though. You understand, don't you?"

"Of course."

"But that doesn't mean I'm not ready to take the next big step in our relationship," he added. Before Victoria could respond, Karl leaned in toward her and planted a sloppy kiss on her mouth.

"Let's go to my room," he whispered in her ear.

"Wait," Victoria said.

"What's wrong?" Karl asked, as if he cared and wasn't bothered by the interruption that would delay the gratification of his sexual needs.

Victoria twirled the fake hair from her wig in between her fingertips. "Well, I—umm..."

Karl gave a look that said 'hurry up already.'

"Well, why can't we be Facebook friends?" Victoria asked. "I tried to add you, but you haven't accepted my request." Karl would hit it and quit it with Sammie now that Victoria asked something like that, which meant that she had no other choice but to end his life tonight. Feeling a high like that of cocaine, Victoria was excited and focused for the kill. She really wanted to kill him right this second. *Patience, this is a marathon, not a sprint*, she reminded herself.

"I didn't see—I mean, I never use my Facebook account. That's why, silly. Come on now. Let's go to my room," Karl insisted.

As Victoria stood up from the couch, she looked at the vase with the flowers. She could slam that vase over the back of his head right now. Get to the good parts. However, Victoria knew that would cheat the entire process. It was important that she followed all the steps. Until the completion. Before she killed the cheaters, Victoria had to sleep with them. It fully confirmed how despicable they truly were and was the final step in the process.

Victoria eliminated the possibility of death by flower vase and instead clutched onto Karl's hand tightly as he led her into the bedroom. It was time to endure Victoria's least favorite part of the process.

In Karl's bed, Victoria lay lifelessly as she suffered through the subpar sex. In comparison to other cheaters, Karl ranked at the bottom in terms of bedroom performance capability. Certainly, the other women he'd cheated with in the past had been chasing after his money, not the sex; that part, at least, had been made obvious to Victoria.

As she'd already uncovered, Karl had a girlfriend. A beautiful and seemingly wonderful one, for that matter. Nonetheless, that hadn't stopped him from putting his dick where it didn't belong. Victoria thought about how Karl's girlfriend would finally break free from a cheater, like Karl. Create a better life for herself. Without a cheater to bring her down. This was all for women like Karl's girlfriend. Victoria was helping them in so many ways.

"Mm, how's that? You like that, Sammie?" Karl asked.

Victoria imagined how the knife would cut into his neck and how the squishy ballsack would feel in the palm of her hand after she removed it from Karl's dead body. "That feels amazing," she replied. Toward the end, she added in a few moans for dramatic effect. Eventually, Karl finished and proceeded to head into the shower.

"Can we cuddle for a bit?" Victoria asked. It was important to appear needy, since that was how Victoria presumed many women behaved after sexual relations. Perhaps, if he said yes, she'd allow him to live a couple weeks longer. His entire life depended on the answer to this question. Victoria enjoyed these little games she played inside her head. They provided much entertainment. Hopefully, Karl answered correctly. Victoria covered her mouth with her hand, to prevent the laughter and cover the smile she had on her face right now as she waited for him to answer the question. Little did he know that his entire life was on the line. The answer to this single question would determine the timeframe of his death. *Best of luck, buddy*, she thought silently to herself.

Karl looked over to the digital clock on his nightstand. "I have a showing I need to get to this afternoon. Maybe another time, Sammie. I need to get ready for work now." *Beep. Wrong answer*, Victoria thought. Not only that but his response was a terrible attempt at a lie. Karl had nothing planned for this afternoon; Victoria knew his schedule.

"Okay, no worries. I'm heading home," Victoria said as she pretended to leave. Once Karl shut the bathroom door, Victoria became showered in excitement. The time had finally arrived, and she couldn't wait to eliminate this next cheater.

While Karl showered, Victoria made all the necessary preparations. In full disguise, she walked to her car and grabbed the extra big purse filled with everything she needed to complete the job. The bag contained cleaning supplies, propofol injections, gloves, knives (castration and regular), metal chains, a gay pride flag, a notebook, a pen, a baseball bat, and the DNA from Big Daddy D (aka Greg), which she'd plant in Karl's house after she cleaned the place spotless. In the past, Victoria had planted sex toys commonly used by gay men at the homes of the cheating men she murdered, but to switch it up, she figured a gay pride flag could work well for Karl. It was critical to throw the homicide detectives off her trail by implementing new ideas into the punishments. The great idea for the gay pride flag had come about after she attended the most recent parade with her brother and Ted. She'd found the flag abandoned in the parking lot and bagged it discreetly with gloves, of course, and figured it could work well as a prop. The flag also reminded her that she'd need to buy a replacement since she'd told her brother the plans to hang it up in the guest room; Victoria made a mental note to order that soon.

Victoria set her bag down on the bed where she and Karl had just recently had sex. Unfortunately for him, that was the last time he'd ever have sex. The shower shut off. Quickly and quietly, Victoria grabbed the baseball bat and a propofol injection from her bag. She headed toward the wall that separated the bedroom from the bathroom. Then she set the injection down on the floor next to her. After she warmed up with a few practice swings, she positioned herself in a stance that would allow her to take a swing at Karl's head like she was trying to hit a pretend home run. Victoria covered her mouth to stifle the laughs as she thought about Karl's head as a baseball. *Batter up*, she thought silently to herself, again, stifling more laughs. The baseball bat was a new tool, but if it went well today, she'd definitely use it another time. Usually, she just shoved the injections somewhere into an open area of skin, but some men had a higher tolerance to them, and took longer to pass out. Her patience had about run dry today, and Victoria figured it would be fastest to knock him out with the baseball bat first. She could then more easily inject him with the anesthesia after.

The bathroom door opened and Victoria aimed high, swinging the bat as hard as she could. Karl moaned in pain from the impact and fell backward. His towel fell off his body, and he lay there naked and passed out. Victoria bent down to get the injection and injected it into his thigh. Upon closer inspection, Victoria realized, as expected, she had hit a home run. The bat had hit Karl straight in the nose, which now looked lopsided and bloody.

While Karl was knocked out and sedated, Victoria got a head start on the cleaning. She vacuumed, mopped, and wiped down furniture and counters vigorously, which reminded her to double check that Karl had renamed Sammie to the contact name of Maid in his cell phone. Following those tasks, Victoria staged the hairs of DNA on the bed and flag in Karl's closet. In combination with the stylish wardrobe, Victoria was sure that the detectives would easily connect this next crime to the Homophobic Killer.

Victoria checked the time. She needed to hurry with the kill just in case Ebony showed up unexpectedly again. The thorough hours spent cleaning passed by fast. Now, Karl lay chained to his bed. In glove-protected hands, Victoria checked Karl's cell phone. He had renamed Sammie to Maid, as Victoria had suggested; she was glad that Karl had listened to her great suggestion.

As Victoria waited for the propofol injections to wear off, she pulled out her notepad and pen to work on some quick dialogue scenes for her novel. At least accomplish something until he woke up. When she began to write, it occurred to her that Karl had been a huge fan. A big smile swept across her face as she decided to remove her wig and wipe off the makeup.

Forty-five minutes later Karl blinked rapidly as he tried to sit up all the way, but the chain restraints prevented any movements. Slowly, he looked around the room. That was when they locked eyes.

He smiled. "Am I dreaming? Victoria Henderson, is that really you?"

Victoria grinned. "It's safe to say this isn't fiction. One hundred percent real life. Isn't it great?"

Karl laughed nervously. "This is really something. I owe my boys big time for this one. My birthday's not until tomorrow, but I guess this day must have worked better for your schedule. I just can't believe it. I'm pretty sure I'm your biggest fan, and here you are about to give me a striptease. I'm in disbelief. Just give me a second here to absorb this—I seriously owe them big time. How much did this cost?"

Victoria smiled and allowed him to say some final words. "Wow, I expected something lavish from them for my fortieth, for sure, but this—this is golden. I'm in awe. You're stunning. Absolutely stunning. I'm sure you see so many fans. But I was at just about every single one of your book signings when you came to Philadelphia."

Victoria reached for her knife.

Another laugh escaped Karl's mouth. "I have myself some good friends. I really do. They're even having you re-enact my favorite kind of role-play. How'd they figure that out? My browser history? Okay, okay—I'll shut up now. I'll just sit here lifelessly and let you work your magic on me."

Victoria walked up to Karl and slit his neck. The way he looked in those final seconds—that look of pure shock—had made this punishment the most enthralling murder she'd ever performed. *Okay, enough fun for today*, Victoria told herself as she quickly got back to work. She untied Karl's limbs, flipped him over, and then performed the castration flawlessly.

55

Victoria

Present Day

On this special evening, Victoria was over at Henry's parents' house. It was the big day. Meet the parents. Victoria was sure that they would love Daisy, and so far, so good, she thought. Henry loved Daisy, so why wouldn't they? Daisy was perfect for Henry, and things were going better than Victoria could have ever anticipated.

As they sat in the living room, Victoria and Henry were in a deep conversation about her boyfriend's busy day at the clinic when his mother interjected, "I know Hens is hungry, so let's go ahead and make our way into the dining room. I already set the table." She looked at them both with glowing eyes. Marilyn led the way as they all followed her into the next room.

During the holidays, Victoria had hired a full staff to put together a setup like what she now observed. There was enough food on the table to feed his parent's entire neighborhood. Marilyn had truly gone above and beyond to make a lasting impression on her son's new girlfriend. It suddenly made sense why Henry adored his mother so much.

"Everyone sit and help yourself." Marilyn smiled graciously at everyone, but her eyes landed on Henry. She then stood behind her son and rubbed his shoulders as he helped himself to the food. Victoria followed Henry's lead and also began to put food on her dinner plate.

Marilyn eventually took a seat at the head of the table. "So, Daisy. Henry's already told us so much about you."

"Aw, really? That's so incredibly sweet!" Victoria said, as she looked lovingly at her new boyfriend. Right then and there, it occurred to her that she could move on from the past. Actually commit to someone. Love someone without it ending in murder. Have a proper relationship with a man like Henry. She looked between her boyfriend's parents. They were perfect. The food looked perfect. Everything was going so perfectly.

Marilyn refilled everyone's wine glasses and then looked at Victoria. "Yes, my sweet boy. It already feels like we're just one big happy family. Doesn't it, Bill darling?"

Bill forked a big piece of chicken into his mouth. "Sure does," he replied in between mouthfuls.

Now seated again, Marilyn turned to look at Henry. "Did you register to vote? Election's right around the corner."

Henry nodded. "I did."

"Good. What about you, Daisy?"

Henry chuckled. "Mom sure knows how to get the conversation started doesn't she. Already bringing up politics. Mom, come on now, Daisy doesn't want to talk about politics."

Marilyn smiled innocently. "Oh, Hens, politics is such a big deal to you. Surely, you and Daisy have already discussed it." Marilyn took a sip of wine and then continued. "Come on, we're all adults here. We can have an educated discussion about it. Politics doesn't have to be a touchy topic. I mean, look at me and my husband. We're on entirely different ends of the spectrum when it comes to politics. And look at the success of our marriage. Twenty-three years now. "

Bill stayed silent, busy burying himself in his meal.

Henry shrugged. "You're right."

"So, Daisy, do you know anything about politics? Have any idea of who you'll be voting for this year? Or not really?" Marilyn asked.

The topic of politics had never interested Victoria much. Besides the serial cheaters, when it came to other things that affected society as a whole, she didn't really care. All she cared about was how certain policies affected her. Well, and her family, too. At present, she didn't even feel like the current political system did much good. At the end of the day, Victoria couldn't rely on the government. They weren't going to fix anything for her. As in every other aspect of life, she could only rely on herself to take care of essential matters that needed her attention. The government better just stay out of her way. Nonetheless, she had enough general knowledge about political party affiliations to know where she stood. Although there wasn't a current party that represented everything she stood for, she supposed the closest one would probably be the conservatives. However, she decided to stick with the safe answer. "I'm a die-hard Democrat."

Bill cheered and held out his hand for Victoria to give him a high-five. "Finally. About time Henry brought home an educated woman."

Henry chuckled.

Marilyn stared intently at Victoria. "So, you don't like to work? What, you like to live off the government? Take advantage of our system? That's lazy and incredibly selfish—if you ask me."

Henry looked at Victoria. "Mom's just passionate about her party. Don't take offense. She's that lady with the Republican Party yard flag, bumper sticker, hat, and T-shirt. She's a very proud conservative."

"Sure am. Both me and Hens are. I raised him with the right values. Taught him how to be a hardworker. Climb that ladder and do whatever it takes to get to the top—you get knocked down, you throw yourself right back up. No time for tears. And look at all his success now. After all those years of hard work, now a doctor. It's truly a success story. What exactly do you do for work, Daisy?"

Henry spoke for Victoria. "She's an aspiring author."

"Psh—what does that mean exactly? You sit in your room all day and aspire to write? That won't work. You'll need to get yourself a real job,

Daisy dear. We can't have Hens here carrying everyone on his shoulders."

Henry turned to Victoria. "Tell her the rest," he nudged her gently.

"Henry and I have also discussed the possibility of opening a bookstore. Together," Victoria added.

"A bookstore?" Marilyn looked at her son.

He smiled and then said, "Daisy loves to read. It's her dream to own a bookstore one day, and I want to help make that possible for her."

Victoria smiled. She liked playing this Daisy character and wasn't sure if she'd ever tell Henry the truth about her real identity. This double life had a lot of excitement to it. She loved the power the secrets gave her.

"That sounds like a money vacuum. Hens, you don't need to be wasting any of your money on that. Daisy can take out a loan for her bookstore endeavor. But, when it all comes collapsing down, just remember—I warned you."

After dinner finally came to a close, Victoria and Henry said their goodbyes. Victoria didn't realize that some families spent such a long time together for dinner. That was the longest Victoria had ever spent sitting down at a table and conversing. Henry's mom sure had much to talk about, and even after Henry insisted multiple times that the hour was getting late, his mom urged him to stay a little longer. "Take a seat. There's no rush," Marilyn said every time Henry hinted it was time to leave.

Now, it was close to two in the morning as they drove back to Henry's place. Way later than Victoria usually stayed up. From there, Victoria would get in her car and head home. She was more than ready for her comfy bed and luxurious house. Marilyn's house had been quite bland. Nothing spectacular about the place. Initially, Victoria had planned to give Marilyn's house a few compliments, but when she'd arrived, she quickly realized that there wasn't anything nice to say about it. All those compliments she'd prepared beforehand would have come across as insincere. It was a shame. Regardless, though, Victoria knew she had done a great job as Daisy tonight.

Henry placed his hand on Victoria's thigh. "Mom loves you. I can already tell. I know Mom's personality can come across as a little harsh at times, but she means no harm with it. That's just the way she is. Beneath all that armor, she has the biggest heart. You'll see soon enough."

"Your mom is so wonderful. She's incredible. I don't think I've ever felt so welcomed before. Your family feels like family to me. I love them so much," Victoria said. Although she didn't mean a word of it, she figured that was what Henry wanted to hear. She grabbed Henry's hand and clutched onto it tightly as they drove the rest of the way back to his place.

56

Victoria

Present Day

Marilyn answered the front door. "About time. I honestly thought you weren't going to show up." She looked at Victoria and then momentarily turned around to yell at her husband. "She's finally here, Bill. I'm heading out. Don't forget to change the light bulbs in the guest bathroom and finish organizing your tools in the garage. I'm tired of looking at that clutter of shit every time I park in there!" Marilyn didn't wait for Bill to respond; she slammed the front door shut and then followed Victoria outside.

Victoria had arrived precisely at 11:55 am, which was well before their agreed-upon meetup time of noon. Since Henry unfortunately had a full day of work at the clinic, Marilyn had agreed to sub in for him and help with the house hunt.

They were halfway to where Victoria had parked her Toyota when Marilyn paused. "Woah, woah, woah," she said, her hands in the air.

Victoria looked back. Marilyn raked her fingers through her short head of hair. "Oh, dear. I forgot who I'm dealing with here." She took a deep breath and then said, "Maybe I better go grab one of Bill's Xanax."

"Yeah—if you need one," Victoria agreed.

"It was a joke. I would never do such a thing; it's illegal to share prescription drugs."

Victoria didn't say anything. She calmly waited for Marilyn to hurry up with her shenanigans so they could get on the way to their meeting with the real estate agent at the first showing.

"You realize we can't just show up to these showings on our own, Daisy dear. We need a real estate agent to let us in."

Obviously, Victoria thought. "I know. That's why I'm driving us to meet her there. We're going to follow the agent in my car—if you're okay with that."

After a more detailed explanations of how Victoria had made the arrangements, Marilyn finally agreed to get in the vehicle. Marilyn opened the Toyota car door and slammed it shut once seated. "Wow, this is tight. I better drive," Marilyn said. She stepped out of Victoria's car and slammed the door shut again. Then, she clicked a button on her keychain to open the garage door. Next, she threw shovels, several pairs of shoes (probably Bill's Victoria thought based on the style), a garden hose, and some other tools outside into the driveway so she could get to the driver's side of her Lexus. Victoria followed suit and proceeded to the passenger side of the vehicle with a big, understanding smile slapped on her face. She wasn't going to let this bitch ruin her day. As Marilyn prepared to reverse the car, she looked back at everything in the driveway.

"You want me to move all that stuff out of the way?" Victoria offered, only because she figured that was what Daisy would ask at a time like this.

"No, it's fine," Marilyn said. She reversed the car, running over everything on the way out. Once they were in the street, Victoria looked back to see the damage. It wasn't that bad. A shovel had a broken handle, and the shoes looked squished, but other than that, everything looked as it should.

Victoria and Marilyn eventually arrived at the first house to meet up with the real estate agent. The agent stood outside near the front door waiting for them.

The realtor introduced herself as Wendy and mentioned how it was great to meet them both officially in person. Then, Wendy led them inside to the interior of the home.

"I like this," Marilyn said as they stepped into the entryway.

"Now, remind me, you're the mother-in-law correct?" Wendy asked Marilyn.

Marilyn laughed and then said, "No. They aren't married. My son, Henry, and Daisy are friends. We're helping Hens out. He's a doctor and doesn't have the time to go on the showings. But I know my son's taste better than he does."

"That's right. I remember Daisy mentioned that on our initial call. Well, it sounds like Mom's going to have the final say then on the house. Is that so?" Wendy asked. She was an attractive woman with straight white teeth, long eyelashes, and plumped up lips. Like Victoria's mom, Wendy was no stranger to cosmetic enhancements.

"You bet it is," Marilyn answered. Victoria allowed Marilyn to have herself a special moment and feel as if she was an important part of this process. Although Victoria knew very well that she'd be the one to persuade Henry about which house they decided on. In time, Victoria would be the number one woman in Henry's life, and Marilyn would need to step down and accept that. Marilyn could have the number two position in Henry's life. Victoria was okay with that, but Marilyn would never be the number one woman; there could only be one winner, and like always, it would be Victoria.

57

Bill Thompson

Present Day

After a long day of cleaning the garage, Bill had worked up an appetite and now sat down for dinner. Although his meal didn't look anything like the extravagant spreads they had whenever Henry came over, Bill was too hungry to care that Marilyn only cooked whenever their son came to visit. At this late in the day, he was ravenous enough to eat a piece of cardboard.

Bill set up the dinner tray with a beer and microwavable dinner on his side of the bed. Marilyn sat next to him on her side. Unfortunately, tonight was the same night that Marilyn watched those late-night celebrity talk shows. For the most part, Bill disliked these talk shows, but when it was his night to pick the show, Marilyn watched without too many complaints. The show wasn't all bad. On occasion, they featured interesting celebrities.

"What did I tell you about the tray, Bill?" Marilyn asked. She had her hair tied up in a bun, and her face looked shinier than usual from what Bill figured was probably her moisturizer night cream. "Over there, please. I don't want you to spill." Marilyn pointed her finger toward the edge of the bed.

"Come on, Marilyn. It's fine. It hurts my back when I can't sit up against the headboard."

"Okay, well, when you spill, just remember what I said."

Bill sliced into the meatloaf on his plate. In a way, the food looked like something you'd find on a school cafeteria menu, but it didn't matter. He'd eat every last bite of it. He was starving.

"How'd the showings go?" Bill asked his wife while the commercials played.

"Terrible. None of the homes had an attached guest house. I told Daisy that was what Hens wanted. Apparently she forgot to tell the realtor."

"Why does Henry need an attached guest house?" Bill asked.

Marilyn gave him a questioning look. "For us. Obviously. Hens wants us close by. He realizes we're getting older. Plus, when—well, if he finds the right woman to have kids with, I want to be there around the clock for my grandkids. Not only that, but Hens and I think the guest home will be the best way for us to take care of you when you come down with Alzheimer's and dementia."

Bill chewed his meatloaf and tried not to grind his teeth together too hard. With all the stress in his life, his teeth had already shrunk in size significantly from that bad habit.

"I'm not going to get Alzheimer's. Would you stop saying that please?"

Marilyn raised her eyebrows. "Okay, whatever you say, Bill. Quiet now. The show's back on."

Bill looked down at the meatloaf as he carefully cut into it so he didn't make a mess. His wife shrieked. "What in the—give me the remote, Bill. Now." With her eyes still on the television, Marilyn swung her hand back for the remote, knocking down his beer can. The beer soaked into what was left of his dinner.

Marilyn looked over at the mess. "Isn't this what I just warned you about? Go clean up. Hurry—hand me that remote first, though."

"I don't have the remote," Bill said. He hurried into the kitchen to get paper towels and multi-purpose spray.

"Bill, get in here! Now! Hurry! How do I pause this? I need the remote—Bill," Marilyn screamed as if she was getting murdered. He was moving as fast as he could. The mess was already made. It wasn't like he could do anything to change that.

"Give me a second, Marilyn. Your show can wait. Let me clean this up first, so I can get in bed and relax now, too. I've been going all day, cleaning the garage. You broke my shovel, by the way. My dad gave me that shovel. It was the best shovel I ever had. They don't make them like—"

"Shut up about the shovel, and look," Marilyn said as she pointed to the television screen. On the screen was an interview with a best-selling author named Victoria Henderson. She looked a lot like Henry's new girlfriend, Daisy.

"What—she looks like Daisy a little. So what?"

"Are you kidding me? What—you have cataracts or something—that is Daisy!" Marilyn persisted. "Give me the remote."

Bill's heart beat rapidly in his chest as he looked under the covers and all over the ground for the remote so Marilyn would shut up already. After a frantic search, Bill finally found the remote under Marilyn's pillow. "Here," he said.

"No. You do it. I don't know how. Rewind it. And then I'll tell you when to pause," Marilyn ordered.

Bill did as Marilyn said. His wife took pictures of the woman on the screen, which apparently she planned to show Henry tomorrow when the three of them went on their hike.

"She lied to us. To Hens. He's going to be devastated over this. I can't believe that bitch. How dare she use our son like this? What the hell does she want? Inspiration for one of her novels? I can't believe this woman."

"Can you calm down, Marilyn. You have no proof of what you're even talking about. All kinds of people look similar to celebrities. It happens all the time."

"I have proof. Right here!" she yelled as she held up her cell phone. "I'm showing Hens the photos tomorrow. I'll let him make of it what he wants."

"Here you go again. Ruining another one of his relationships. When are you going to stop, Marilyn? When?" Bill asked. Although he'd already showered this evening, he could feel sweat beneath his armpits and along his back. It was a workout being in a relationship with Marilyn. Bill didn't know how much longer his body could sustain it.

"Me—ruining their relationship? You're crazy, Bill. This woman—Victoria or Daisy—whatever the hell her name is—she's a liar. She lied to Hens, and you think I'm the one ruining the relationship? You don't care about our son in the same way that I do. It's like you're jealous of his life, so you want to ruin it. It's insane, Bill. So ridiculous. You really need to get in with that therapist. The card's in the junk drawer in the kitchen—which reminds me, that needs a cleaning, too. Maybe you can finally get to that tomorrow, and then set yourself up with some therapy. Please. For all of us."

At this point in the evening, Bill was fed up and still hungry. He'd have to wait until tomorrow to talk some sense into his wife. Right now, he needed food. "You're right. I'm sorry."

Marilyn suddenly appeared more peaceful.

"Do you mind if order a pizza since you knocked over my beer?" Bill asked. "There was nothing to salvage from my frozen food meal. I had to throw it all away."

"Don't blame me for that, Bill. That was your fault. Own up to it. You're always trying to point the finger at everyone else. Man up and take responsibility for once."

"You're right. My fault. Now, can I order that pizza?" Bill asked, grinding his teeth together.

"You really don't need the extra calories, darling. You should go on that *Naked and Afraid* show. Let your body starve and eat all that fat off for a while—you don't need to eat every second of the day to sustain yourself. But if you're that starving, I guess. Go ahead and order it. Put it on your credit card, though. Not mine."

58

⤿⧤⧥⤾

Victoria

Present Day

Victoria and Henry rode in his car on their way to a hiking trail near his parent's house. "I can't wait for you to see how beautiful it is. When I was a Boy Scout back in the day—"

"Aw, a Boy Scout. I love that," Victoria said, smiling at her boyfriend.

Today, Henry was taking her someplace special to propose. It seemed like Henry had done everything in his power to keep it a secret from her, but he didn't understand that secrets never worked with Victoria. She'd always find out. What had given this secret away was Henry's browser history—all the wedding ring searches. Victoria was able to confirm that he'd purchased a ring for her after she went through his phone and clicked on the banking app. Upon inspection of his credit card statement, she learned that her boyfriend, and soon-to-be-husband, had purchased a thirty-thousand dollar ring. Victoria was a tad bit concerned over the ring's quality, considering the cheap price tag, but regardless, she was still delighted over the proposal. Today was going to be a great day, the best day.

"Yep. A good ole Boy Scout. Mom has a bunch of pictures. I'll have her show you all of them later—once we're back from the hike."

Victoria zoned out while Henry talked about his time as a Boy Scout. Meanwhile, she thought about how perfect of a guy he was for her needs. From the time Victoria had spent with him—as Daisy, of course—she was certain that he wasn't a cheater. He was everything Victoria had ever imagined her husband would be. Victoria would continue with this secret life. She could maintain it while writing full time. She could write from anywhere. *Till death do us part*, she remembered what Henry had said on their first date and smiled.

After a thirty-minute drive, Henry and Victoria arrived at Meadow Woods Park. "Oh look, Mom's already here. She's an early bird," Henry said. Victoria looked to where Henry pointed. His mom had her hair pulled up tightly in a ponytail with the little strands poking out at the top of her head. She wore a North Face windbreaker, leggings, and hiking boots. Unlike Victoria's hiking boots, it looked like Marilyn's had treaded all the way up to Mount Everest, which made it seem like Marilyn and Henry went on these hikes frequently. Well, Marilyn was in for a surprise. She'd need to find a new hiking buddy, because Victoria was Henry's soon-to-be wife and permanent hiking companion. On second thought, Victoria wasn't sure if she even liked hiking. If the hike didn't provide enough excitement for Victoria, she'd allow Marilyn to maintain her regular hiking schedule with Henry. However, if Victoria enjoyed the hiking activity, she'd need to find a way to slide into the number one spot as Henry's hiking companion. Again, Marilyn would need to step down and gladly accept position number two in most areas of her son's life.

Victoria figured after the proposal, Marilyn would more than likely do just that. Wasn't that what mothers did after their kids got married? Victoria wondered. Marriage was an entirely new concept and experience. She had been too young to remember what married life looked like back when her biological father was still in the picture, and her mom hadn't remarried since. Victoria wasn't certain how a healthy marriage worked. But she was absolutely sure that despite Marilyn's overly-involved personality, she'd step down into her place once she saw how happy Henry was with Victoria. That was what all mothers wanted for their son. Happiness and marriage. And Victoria—well, Daisy—was providing Henry with exactly that.

"Henry. I missed you. Come here," Marilyn pulled her son into a tight hug and at the same time gave Victoria a rude look. *What is her deal today?* Victoria wondered. "Come on let's go. I need to talk to you. It's an emergency." Marilyn grabbed her son's hand and tried to get a head start with him on the hiking trail.

"Hold on, Mom. Wait, speaking of emergency. That reminds me. I need to call the clinic to make sure the new doctor showed up today. You guys go ahead. I'll catch up here soon."

Victoria and Marilyn did what Henry suggested and began the hike. "So, Daisy, how's the writing going?"

"Good," Victoria said. She took in the beautiful landscape. Trees of all shapes and sizes engulfed the landscape. Unlike Texas, Pennsylvania had giant trees that looked centuries old. In an opening between the branches and leaves, Victoria could see an overlook of the entire landscape in the distance. Victoria and Marilyn walked toward the cliff to get a better view.

"This is beautiful." Victoria admired the scenery. Henry was going to propose to her on this gorgeous cliff. Hopefully, Marilyn had brought her camera. For the special occasion, Victoria had even put on more makeup than she usually did. If Victoria and Henry ever had kids one day, she wanted to show her kids these photos so they could see how stunning and beautiful their mom was and why their dad wanted to marry her.

Marilyn stayed silent. She had her attention focused on something on her phone.

"What, you've never seen anything like this before, Victoria?" Marilyn asked. Victoria remained calm, but she didn't like how Marilyn knew her real name. That would ruin the whole plan, the entire marriage. Victoria wanted this secret life that came with real love. *Why is Marilyn trying to ruin everything?*

Victoria would play it off. Marilyn was getting old. Perhaps, her memory was fuzzy, and she wasn't good with names. "You mean Daisy. You called me Victoria."

Marilyn held out her phone. "No. I mean, Victoria. I know who you are, you little bitch."

Victoria looked at the photo. It showed a picture of Victoria at a talk show interview. *Damnit.* This was why she hated it when she had to make those appearances. Victoria tried not to clench her fists as she absorbed the information. This would ruin everything. The proposal. The marriage. The love.

"I'm telling Hens. You lied. To him. To all of us. He'll want nothing to do with you after this," Marilyn said.

"Let me tell him. I'll explain it all later. He needs to hear it from me. Not you. Stay out of this. He loves me, and he's going to propose to me. Today. Right now, actually. As soon as he meets us over here."

"Oh no, he isn't, Victoria or Daisy. Whoever the hell you are. I don't know what fantasy land you're living in, dear. But my son won't marry a lying bitch like you. I won't allow it, and once he sees these pictures. It's over for you."

Victoria tried to reach for Marilyn's phone. If she had to tell Henry the truth, she would eventually, but today was a special day. This bitch was trying to ruin it with these stupid photos.

"Daisy, Mom," Henry's voice called from the distance.

"Give me the phone. Now," Victoria demanded. She clasped onto Marilyn's hands and tried to pull the phone away from her. Marilyn maintained a tight grip and pulled away, closer to the edge of the cliff. Victoria followed. Henry would be over here any second. If Victoria didn't get that phone and delete those pictures right now, Marilyn would ruin this special day.

"Give it to me." Victoria reached in fast this time, and with all her strength, tried to rip it from Marilyn's hands. Marilyn stepped back farther and farther away. They now stood on the very edge of the cliff. Victoria got closer and again tried to grab the phone. It was a tug of war match.

"Mom, Daisy. Where are you?" Henry's voice called. The proximity of Henry's voice made Victoria release her grip. She couldn't let Henry see her getting this aggressive with his mother.

The sudden release of pressure caused Marilyn to tumble backward. Her hiking boot hit a tree branch, and she fell back all the way. "Hen—ry!" she yelled as she flew off the cliff.

Victoria's perfect day was ruined. The bitch fell off the cliff. *How am I going to explain this to Henry?* Marilyn was an experienced hiker, but she was old. Could Victoria make up a lie about her vision being off? Perhaps Marilyn didn't see the edge of the cliff very well. Or would a lie about suicide work better? *Damnit,* Victoria thought. She suddenly regretted not looking into Marilyn's history more.

Marilyn had been the real enemy here, and Victoria had failed to study the enemy's ins and outs. Had she done that, she would have been prepared for a situation like this. However, she didn't know if Marilyn had any previous suicidal behaviors. How would Victoria explain this to the love of her life? Would he even be the same man she fell in love with after all this? Henry talked about his mother all the time. Would he ever recover from this incident?

Right then and there, Victoria was hit with the realization of how to fix this. Now that Marilyn had fallen off the damn cliff, the police would need to get involved. They'd need to ask Victoria questions. Perhaps confirm her real identity. Get a statement. Then, the truth would come out about how she wasn't actually Daisy. If the media caught a hold of this story, she'd be screwed. *Best-selling Author, Victoria Henderson, Stands Nearby as Old Woman Falls Off Cliff.* That didn't make Victoria look like any kind of hero. Although Victoria knew that sometimes negative press was helpful with marketing, she didn't need any extra attention right now. Her books sold better than everyone else's, and her author platform and marketing strategy was top of the line.

Victoria needed to get rid of all the evidence. All witnesses. *Till death do us part,* she remembered what Henry had told her, which was what she had to do.

As much as she didn't want to, Victoria now needed to kill the love of her life...